HOME IS NOT
A COUNTRY

HOME IS NOT A COUNTRY

DAVID BLACKIE

The Book Guild Ltd

First published in Great Britain in 2022 by
The Book Guild Ltd
Unit E2 Airfield Business Park,
Harrison Road, Market Harborough,
Leicestershire. LE16 7UL
Tel: 0116 2792299
www.bookguild.co.uk
Email: info@bookguild.co.uk
Twitter: @bookguild

This work is entirely fictitious and bears no resemblance to any persons living or dead.

Typeset in 11pt Adobe Jenson Pro

Printed on FSC accredited paper
Printed and bound in Great Britain by 4edge Limited

ISBN 978 1915122 339

British Library Cataloguing in Publication Data.
A catalogue record for this book is available from the British Library.

In memory of my mother,
Ella Blackie

I

Adelaide, 1997

Whenever I think of that time in my life, I always picture a pelican. I remember sitting on the parched grass, shading my eyes from the afternoon sun, when the bird rose clumsily from the riverbank. Its slow-motion wings strained to take flight and seemed to reflect my own lack of energy.

Friday night – that was when I slept last and it was now Monday afternoon. Was that right? But thinking about it, it was eight hours already since the flight landed in Adelaide. And seven hours since Archie met me in arrivals. Laughing to myself now, I recalled worrying that I wouldn't recognise my uncle. But how could I have missed him? The wiry build, the patterned golfing jersey, the thin, drawn face with the permanent frown of a Thomson male. We shared a family resemblance except that he was twice my age and his face had been weathered by the Australian sun. That was Archie alright, Archie as I seemed to remember him from my childhood.

My mother, though never explicit, regarded him as her favourite brother. He keeps in touch, she said, unlike some of the others whose snooty wives, with airs above their station, didn't like to slum it with folk from a council estate.

A few months before my trip to Australia, we were sitting in her living room sorting through boxes I had brought down from the loft.

The family home of more than forty years had been sold and she was preparing to move to a new retirement apartment. Better to make the move now, she said, while I still have the energy for it. As her only child, it was my responsibility to help her get ready. I picked a pair of tiny leather slippers from the box in front of me.

'Where did these come from?' I said, repeating the question in a louder voice as usual.

'Archie. Archie sent them from Aden.'

'Aden? What was he doing in Aden? I didn't know he did National Service.'

'He didn't. His ship stopped in Aden when he went out to Australia and he sent them from there.'

'So that would be... nineteen fifty-five or something?' I heard myself shouting the year.

'I'm not sure. About then, yes. It was well before you were born.'

'And didn't he meet Nesta on the ship?' I had no idea where that came from. Perhaps one of my aunts suggested it.

'Oh, you could never get any sense out of him about that.' There was a tetchiness in her voice, an unwelcome reminder of my childhood. I put the slippers to one side and returned to sorting through the box.

Archie and I shook hands in the arrivals hall. He offered a thin smile and a tight, 'you got here okay then'. His accent was a strange mix of Edinburgh and Australia as if he couldn't quite lose the former and commit to the latter. I picked up the rental car and followed close behind him, round the ring road and up into the hills above the city. The roads seemed bumpy and potholed and were lined with rows of wood-framed houses and their corrugated roofs. Eventually, we crested a hill and swung into Belair where the houses were more substantial, more individual, more stylish. Archie parked on the driveway of a low, broad house, all white walls and slate roofs running off at odd angles.

Nesta came to the door wearing a dressing gown, her wispy hair unbrushed. Fair enough, I thought, it's barely eight o'clock in the morning. She smiled toothily and we hugged. I didn't linger, aware of my sour smell after so long without washing.

Half dozing on their terrace, I drank a mug of cheap instant coffee and watched a possum asleep on the roof of a neighbour's shed. They didn't ask about my flights, in fact they didn't ask me anything. I was so tired I couldn't think of anything to say either but the silence was unbearable.

'I'm surprised the roads are so bumpy,' I said.

Archie's eyes lit up a little, but his face remained stony.

'What did you expect? Bloody billiard tables like you have back home? Can't afford that kind of thing out here, not when it's nearly six hundred miles to Melbourne and five hundred more to Sydney. They're bumpy alright and you better get used to it. And wait till you start driving through the bush, it's bloody kangaroos and wombats you'll have to worry about, not road surfaces. How's your mother anyway, Jim?'

My mother was bearing up, still dealing with the trauma of leaving the family home and trying to settle into her new surroundings. But I sensed that neither of them wanted the long version.

'Mum's fine, thanks.' My eyes followed a streak of orange and green flying across the garden. 'Just taking time to get used to the new apartment. It's been a big upheaval for her.'

'Yes, yes we heard about that,' Nesta said, smiling briefly as she stood up. She collected our empty mugs and disappeared inside. Archie stubbed out another cigarette and rose from his chair.

'Anyway, you'll be wanting to get yourself sorted out at the university, see what your room's like. And catch up on some sleep, no doubt. Follow me down the hill when you're ready.'

Driving back, I tried not to think about the bumpy roads as we wound down the hills to the riverside campus. So much for trying to make small talk. I made a note to bite my lip in future.

*

The pelican had returned to the riverbank, folding its wings carefully. I raised myself from the grass, stretched my back and headed for a footbridge which led to the city centre. Despite my tiredness I felt a little thrill at being here at the other end of the world. So far Australia seemed a mix of the exotic and the familiar which I reckoned would suit me well. I had three weeks ahead of me, three long weeks of exploration.

I was here on a travel fellowship. The award came as a surprise. Three thousand pounds, on the back of a half-hearted, why-the-hell-not proposal based on my interest in convict transportation. Or more specifically, my interest in one Walter Avery. In eighteen thirty-three, Walter was transported for fourteen years to the penal colony of New South Wales. Years later he wrote an account of his eventful life called *Reflections of a Condemned Man*. Ever since its publication the book had caused arguments over its authenticity and it was often ignored by recent historians. But I had stood by Walter ever since my student days. In amongst his tall stories and bleating victimisation I felt there were fragments of truth worth pursuing. Despite his faults, I liked the man. And after all, I had Walter to thank for being in Australia in the first place.

When the funding letter arrived a few months earlier, it felt like a lifeline. At that point I was fed up with being a slave to work commitments; fed up with forcing myself to maintain a social life which did nothing except provide some relief from the boredom of my own company. The divorce from Ann a few years back still had a lingering effect on my moods, my sense of failure. And underlying it all was a restlessness, a feeling that somehow my life should be lived somewhere else, that *there* was better than *here*. But, when I was being honest with myself, I admitted that I'd pretty much always felt that way. What I wanted was a catalyst, some opportunity for a fresh start.

So here I was, walking in warm, late summer sunshine through Adelaide University. I had a strong sense of being alone and invisible. There was no chance of meeting anyone I knew. It felt exciting but there was also a lurking feeling that I might be found out at any moment. As if a stranger might come up to me and say, 'Hey, who are you? What are you doing here? You're not from round here.'

A fingerpost for the South Australia Museum caught my eye. Walking slowly through the Pacific Cultures galleries, I stopped for several minutes to study a shrunken head from Papua New Guinea, marvelling at its compact, sad beauty. Not that Archie would think so, I told myself. I felt like Archie was with me as I strolled round the galleries, constantly hearing his unprompted running commentary. Bloody barbarians, tried to drag them out of the dark ages and what use was it? Might as well have left them in the bloody jungle. But Archie hadn't said that, I reminded myself. Archie hadn't said anything. Not yet anyway. All the same, I made a note to avoid the subject of native culture when I headed back to my uncle's for the weekend.

Over the following days I attended a few meetings at the university and got over my jet lag. I also spent some time at the state archives. Walter Avery claimed he had settled in South Australia and bought a parcel of land with the proceeds from his memoir but I found no evidence that he had. I hoped it wasn't a sign of things to come.

*

When I arrived back at the house in Belair a few days later Nesta answered the door, this time wearing day clothes and looking brighter than earlier in the week. She had that toothy smile again. It seemed slightly forced, as if she were hiding something.

'Archie's in his den. Pop down – end of the corridor and down the stairs.'

I made my way down the wooden stairwell and told myself to stay calm, everything would be fine. My uncle sat in a well-worn armchair, legs crossed and a cigarette held slightly aloft and away from him. The room reminded me of a scout hut, all varnished wood panelling and scuffed old furniture. The walls were bare apart from a dartboard in one corner, its surface bristly like a doormat.

'So, you found your way alright?'

'Yes, sure, I think I've got my bearings now.'

'Good. Thought you might like to go for a drive, we can stop off at the club for a beer maybe?'

'Sounds good.'

There was no polite enquiry about how my first few days had gone and what I had been doing at the university. In some ways I felt relieved; I didn't have the energy to explain about student exchange programmes and reciprocal funding agreements. But I also felt disappointed. There was no chance to let Archie know what I did and what I knew; that I had a proper job.

As he drove, Archie explained about the club. I was content for him to talk and let his words wash over me. About twenty years ago, he said, he and a few cronies had purchased some land with a plan to build their own golf course. They did much of the clearance themselves, some by hand, but mostly with heavy plant which one of the cronies, a builder, owned already. With a long-term loan they developed a course and clubhouse.

'And it's just grown and grown,' Archie said. 'We're hosting the South Australian Open next year.' He turned into a long, brick-paved driveway lined with waxy shrubs, and parked in front of a small brass plaque embossed with the words 'Club Captain'.

I knew Archie played golf, knew he was fairly wealthy, but Club Captain of this place? I seemed to shrink into myself as we walked up a few steps and entered a long corridor. The green carpet was thick and expensive-looking with a patterned logo of two crossed golf clubs and some red lettering. On the left-hand wall was a series of photographs in gold metallic frames. I slowed my pace to look at them, noticing the similarities: all men, white, sixtyish, green blazer and gold tie. None of them looked distinguished, but their tight smiles said hard graft and ruthlessness. Look at me, they seemed to say, this is what a self-made man looks like. Below each photograph was the person's name and a range of years. The last frame was of my uncle: *Archibald Thomson 1994 –*.

Archie beckoned me into the bar where open French windows led onto a spacious, dark-wooded terrace with cushioned wicker chairs and glass-topped tables. The view overlooked a weed-free green; in its centre was a flagpole with a red number 18 stamped on a yellow flag. We sat side by side on a low sofa. A waiter appeared wearing a gold waistcoat and black bowtie.

'Good afternoon, Mr Thomson, what can I get for you, sir?'

'Jock, meet my nephew Jim – my favourite sister's son.'

We exchanged a few pleasantries and Archie ordered two bottles of local beer. I caught myself fidgeting with my watch strap and staring too intently at the list of club champions hanging on the wall in front of me. There was a dryness in my throat.

'So what do you think of it all?' I assumed Archie meant the golf club but I wasn't sure. In any case I couldn't tell him what I really thought. Not now.

'It's impressive. Different from what I was expecting.'

'In what way?' He knitted his brows.

'It's more, it's more… affluent. Distinguished maybe.'

'So what were you expecting – a public park hackabout?' Archie laughed but he wasn't smiling.

'No, not at all. But it seems… I don't know… the terrace, the furniture, the flower beds. Jock with his uniform. It's like how I imagine some fancy American country club.'

'Good, that's exactly what we set out to do.'

When I look back on it now, I wonder if I was more impressed than I admitted to myself. It was too easy for me to simply dismiss it all as vulgar. Yes, I'm sure there was a rush to judgment about self-made white men. All I could see was the club, the photographs, the waiter, the too-perfect golf course. And a sense that Archie had got it all by climbing over people, by pushing their faces in the dirt. I began to dislike the man. But it wasn't fair, it really wasn't fair at all.

Archie sipped his beer and sat back. 'So, you're staying until Sunday, then you're off to Melbourne, is that right?'

'Yes, I've got a meeting first thing Monday morning.'

'It's a long drive, you'd better set off early.'

'I'm looking forward to it, chance to see some of the country.'

Archie snorted. 'Nothing to see – unless you're fond of fields and sky. Still, it's a damn sight easier than driving through the outback.'

I tried again. 'Melbourne should be interesting though. Is that where you stayed when you first arrived?'

'That's right,' he said. 'But not for long.'

'And Nesta. Am I right in thinking you met on the ship?'

He put his glass down on the beer mat and licked his top lip.

'You'd best ask Nesta about all of that stuff – she's the family historian.'

He gave me a jaw-clenching smile and squeezed my shoulder. The pressure he applied was too much.

'Anyway, I'll show you some country worth seeing tomorrow. We'll head south, take a drive down to Victor Harbor. Last stop before you reach Antarctica.'

As we drove back to Belair in silence, all I could see was Archie's photograph staring back at me from the clubhouse wall.

*

Ewan returned from the fridge with two more beers. I was still struck by my cousin's appearance – six-two, six-three maybe. Not fat. Yes, a bit of a beer gut, but big and solid looking. And fair, very fair. I wondered where those genes came from. Not from Archie's side of the family. All the Thomson males I'd ever met were dark and slim.

We'd been sitting on Ewan's porch for a couple of hours in the dimming evening sun. It didn't take long to work out we had little in common. Sport was never going to be an easy option. Like Americans, most Australians don't do football and I had no interest in cricket or rugby. Neither did Ewan really. When he got the chance, he liked to drive north into the desert with his mates. They'd spend the weekend camping and spinning their utes over the gritty sand. 'I'm a petrol head,' he said, smiling shyly.

Ewan seemed a lot different from how I had imagined him. He was Archie and Nesta's son, after all. Shouldn't he be a corporate lawyer or a television producer or something? As if life were that straightforward. As if careers were simply a genetic progression from one generation to the next.

We were both divorced and Ewan had a ten-year-old son who he saw most weekends. I had no children. We drank more beer and the conversation loosened a little. I chose my words carefully.

'Your dad's certainly a character.'

Ewan laughed. 'That's putting it mildly.' Like his mother, his smile showed a row of even teeth. His voice was soft for a big man. 'You mean last night's performance?'

I began picking at the foil label on the neck of my beer bottle. 'Well, yes, I suppose so. I guess he's used to getting his own way.'

'Sure was – work, kids. I think he struggles now he's retired, and Hannah and I are all grown-up. No one to order around apart from Mum and she's so used to it, just humours him most of the time.'

'Not last night though.'

'No, not last night.'

When Archie had driven us back from the golf club I made an excuse about needing to write up some notes from my university meetings. It sounded plausible, I thought, as I headed to the granny flat, down a few stairs off the kitchen. I showered, dressed and lay on the bed trying to empty my mind. I wasn't used to socializing so much with people I hardly knew. My head throbbed a little and I felt myself dozing off when I was startled by Archie's raised voice through the wall. Shamelessly, I crept from the bed and cocked my ear to the door frame.

'For Christ's sake not a bloody Chinese takeaway. I've already booked a table for five at the club.'

'But, Archie, the kids hate going to the club, you know that.' Nesta's voice was gentle but weary. 'They just want something informal. Something fun. A chance to relax and get to know Jim. And anyway, it'll be six, Hannah's bringing Ross.'

'Not that bloody parasite. Freeloading as usual. Well he'd better bring his own beer because he's not drinking mine. The sooner she gets rid of him the better. Complete waster.'

'He's good for her Archie, for now. Yes, she'll grow out of him but he's helping her confidence.'

A door slammed and I lay back on the bed. My head throbbed more strongly and I felt that dryness in my throat again. For a moment I toyed with the idea of feigning illness. But I couldn't make excuses; this was an occasion I would have to deal with. Give it half an hour, I told myself, let things settle before you go through.

Ewan arrived first, parking his enormous silver ute on the kerbside. He seemed genuinely pleased to meet me and we spent a few minutes trying to remember when we had last seen each other. We reckoned it was about twenty-five years ago but neither of us was really sure. Some grand family tour of Wales and Scotland they'd done in a motorhome, I thought, but Ewan had been too young to remember.

Hannah turned up a few minutes later with her boyfriend. Ross was short and stocky, slightly hunched, with a weasely face and long, dark hair scraped back in a ponytail. He wore a white vest and baggy, patterned beach shorts. Hannah appeared nervous and I wondered if I was the cause of it. She bit her cracked, broken nails and rocked on the balls of her feet, pushing strands of thick dark hair behind her ears. The four of us stood making small talk in the lounge when Nesta appeared holding a laminated takeaway menu.

'Best get our order sorted if we want to eat this evening.'

Hannah grabbed the menu. Ross peered over her shoulder.

'We could start with some ribs, girl. What d'you think?'

My stomach lurched and I looked around the room for Archie. There was no sign of him. Hannah looked up from the menu.

'Let's just get a couple of big set meals. That way there's usually something for everyone.'

Ewan put his arm round his younger sister. 'Good idea, sis, I'm okay with that.'

'Where's Dad with all this though?' said Hannah, shielding one side of her face with the menu.

'Don't worry about him,' her brother said, 'he'll be fine with it.'

When the food arrived we sat around the long dining table unwrapping cartons. Nesta brought through paper plates, napkins and plastic cutlery. I heard Archie's footsteps on the wooden stairs coming up from his den. Hannah looked at her mother. A pleading look.

'Oh good, you've come at the right time, Archie. Pull up a chair, dear.'

He crossed the room and stood over the table, hands in pockets.

'So, you can see how the other half live. Eh, Jim?'

I felt everyone looking at me. My mouth was dry. I croaked, 'How lots of people live these days, I guess. It's fine with me, honestly. The food looks good.'

'Yes, and no doubt I'm the one paying for all of it.'

Nesta stroked her husband's arm, holding it gently by the wrist.

'Any chance of a drink, Archie? I'm sure we can stretch to something more than water from the tap.'

Archie became animated. 'What would you like, Jim? Beer? Victoria Bitter? Yes? That'll be four beers and a glass of white wine for Nesta.'

I felt very thirsty. I wanted that beer now. Archie returned from the esky and made a show of setting the drinks down before each person, reciting the order as he went.

'Dad, you've missed out Ross,' Hannah whispered.

'Did I? Well that's funny. I thought Ross was bringing his own beer. In fact, I thought Ross was restocking the esky after he drank a whole bloody case the last time he was here and not a word of thanks. Isn't that right, Ross?'

I wanted to laugh. A nervous laugh. I covered my mouth with my hand. Ross looked at Hannah, then Ewan, then his food. I fixed my gaze on Ross. Don't look at Archie, I told myself.

Archie leaned in towards him, spittle forming in the corners of his mouth. 'Has Ross lost his tongue? Or is he too busy eating my food to answer me?'

'Dad, please! Give it a break!' Hannah's voice sounded desperate.

'Okay, okay, fair enough. Only because I have a guest in my house. You see what I have to put up with, Jim? Me, that worked himself into the ground for this family.'

Archie took the plate of food offered by Nesta and walked back downstairs to his den. Hannah fetched Ross a beer from the esky. Nesta began to talk about an art exhibition she was involved with. The rest of us ate quietly and appeared to listen.

*

Ewan rocked back in the cheap plastic chair. Darkness had closed in. Large insects buzzed noisily around dim lights set into the tin roof of the porch. The huge, silver ute stood in silhouette on a worn patch of grass in the yard. I leaned back, shaking my head.

'And yet today, when we went to Victor Harbor, he was… generous.'

'Because you're special to him, mate.'

Well, he has a funny way of showing it, I thought.

Ewan went on. 'It's your mum. Dad's always looked up to her, used to talk about her a lot when we were growing up. How she always took care of him when he was a kid. And there's something else. I'm not sure, I guess you're an example of what he expected me to be – educated, successful, doing a professional job.'

I snorted. 'I hardly think so. I'm just an average academic. I'm not a merchant banker or something.'

'No, but you're not a truck mechanic who went to a private school, either.'

'So long as you're happy, what does it matter what you do?'

'Try telling Dad that. No seriously, it might help me a bit.'

Throughout my childhood I heard bits and pieces about Archie's life from my mother and aunts. He wrote regularly and Christmas cards arrived with long, round-robin letters from Nesta. They always seemed to be doing exciting things. I used to make up stories about Archie flying on business trips to Japan where the people wore traditional costumes and bowed deeply to my uncle when he stepped off the plane. Or I imagined Nesta singing at the new opera house in Sydney; there were endless encores with her clutching huge bouquets and waving to the beaming audience.

And the climate. Their letters were always full of sunshine. From these scraps I built a whole fantasy world in far-off, exotic Australia where Uncle Archie had made a good life for himself. It all seemed such a far cry from an Edinburgh council estate.

I had met him a few times. How many, I couldn't say. Mostly he was on his own, travelling to Europe on business, making time to stop off in Edinburgh for a day or two. And I had met Nesta and the children once when they did their grand tour of Wales and Scotland.

So, by the time I travelled to Australia, I knew some facts. Archie had trained as a butcher in Edinburgh and sailed to Australia in the mid-fifties on the Assisted Passage Scheme – he was a ten-pound Pom. His ship docked in Melbourne and at some point he married Nesta. Later, they moved to Adelaide where Archie became sales director of a large canned food business. He played golf. And he smoked. That was about it as far as the facts went.

There were other stories, but I wasn't sure how reliable they were. I'm a historian so I need to be sure about sources of information. Primary sources, checking and cross-checking the facts – all part of my stock-in-trade, after all. I can't afford to go speculating about things.

I took another swig of beer. A large moth, too large for my liking, fluttered around one of the lights.

'So, is it true your mum and dad met on the journey out to Australia?'

Ewan laughed. 'I've no idea, mate. They've never really talked about it. I think I asked them once but couldn't get any sense out of them. So I lost interest.'

'I heard something about your mum going out to Australia with her fiancé?'

Ewan rocked back again and puffed out his cheeks. 'Who knows. Dad said something about telling Mum he was going to make his fortune and her being impressed. But that might have been after they arrived here. And Mum was coming out to start a new life anyway.'

'As a singer?'

'Yes, apparently she'd been offered a place to study at the university in Sydney. The conservatorium or something.'

I tilted my head back and stared at the stars, bright against the inky sky.

'How on earth do you begin to know the truth?' I said.

Ewan threw his hands up and shrugged. 'Who knows, mate. And what does it matter anyway? However they got together, we're still here drinking beer on the porch.'

It was getting late and I needed to make an early start for Melbourne in the morning. Ewan called a taxi and we stood on the pavement waiting. We shook hands and I waved briefly as the taxi driver reversed and headed up to Belair.

Before I went to bed I packed my bags. I felt a little guilty about my sense of elation at leaving. The last two days had been draining. I also felt dissatisfied. Archie and Nesta were nagging at me. I'd barely had a chance to get to know my uncle. Yes, he'd been generous with his time and with his money. He'd also been abrasive and rude on occasions. My cousin's words about how Archie and Nesta met came back to me: what does it matter, anyway? But it did matter, it mattered to *me*. They were such an odd couple – the philistine, self-made businessman and the sophisticated, arty opera singer. There was also a huge gulf between the uncle I'd just spent the weekend with and my childhood fantasy of the man. I wanted to piece together his story.

Nesta too. Always in the background, appearing to defer to Archie. But how she behaved on the bluff at Victor Harbor earlier in the day, that was a whole different matter, as if she wanted to confess something.

Still, it would be good to hit the road. As I lay in bed all I could see were miles and miles of fields and blue sky.

*

The Dukes Highway was deserted at seven o'clock on that Sunday morning. I cruised through the flat grassland under a low, baby blue sky. It felt good to be eating up the road, on my way to somewhere new. I knew little about Melbourne except that it was a hell of a long drive from Adelaide. There was no practical reason for me to drive there at all. I could have taken a flight but the lure of the open road was too great.

I passed through small towns whose names – Tailem Bend, Coonalpyn, Tintanara – promised more than they delivered. They all looked the same to me with their roadside petrol stations, bakeries and cafés. The local radio station pumped out country music punctuated with farming and weather news. I stood it for a while then switched off. My thoughts turned to Walter Avery even though I was a long way from where I would do my research. Part of me was impatient to get to Canberra where it would start in earnest. But I was also content to ease my way into Australia, to let my senses absorb the place.

My earlier elation on leaving Adelaide had waned and the endless flat road, flat sky and parched roadside scrub seemed to affect my mood. Fragments from the past few days flitted in and out of my mind and, slowly, I began to piece them together. I thought about the big scene on Friday evening when Archie tore into Ross. I thought about Ewan and felt sorry for him. And for Hannah, too. They seemed damaged somehow, like they were struggling to find their own way; that whatever they did would never be good enough, at least not for their father.

And then I thought about Archie, my exotic uncle from far away Australia. How little he lived up to my image of him. Those rare occasions in my childhood when he turned up in Edinburgh for a few days, interrupting some important European business trip to make time for us. In my mind he was driving a sporty Ford Capri, which I guessed he picked up at the airport. Then he would park the car at a swish hotel where some bellboy in a smart uniform greeted him and called him sir. Flying into an airport, hiring a car, staying at a smart hotel – these things sound ordinary enough now but back then, where I came from, it was definitely exotic. It was an event, something you could use to gain points for credibility but only if word spread far enough. *There's Jim*, I wanted my schoolmates to say, *Jim with the uncle in Australia.*

Compared with a pebble-dashed semi in an Edinburgh council estate, Australia seemed almost mythical. I felt I knew so much about it from my book, the one Archie gave me. I knew the shape of the country – like the head of a West Highland terrier in profile; its remoteness, stuck in the bottom right-hand corner of the world map; its unique fauna and flora – eucalyptus trees, kangaroos and koalas; the sheer enormity of its landmass. It may as well have been another planet. Lying on my candlewick bedspread, chin resting on my palms with the book open in front of me, I devoured information about population, political systems, major industries, infrastructure projects, leisure and tourism. I understood none of it, but it must have seeped into my consciousness.

The book was called *Spotlight on Australia*. Archie gave it to me on one of his visits to Edinburgh in the late sixties. I have kept it ever since. I even skimmed through it shortly before flying out to Adelaide. Let's just say it was 'of its time'. In the entire book there is one photograph of an Aboriginal person, a head and shoulders shot of a man with the caption: 'the striking features of the Australian aborigine are clearly shown here.' Uluru was still labelled Ayers Rock and an aerial photograph of Sydney showed the site for a daringly designed opera house to be built on Bennelong Point.

I wished I had dug out the book earlier and spent more time studying it before I left Sheffield. It had no relevance to my research here. But something in me connected the book with Archie. Not because he gave it to me, more that it seemed to capture a point in time; a confident white man's sense of a country caught up in the great sweep of modernism, just when Archie was making his way here. And perhaps because the book helped shape my childhood imaginings about Australia, that life could be far more exciting somewhere else.

I spent ages studying details of the photographs in the book: busy street scenes in Adelaide; modern restaurants in Melbourne; riverside shopping malls in Brisbane, and Sydney ferries docking at Circular Quay. And always, I peered at the people in the shots, trying to catch sight of Archie.

2

Mediterranean, 1955

Late afternoon clouds gathered over Vesuvius as the ship made its way south, the white mass of Naples shrinking with each shudder of the engines. Even this close to shore the wind was picking up. The *Fairsea* started to roll a little, sending groups of passengers inside. Some headed to their dormitories, others went in search of something to pass the time for a few hours before the restaurant and bar opened. A game of cards or skittles if they were lucky; there wouldn't be any organised activities on deck, not when they'd just left port.

Archie stayed on the promenade deck, resting his forearms on the rusty white rail. A fruity voice whispered loudly in his ear.

'Leaving Naples, end of the known world. What now, eh?'

He turned to the short, stocky man in khakis who waited expectantly as if Archie had an answer worth hearing. Archie said nothing and shifted his gaze landwards again. After a while the man shrugged and walked towards the stern.

What now, indeed? Port Said the itinerary said, then through the Suez Canal and the Red Sea to Aden. They were six days in and still had four more weeks at sea ahead. Too early to go speculating about what lay in front of them. You had to play the long game. But it wasn't easy with so much time to kill, even more so with Billy laid on his bunk day after day, groaning and heaving into a tin pail. He wasn't the only one. The stench of sick hung in the stale air of the dormitories, the toilets and the corridors, mingling with diesel fumes from the engines.

The *Fairsea* was an old troop ship hastily and cheaply refitted after the war for its new life ferrying thousands of ten-pound Poms to Australia. Open dormitories segregated men and women. Husbands and wives split up, families split up. And the toilets – best not to think about them. Worst of all, the ship had no stabilisers. Crossing the Bay of Biscay had been carnage, dozens still laid low, recovering slowly in the calmer waters of the Mediterranean.

Laughter. Archie glanced along the deck. A man and a woman arm in arm, her leaning into him, sheltering from the wind as they walked his way. She had a heavy-looking scarf at her neck in spite of the warm spring sunshine. He'd seen them before in the restaurant, caught the sound of their voices. Welsh, he thought. She had a round, open face with prominent teeth when she spoke. The tooth fairy, he called her. Early twenties, Archie's age, but the man was older. Not old enough to be her father but old enough to draw attention. The odd comment maybe. No rings on the important fingers so Archie wasn't really sure what their relationship was. But now, arm in arm, her laughing and leaning into him, it was crystal clear. Pleased with himself, Archie thought. He turned his gaze back to the land, avoiding any chance of eye contact as they passed.

Why did it bother him? None of his business. If he was honest with himself, he would admit to feeling envious. Not jealous, that would come later. Going out to start a new life in Australia was hard. Sure, he was with Billy, his best friend since childhood. They had made a joint decision to give it a go. What was there to lose, after all? Archie working all hours hacking carcasses in the butcher's, Billy eking out a living as a jobbing plumber. No wives or girlfriends, both of them living at home with their parents. But the prospect of going out there with a woman – a wife or fiancée, even – that was a different matter. You would be sharing an adventure properly, certain that you were starting new lives together.

He didn't envy the husbands and wives with families in tow. Every day he saw them struggling to keep an eye on the children, trying not to lose patience in face of their constant demands. But he could picture himself standing at the rail with his arm around someone, gazing out to sea, excited as they made plans. Archie stubbed out his cigarette on the rail and flicked the butt overboard.

When he got back to the dormitory, Billy was awake, sitting up in his bottom bunk. He looked better than he had since they entered the Bay of Biscay.

'How are you feeling, big man?'

'Aw, a bit better. Might manage something to eat later. What have you been up to?'

'Just enjoying the sea air. Saying goodbye to Naples.'

'And making plans no doubt, if I know you.'

'Aye, maybe. I'm thinking things might be about to take a turn for the better.'

'Is that right? Well, calmer waters would help for a start.'

Yes, calmer waters would be good. Archie felt a flutter in his stomach. Once again, that image forced itself to the front of his mind: Ma and Pa on the platform at Waverley station as the train pulled out. Her heavy coat flapping in the wind, one hand over her mouth, the other half-raised in a solemn wave. Was it guilt he felt or was it just part of the adjustment out here in this watery no man's land, caught between the known and the unknown? Try as he might, he couldn't picture Australia at all.

But he could picture Leith alright, in all its dirty-sooted drabness. He did not miss it one bit. But maybe that isn't surprising when you're sailing across the Mediterranean on a fresh spring afternoon. Missing it would come later, he thought, if at all.

*

Archie recognised the sound of Johnnie Ray's voice, a tinny crackle as it came through the speakers in the sun lounge. Some crew members moved tables and chairs closer to the walls, freeing up the centre of the room as a makeshift dance floor. Archie sat waiting for Billy at a table next to the toilets. Just to be on the safe side – Billy was getting better but you never knew. The bar area was lined with men speaking in English accents. More south than north, Archie thought. One or two of them wore ties and were drinking shorts even though it was just after seven thirty.

Johnnie Ray kept on crying about his heartaches. The last time Archie heard the song was at the Eldorado three weeks ago. He thought Johnnie wouldn't have been too impressed by the resident crooner that night, whose Leith vowels chewed the lyrics to shreds. The evening was meant to be a kind of send-off for him and Billy. Archie half-expected a decent turnout. There was a lot of talk about them signing up as ten-pound Poms, after all. But when he thought about it now, most of the talk had been at home or came from customers in McKay's, the butcher where he worked. And there was some talk at his local too, but that tailed off pretty quickly. Maybe it was envy, maybe people had their own lives to be getting on with. Or maybe they all kept their thoughts and feelings to themselves. That's what people did in Leith, didn't they? Christ, you could have set most of them down at the gates of Belsen and they would have said, 'Aye, that's no' sae good,' and carried on with their business. Most of them needed a good shake, Archie thought.

On the night of the send-off the Eldorado crowd broke up at ten o'clock as usual. Most of them were heading up town to the Palais de Danse in Fountainbridge for the late session. Archie remembered standing in the damp, dark toilets, inhaling the reek of stale beer and piss, and thinking how glad he was to be leaving this place. All of it. How Australia would be like starting a new life altogether.

The sun lounge was filling up. Younger couples drifted in after their evening meals and gentle strolls on deck. They joined the core of men who stood at the bar or sat at tables nearby. Later, some of the older couples might make it after the children had settled or if they managed to arrange a sitter.

The music stopped, ready for Bastoni's Quartet. The band did some final soundchecks and tuning. People talked quietly at their tables. It was too early for raised voices, even from the crowd hanging around at the bar. It seemed that calmer waters had improved people's moods, for now.

Billy stepped into the room. Archie, with his back to the wall, gave him a short wave. His friend walked up to the bar, looking at Archie and waggling his fat hand round an imaginary pint glass. Archie nodded.

Billy lowered the pints on the table and sat down facing Archie. The band started up with Glenn Miller's 'Little Brown Jug'. Billy leaned over.

'Bloody hell, you'd think it was still war time.'

Archie caught the words but he was looking across the room at the tooth fairy. She sat down in the opposite corner at a table near the band. Her companion, the older man, leaned over her then headed to the bar. She reached for her handbag and took out a compact. She gave her nose a quick dab then snapped the compact and put it back in the bag. Her slender neck moved slightly as her eyes took in the room. Then she turned sideways and joined in faint clapping for the band as they stretched the final chord.

Archie forced himself to switch his gaze to the bar. The companion pocketed his change and strode confidently back to the table. He carried a small glass in each hand. Not a beer drinker then.

Billy put his glass down and tapped it. He raised his voice above the music. 'I see you find my conversation riveting as usual.'

Archie stared at him, cleared his throat. 'Sorry, Billy. I was just thinking.' The sound of the brass was beginning to make his head ache.

Billy snorted. 'More like looking than thinking from where I'm sitting. What's caught your eye? And don't say "nothing". Or maybe I'll just turn round and take a look myself?'

Archie nudged his glass to the side, leaned forward with his forearms on the table. He shouted confidentially.

'Alright. I'm curious. There's a couple just sat down, over near the band. I've seen them on deck a few times and in the restaurant. She looks about our age but he's much older. No rings on their fingers. I thought maybe he was her old man or her uncle. But then I saw them on deck all cosied up like they were an item. That's all.'

Billy took a deep breath as if he was ready to make a speech. 'I was going to say, "and what's it to you?" but something tells me you're taking more than a passing interest. Something tells me you've taken a shine to the lass. And that's why you said things might be about to take a turn for the better. Am I right?'

'Aw, come on, Billy. I'm allowed to look am I not? As I said, I'm just curious.'

'Well make sure it doesn't go beyond curiosity. I'm just starting to feel better and I want to try and enjoy the rest of the voyage. I don't want any hassle.'

Archie nodded but when Billy headed to the toilets, he couldn't resist looking across the room again. She wore a square-necked, sleeveless cream dress, with what looked like a pattern of small blue flowers. It went well with her wispy, fair hair, he thought. A pale blue cardigan was draped across her shoulders. The heavy scarf had gone and Archie's eyes lingered on the curve of her neck. She fingered the short glass but didn't drink from it. Stylish. Too young for the companion, too good for him. But maybe too good for Archie too? Something different stirred in him. He knew it wasn't lust. Or not only lust. A tingling in his stomach. His heart beating faster and louder as if he was nervous. He almost felt sick.

The band eased their way into 'Moonlight Serenade'. The companion stood up, took her hand and led her to the edge of the dance floor. They waited for two couples to waltz by before taking the floor.

Billy came back to the table, sweat trickling down his cheeks.

'Sorry. I'm not feeling too good again. I think I'll call it a night.'

Archie stood up, made a show of finishing his pint and rapped the empty glass on the table. It made no sound above the music and the noise of people's voices. But he heard it clearly in his mind.

'Aye, me too. Let's get out of here.'

*

It was still early. After Archie had seen Billy to his bunk he climbed the stairs to the boat deck. Occasional bursts of laughter from the deck below. A metal door banging. But up here, nothing. If there were other people around, they were staying quiet. Not even a giggle from the lifeboats but it was probably a bit early for that. The wind had dropped to a whisper. Low clouds moistened the air.

He lit a cigarette and listened to the engines droning, pushing the ship through the darkening sea. What were these new feelings? A sense of wanting something like he had never wanted anything before? Yes, but more than that. A sense of purpose, a clear view? Like watching a film of the rest of his life unfolding. Possibilities. He couldn't find the words to express it but he tried again. Maybe it was fearlessness. Or? He laughed inwardly, looked left and right in case someone heard his thoughts. Or love? Now there was a word never spoken. Not at home, not at school, not in the pub or the dance hall. Or rather, it was spoken at home but only about God and Jesus. Nobody said they *loved* another person. Nobody would *love* to see that new film at the pictures. Nobody would *love* another helping of Ma's clootie dumpling. Nobody has prepared me for these feelings, he thought.

Archie felt his childhood had been ruled by don'ts as if life was something to be avoided. Or something to be endured. Ma and Pa seemed afraid of everything. They were afraid of God, afraid of the Devil, afraid of the church. They were afraid of losing face, afraid of saying the wrong thing in front of their betters. They were afraid of want, afraid of showiness, afraid of disease. He knew he was being unfair about some of it, at least. Sometimes he envied his parents' faith, their certainty. But all the same, it was a God-fearing faith which suffocated you if you let it. Ma's favourite sayings rang in his ears: may God strike you down; the Devil will get you for that; wash your mouth out.

A couple of years back, word got about when Archie started dating Irene Kay who worked in Galbraith's draper's shop in the Kirkgate. They knew each other from school and mingled with the same crowd at the Eldorado most Friday nights. When Ma found out, she had her opinions on the Kay family readily to hand: infrequently seen at the kirk but Elsie Kay was known to work hard and keep a clean house. All the same, Ma wanted her three daughters who still lived at home to provide chapter and verse on the girl Irene. And when they did, Ma's judgment was blunt. Irene was a Jezebel, she said, known to wear make-up to work, the clarty so and so. Fortunately for Archie, and for Ma, his relationship with Irene was going nowhere and ended on friendly terms after a month or two. Fortunate for Irene too, he thought.

Archie was the youngest of five brothers and five sisters. By the time he was born in the early thirties, Ma had been pregnant off and on for more than twenty years. When Archie appeared, his eldest brother was already married, and Archie had a niece who was two years older than himself. Sometimes he wondered why he had been conceived at all. The first four children to survive infancy were boys, followed by the five girls. They had all been born at regular two-year intervals but there was a five-year gap between Archie and his sister Mary. What were Ma and Pa doing? Were they trying to even the score between boys and girls? That would be strange enough, but stranger still with eleven of them squeezed into a three-bedroomed, first-floor tenement, albeit in a decent part of Leith.

When Archie was eight, all four of his brothers were called up to serve in the army. From wartime until he left for Australia, his home life was dominated by women.

The boys all survived their wars in North Africa, in Italy, in France and Germany. Looking back on it, he thought his brothers might have been changed by the war, by having to confront fear, by having lives full of do's rather than don'ts. Three of them got white-collar jobs and the chance to build careers in engineering, insurance and surveying. They came back, settled down again, thanked their lucky stars and never, ever talked about the war, or not to him. The fourth son, Bob, couldn't settle into anything except marriage and having children with his wife, Jessie.

Maybe his brothers *had* changed but Archie was much too young to talk to them in that way. By the time he left for Australia he had never even drunk a pint in a pub with any of them.

Archie lit another cigarette. There was a chill in the air now. A light wind allowed a waxing moon to glow behind a thinning curtain of cloud. He leaned over the rail and looked beyond the bough at the endless, inky sea and darkness. The whole world was ahead of him, and he was racing towards it, ready to grab it. There it was again, that tingling in his stomach, and a steeliness in his gut, too. The corners of his mouth turned upwards for the first time in weeks. There was nobody there to see it. Not yet.

3

Adelaide, 1997

Some mornings, like this one, she wakes early and thinks of the ship. In half-sleep she pulls the duvet up under her chin and lies back. She imagines her head tilted to the stars under a heavy blanket of sky. If only. If only she had headed straight to bed instead of going up on deck, unable to resist the silver dark sea. Unwilling to resist the sparkling sky, unwilling to resist anything. And later, if only she hadn't lingered, both hands on the rail, feeling the motion of the ship sailing across the map just like he said. But she had done all that, and more, and lived with the consequences for forty years.

Shuffling the duvet, Nesta kicks her right leg clear and lets it dangle over the edge of the bed. What other life could she have lived? It is comforting to doze a while and let her mind roam. But her speculation never leads her very far. Perhaps life hasn't been so bad. After all, sooner or later she would have had to marry someone once she got here. In those days you couldn't arrive as a single woman and expect to make a decent life for yourself. Not even in her position. No, you needed to get hitched as soon as possible and she knows it could have been worse. He'd never hit her. And in a funny way, he'd never really tried to control her. It was like an unwritten agreement between them – you do your thing and I'll do mine. Over the years, they had ploughed their own furrows, meeting occasionally to have children, to move home and to take family holidays. She is exaggerating, of course, but there is precious little glue left between them. Just enough to stop the core of their lives from coming apart. And if, as time passes, he has become more of a burden, isn't that to be expected of most husbands?

She hears his rasping cough, his slippers slapping on the floorboards. The sound of him hacking up a night's worth of phlegm into the wash hand basin. Harder to doze now but plenty of reasons for pretending to. Her train of thought is lost so she tries a different tack. What is the real story then, the one they never tell at dinner parties, at business functions, at charity balls? We met on the ship, you know. We were both gazing at the stars as we crossed the Mediterranean and it was love at first sight! No, not that one. Or, the ship lurched, I almost fell overboard, and this handsome stranger saved me. Said it must be fate, we could make a wonderful life together! No, none of that, none of that at all. And there's the story she's never told *him*, the one she thought she'd buried for good. Strange though, how the tales we tell ourselves, and others, grow with the passage of time. We rewrite them and edit them until they become settled, published versions in our minds. And the more we do that, the more we lose sight of the real stories, what really happened.

Sighing deeply, she swings her other leg out of bed, puts on her dressing gown and slippers and shuffles down the hall. In the kitchen she fills the kettle and rolls up the blind. Outside, a thin, milky sky bleeds into the darkness. How she hates this time of the morning when other people's words and actions and demands are about to break into her day. At least today will be different, she will make sure of that. A chance to make amends, for a start. A chance for Archie to redeem himself after last night's performance. Poor Ross, why did Archie have to pick on him like that? Maybe he did have a point. Ross was a bit of a freeloader, after all. And then there was the letter too, of course. Understandably, Archie was on edge after it arrived at lunchtime. But nonetheless, there were better, more subtle, ways to deal with Ross and not least with Jim there. Yes, a chance to make amends. They had promised to take Jim on a trip down to Victor Harbor today.

These days the old whaling station is all cafés and seafood restaurants in carefully weathered shacks strung along the waterfront. You can sit in the shade on a verandah watching pelicans and listening to the breakers roll up from Antarctica. And walk up to the bluff at the southern end of the bay. Rosetta Head it's called, where the women used to keep watch for schools of Southern Right whales and signal down to the men in the harbour, ready to launch their boats. How the sea must have turned red, she thinks. How the waves must have broken on the shore like frothing blood.

She would like to climb the bluff today. Archie won't. Or rather, Archie's lungs can't. But Jim might like to stretch his legs and admire the view. It will be a chance to talk to him alone, to get to know him better. When Archie is around no one else gets a look in. From what she's seen so far, Jim appears pleasant enough but a bit reserved. A bit po-faced perhaps, like his mother. But that's being unkind and last night wasn't the time to judge him. It will be good to find out more about Jim and his life back in Britain. How odd to meet someone again after more than twenty years. Jim must have been no more than ten or eleven when she last saw him in Edinburgh. Yes, she looks forward to getting to know her nephew better.

She waits until she hears Archie whistling in the hall, her signal to slip the teabags into their mugs.

*

On the way down to Victor Harbor she sits in the back of the car, tries to switch off from Archie's running commentary to Jim. She has heard it all before on this journey. It has been told to her distant cousins, friends, cousins of friends and friends of cousins. The vineyard in McLaren Vale, the boat on the Murray estuary. Only this time, she detects something different about Archie's voice. Usually, it's laconic, trying a little too hard to be casual. As if it's all nothing – after all, who wouldn't own a stake in a vineyard or moor a boat on the Murray river? But, with Jim, he sounds more earnest. He's telling Jim a story so that his nephew can take it back home and tell it to his mother, to his aunts, to anyone else in the family who Archie wants to reach.

She is not surprised. After all these years, Jim is the first of Archie's family from Britain to visit them in Australia. There is a lot to show, a lot of information to get across to Jim – Jim the messenger. But how do you cover it all? How do you curate this exhibition of their lives over the past forty years? Well, Archie knows only one way: he uses material wealth, real things. You can't touch all of them. You can't touch the vineyard but you can drive past it through the rolling country. You can't touch the boat because it's been sold now. But you can look out of the car window at the widening estuary and see other boats, wonder how Archie's compared – bigger or smaller?

She thinks Jim looks intimidated by how relentlessly Archie talks about their successes. Or perhaps Jim is bored, it's hard to tell. He doesn't give much away.

She wonders: if I were curating our lives, what would I choose to put on display? She starts with what Archie has left out. He has left out the children. Her eyes moisten a little and she runs her index finger across her eyelashes. Ewan and Hannah are not broken exactly but they're certainly not whole. Archie assesses them by using his own favourite measures: status and money. In both cases the children are a disappointment to him. She is familiar with his bewilderment. She's heard it often enough. How do we spend a fortune on private schools and end up with a truck mechanic and a secretary? Because you fucked them up, that's why. She has never said as much, or not in those terms. But she has been consistent in telling him where he went wrong and the effect it has had on their children. She traces it back to the factory lock-out. 'That's where it all started, Archie,' she's told him more than once.

The children were old enough to know what was going on. Archie was manager of a canned fruit factory in upstate Victoria. It was a small town and the plant was the largest employer. In those days, Ewan and Hannah went to the local school where many of their classmates were children of factory workers. There was a labour dispute, something to do with reductions in guaranteed overtime hours. Archie told her the changes were necessary, too many people were getting paid for too many hours. The whole plant could be more efficient and needed to be.

After a stand-off between Archie and the local shop steward, a strike ballot was called, and the workers walked out on a Friday morning. The end of the week was pay day, of course, and Archie locked up the factory late Friday morning, after handing out the wages due for that week. Over the weekend, men from the factory – they were mostly men – gathered outside pubs and bookies to shout the odds and stiffen their resolve.

At school the following Monday, Ewan and Hannah were name-called, spat on and threatened by their classmates. She can still see the scene clearly. The children in tears, burying their heads in her chest as she sat on the sofa. Her shouting at Archie that they must take the children out of school until the strike is over. And his response: what, and let them think we're scared? Let them win? Over my dead body!

Every day, Ewan and Hannah endured the abuse walking to school, at playtimes, lunch breaks and walking home. The strike dragged on for two more weeks until the union conceded and accepted the new conditions.

She laughs silently. And who won in the end? Well Archie won, of course. Within months they were on their way to Adelaide on the back of Archie's promotion. She remembers the journey to their new home, her driving all the way. In the rear-view mirror, she sees the children on the back seat clutching their favourite soft toys much too tightly.

Archie and Jim laugh briefly, trespassing on her thoughts. Her husband catches her eye in the rear-view mirror. 'Penny for them,' he says.

*

A galah's strangled whistle pierces the silence and wakes her. She spots the bird's pink plumage in the blue gum which shades this side of the terrace. The magazine she was reading lies on the liver-coloured tiles as if it's been thrown there or fallen from a tree. She looks at her watch. Goodness, just gone eight, how long was that? Half an hour or more. Must have needed it.

They only wanted a snack after eating well at Victor Harbor. Archie has gone to the golf club. He dropped Jim at Ewan's house on the way. They're probably out on Ewan's porch, making free with the beer. She hauls herself upright using the arms of the chair. Her right knee cracks a little as she straightens up and she pushes her shoulders back, hands on hips. And the fronts of her thighs are stiff too. Must be from the walk up to the bluff.

She fills the pink watering can at the outside tap and begins to sprinkle the pots. It's not a steep walk up to the bluff. Still, she did take Jim's arm on the first section. I'm not sure what to make of him, she thinks. Good manners, civil, quiet. Is that it? She wants a bit more from her nephew but she is struggling to find something. At times, it felt like having a conversation with her bank manager. He didn't want to talk about his marriage, he made that clear enough.

But on the other hand, when the chance presented itself, he was quick enough to ask about how she and Archie met. According to Jim, Archie had appointed her as official family historian. 'I heard somewhere that you met on the ship,' her nephew said. His remark caught her off guard. Perhaps it was being on the bluff with its views of the deep, dark ocean or perhaps her early morning memories were still fresh in her mind. Anyway, it was unlike her to get upset. And then to… what?… to almost confide in this young man. He seemed embarrassed by what she said.

She has watered all the pots and returns the can neatly to its place by the conservatory door. Time to flush these thoughts from her mind. As it is, she spends too many hours going over the past. But then, that's what Louise tells her to do, isn't it? She hears the phone ringing in the conservatory. It's Hannah, in tears. Ross has dumped her after last night's shenanigans. Or rather, Ross has dumped Hannah's family, by which he means Archie. 'It's them or me,' he told her. So Hannah chooses her family. 'I like Ross, for all his faults,' Hannah says. 'But.' There's a pause. But what? *But Dad pays the rent on your apartment downtown*, she wants to tell her daughter. 'But he's not worth sacrificing my family for,' Hannah says. Her mother nods at the wall but says nothing.

Later, she pours a glass of wine and sits at the table in the conservatory. It's hard for her to believe that Hannah will be thirty in a couple of years. How can she almost reach thirty and still be financially dependent on her parents? Archie's too soft. Surely Hannah would learn quickly enough if she was forced to rent some run-down place up in the northern suburbs. That would sort her out. At her age I was... she has to think. At her daughter's age she was touring the state capitals with the Elizabethan opera company. Where was Ewan? she wonders. Then she remembers that he came along later, after Archie tried to put his foot down.

4

Melbourne, 1997

I first caught sight of Melbourne from twenty miles away. Across the plain its cluster of high-rise buildings shimmered in the afternoon haze. From this distance, the city announced itself as bigger, taller and ritzier than sleepy, dignified Adelaide.

By the time I got onto the central ring road I was flagging. More than ten hours on the road and three since my last stop. So it was no surprise when I took a wrong turn. I cursed my poor navigation as I drove aimlessly, looking for a place to park up and check the map. Eventually, I pulled over at the side of the road next to a café. A large man with a thick grey beard sat on a plastic crate outside. He wore a white vest and a pair of formal-looking trousers.

I turned to the pages at the back of the road map where they have street plans for the centres of major cities. But the turn-off where I'd gone wrong was too far out from the city centre to be on the plan. I heard three raps on the passenger side window, leaned over and wound it down.

'You need some help?' The man poked his head in, grey chest hair spilling out of his vest.

I nodded and got out. A painted sign above the door read Kangaroo Café and underneath, in smaller letters: *Fasoulakis Bros, proprietors.* The man opened the door into the café. 'Please, please,' he said, sweeping me in with his hand.

'You like a drink? You want to use the toilet?'

'Just a coffee, please. And yes, I would.'

When I came back, he was standing behind the counter with a mug in his thick, fleshy hand. 'What do you like? Glyko? Metrio? Sketo?'

'No sugar, please. Sketo.' I sat down at the nearest table.

'Ah, bravo. You speak Greek. Kala.'

He set the coffee down on the table along with a tumbler of water and sat opposite me. 'So, where are you going?' he asked. After I told him, he reached across, took a pen and a paper bag from the counter and drew a map. First left, straight on at the traffic lights then left at the junction. Back to the inner ring road.

And then the real questions began. Where are you from? Where are you going? Do you have a family? A wife? Children? What work do you do? It struck me that he showed more interest in me than Archie and Nesta had. I asked about his own family, how long they had been in Melbourne. 'I am second generation,' he said. They came out from Crete in nineteen fifty, after the civil war. He was fifteen years old. His wife died of cancer ten years ago and his brother had dropped dead from a heart attack last year. But his children and grandchildren were close by.

'You must like it here if you've stayed for this long,' I said.

'Here is home,' he said, looking around and spreading his arms like some ancient orator. He leaned towards me, his massive forearm spread across the table. 'I love Crete but I could never have gone back there. This country took my family in. Of course it was difficult at first with nothing. Nothing. But you work hard and you find something. You find a way to live. I am happy here.'

He stood up and clapped me on the shoulder. 'So,' he said, 'you must enjoy your stay in Australia. Look around, make the most of it.'

I asked how much I owed him for the coffee but he just squeezed the top of my arm. 'When I come to visit you,' he whispered, 'you will make me coffee too.' I promised him I would.

*

Later, after checking in at the hotel and showering, I walked down King Street towards the Yarra river. I was surprised by the seediness of shops and cafés but perhaps they were made to look worse by the adjacent massage parlours. It was a long way from the picture I had imagined back home of colonial buildings, trams and leafy, manicured parks. A long way too, from the photographs in the book Archie had given me. I caught a glimpse of some of that old Melbourne when I turned into Flinders Street, heard a clanging tram bell and saw the yellow façade of the station. After sitting in the car for so long, I needed to stretch my legs. I walked steadily up St Kilda Road in early evening sun and into the botanic gardens. I had an urge to find some flying foxes and when I did, I sat alone on a bench watching a group of them hanging from branches like giant, grey aubergines, seemingly oblivious to the sights and sounds of the city.

Back at the hotel, I dined early in the restaurant, too tired to head out into town again. I got a little drunk on a bottle of chardonnay, went back to my room and lay on the bed.

I found myself drifting back to the day before when Archie and Nesta drove me down to Victor Harbor. We ate lunch in a fish restaurant right on the seafront. From our table on the scrubbed, wooden terrace, we watched waves roll in from the breakwater. Groups of pelicans bobbed in the swell and sat on wooden posts drying their wings.

On the road down from Adelaide we had passed through McLaren Vale where Archie said he owned a stake in a vineyard. And when we skirted the estuary of the mighty Murray river, he talked about the boat he used to have moored nearby and how he sold it a couple of years back. Nesta tried to make a joke about him not having the energy for sailing anymore but Archie didn't laugh. My mother, or perhaps one of my aunts, had talked about him having treatment for skin cancer but it wasn't something I felt I could mention.

I let Archie lead the conversation at lunch. Maybe I felt overwhelmed by it all – golf club captain, vineyards, boats; not to mention the scene with Ross the previous evening. And whatever I said seemed to meet with little interest, so why bother? I may as well sit back and let him hold court. He talked a lot about Australia or so it appeared. I felt like everything he said was followed by a criticism of Britain. Little digs about class and privilege and the inverted snobbery of the working class. God knows, I wasn't one for singing the country's praises but I still found it irritating. At one point I made a remark that at least Britain didn't have a big hole in the ozone layer directly above it. This was met with scornful laughter from both of them, so I left it there. Was I trying to make a subtle point about Archie's alleged skin cancer? I can't be sure.

After lunch, Archie drove a couple of miles south along the bay and parked in a lay-by at the foot of a bluff. I asked if he would like to walk with us but he brushed it aside, said something about having a quiet read of the paper. Nesta and I crossed the road and started up the broad, grassy path, worn brown with footfall and a rainless summer. Above and to the left I caught sight of the top of the bluff. It looked like a gentle walk, no more than twenty minutes or so and Nesta slipped her arm through mine. She wore a light pair of jeans and one of those French-looking tops, white with thin, blue bands. She looked youthful with her unlined face and easy smile. I wasn't sure of her age but I guess she must have been in her mid-sixties then.

After a few minutes the path levelled out and Nesta's breathing eased. She asked about my marriage. I wasn't expecting the question. I mumbled something about being too young, that within a few years we both realised we had made a mistake. The split was amicable or as amicable as these things can be. I said I moved to Sheffield to take up a junior lectureship. Ann stayed on in Edinburgh. No, we didn't stay in touch, why would we?

God, I must have sounded defensive. I remember feeling very young, like a schoolboy who had failed his exams and didn't want to talk about it. Nesta said something about things being different now. How in her day, you stuck it out, made the best of it. I felt like she was inviting me to ask her: so have you and Archie made the best of it? But I didn't accept the invitation. I was thirty-three but felt she was too grown up to be asked such a question. Or was I too immature?

We reached the head of the bluff. I expected a wind off the sea but there wasn't a breath of it. We stood side by side, shading our eyes and looking south beyond the sweep of the bay to the endless, blue-black ocean. Next stop Antarctica, Archie had said. After a few minutes we sat on a bench. Nesta turned to me.

'Anyway, I'm sure you did the right thing. About your marriage, I mean. Sometimes you just have to be brave and do what feels right even though it's painful. Archie's brave, you know,' she said. Her accent was Australian but cultured, like a newsreader.

Come on Jim, she wants you to engage here. I said, 'I'm sure he is. You mean, what he's done to achieve everything out here… for himself… for you and the children too.'

Nesta gave me her wide-open smile but I detected a note of irritation in her voice. 'Not for me. Whatever I've achieved, I've done myself. But we're a team, I suppose. No, I mean he was brave in coming to Australia in the first place. People see us, the successful careers, family, nice house, boats and so on. But they don't stop to think of what it took to give ourselves the opportunities. More so Archie. I came out on a music scholarship. He came out on a wing and prayer. He grabbed life with both hands.'

It was out before I knew it. 'I heard that you met on the ship?'

Nesta shifted to face me. 'Who told you that, Jim?'

I scratched at a bubble of peeling paint on the bench. 'I don't know really. One of my aunts maybe.' I said how Archie had told me to ask her about how they met.

She lifted her head and looked out to sea as if she was searching for something.

'I wish I could tell you about it.' Her voice was a murmur.

'But it's not a big secret, is it?'

'No, not all of it, I suppose. One day perhaps.' Nesta fished a tissue from her sleeve, blew her nose and dabbed her eyes.

I looked away, trying hard to think of something to say.

'I love it up here,' she said, 'all that ocean just stretching out forever. Anyway, Archie will be wondering where we've got to.' She stood up briskly. 'Shall we?'

I woke with a start and looked at the bedside clock. Nearly midnight. I really needed to get some sleep before my nine o'clock meeting at Melbourne University.

*

Michael Shearsmith closed the window which faced onto the quad and flicked a switch on the fan. The sound of angry shouts was muffled now, replaced by mechanical whirring and occasional clicks. I was already feeling uncomfortable. Perhaps the breeze from the fan would staunch my sweating. Michael explained that a group of students was occupying the Humanities building in protest at a big hike in tuition fees. And that's where I was meant to be, in the Humanities building with Cora Bracewell, agreeing details of an exchange programme. But Cora was locked in her office along with her staff. So, here I was sitting opposite the academic registrar, a late substitute and a busy man. He was tall with stylishly greying hair and he wore a well-tailored navy suit.

Michael talked about the sit-in the way Australians seem to talk about a lot of things: with a mix of dismissiveness and optimism. She'll be right, he may as well have said. Without all the relevant information to hand, we realised there was no way he could agree to the details of the exchange programme. But coffee had already been brought in and poured at the low table between us. He looked at his watch and said he was happy to give me twenty minutes of his time.

Michael leaned back, spread his arms along the sofa and asked, 'Any family out here?'

Where do I start? I thought. I told him about Archie and Nesta, how they came out in the fifties, what they did, where they lived. I was surprised when Michael told me his family were ten-pound Poms too. 'Came out from Birmingham in nineteen forty-nine,' he said, when he was three years old. His parents started off in Sydney, his father driving a bus, his mother scalding and skinning her hands in a laundry. Never regretted it. 'They're retired now,' he said, 'living up on the Gold Coast.'

'And the history of post-war migrants is fascinating,' he said. 'It's early days but they reckon in a few years all the records for migration applications and ships' voyages and so on will be digitalised. They'll all be there on the World Wide Web for anyone to look at.'

Had he forgotten I was a historian? That Australian convict transports were my research specialism? Or perhaps I hadn't mentioned it. But fair enough, he wasn't talking about convict ships anyway. In the meantime, I asked him where the post-war migration records were held and if the public could access them. 'You can view them in Canberra,' he said, 'at the National Archives.' I was due to arrive in the capital later that week.

*

I needed to get out of Melbourne. The streets were too wide, the traffic too noisy, the buildings too tall. It all felt a long way from the Kangaroo Café and Mr Fasoulakis. In any case, I had no more business here, and I knew nobody, so I may as well enjoy my own company elsewhere. I had a craving for peace and quiet, fresh air, a walk in the mountains.

Back at the hotel I studied my guidebook and checked out a day early. After a few goes at trying to negotiate the inner ring road, I got clear of the city and headed for Mount Buffalo, a couple of hours drive to the north east. I turned off the highway at Wangaratta and headed south. At Porepunkah I stopped to pick up a packed lunch then drove slowly up and into the forest. The road climbed in a series of sharp switchbacks. All around me, granite tors stuck up through a sea of eucalyptus. I parked up where the tarmac road ended in a rough lay-by. There were no other cars.

A strong, minty scent from the trees filled the air and I started up a rocky trail signposted for the Horn, the high point in the park. Two parrots, with dull markings, fluttered up from a rock in front of me. I shaded my eyes and watched their silhouettes against the sunlight before they disappeared from view further up the trail. The eucalyptus scent seemed to thicken the silence and any sounds, of insects or small birds, were louder than I had ever heard. For the first time since I arrived in Australia, I started to relax.

Of course, the journey all the way from Sheffield had been tiring and it took me a while to recover from it. But I knew it was more than that. Too much contact with people I didn't know – at universities, in hotels and restaurants. And with my family too. I hated having to pretend to be interested in other people and their lives. Or maybe I *was* interested in their lives but I was no good at talking to them.

Sometimes I felt it would be so much easier if everyone simply wrote me letters. Perhaps I was born in the wrong century. In any case, I found talking to people tiring.

I reached the lookout point more quickly than expected. It jutted out from a rocky outcrop on top of a sheer cliff. At the edge, an iron railing curved inwards, almost in a semi-circle. I stood there gripping the rail as if I was on the prow of a ship, looking out on an endless, calm sea of eucalyptus trees. I had one of those moments when you feel an urge to jump off. Like this is as good as it gets so why not just end it right here?

For a moment, I seemed to merge with the landscape. My whole body absorbed the feeling until the silence began to prickle my skin. I moved away from the rail, sat down on a flat rock and started to eat my sandwiches. The only sounds I heard were my jaw chewing and my throat swallowing. I threw the rest of the sandwiches over the edge of the cliff, picked up my backpack and raced down the trail to the car, the silence chasing and snapping at my heels. Even now, I remember how I felt when I started the engine and snaked down the switchback road. Safe again after a narrow escape.

It was still early, so I took the scenic route over the Tawonga gap and headed down the broad, green Kiewa valley. A snake slithered swiftly across the road at one point. I wound down my window to savour the scent and sounds of the bush and eased my foot off the accelerator. Eventually, I reached Wodonga and crossed the bridge over the Murray river which separates the city from its twin, Albury, on the New South Wales side.

The motel was quiet. I had no problems checking in for an extra night. My time was free until the following evening when I had arranged to visit Archie's older brother, Bob and his wife Jessie. They were retired now and had moved to Albury from Wollongong to be nearer their children and grandchildren. Bob and Jessie came out to Australia the year before Archie did, but their lives turned out very differently from his.

5

Port Said, 1955

The fishmonger stretched his vowels like a call to prayer: *barboooony Shabaaaar... kaboooooryaaaa*. The man's thick, scarred hand flicked at the flies with a short stick, tied at the end with sugar-cane bark. A pillar of ice shattered over the sad-looking fish, their shimmering scales dead but still smelling of life. Archie moved into the sunlight, shaded his eyes and shifted his gaze back to the tooth fairy thirty yards away. She stood with the companion. Both of them seemed deep in conversation with a shopkeeper who wore a dusty, black galabeya; on his head, a white turban. They moved closer into the half shade of the shop, allowing other people to squeeze past, going deeper into the souk. The shopkeeper let his fingers ripple over a jade green fabric as he unrolled it expertly. Archie watched her reach out to feel the material, her bare arm caught in a shaft of sunlight.

After the ship had docked on the west jetty of Port Said, small groups of passengers made their way along the Quai Francois Joseph, their heads throbbing from the late morning sun which reflected off every surface. Archie tagged along, on his own again, with Billy still recovering in his bunk. 'Head for the Arab Quarter,' the Italian crew members said, 'you'll find the souk there.' Why only a quarter? Archie wondered. Weren't they in Egypt now? But he knew things were in flux here. The main streets still had their French names but Nasser had been in control for over a year and the first British troops were starting to leave the Canal Zone. The Arab Quarter would become an Arab Whole soon enough, Archie thought.

Some passengers whispered loudly about the absence of British troops, of French police. 'Egyptian police with guns,' they said, 'I'm not happy about that at all.'

'Not to worry,' the Italians said, 'the Arabs want your money, not your life.' At the end of the Rue Quai du Nord, the groups of passengers merged, herding as they left the wide street and the comfort of its solid, stone facades. They funnelled into ever-narrowing alleys where surprisingly tall, wooden buildings with lacy balconies loomed over them. Odours of garlic and coriander, stronger than in Naples. Unfamiliar clucking voices. Women covered in black from head to toe, dragging small bare-footed children. It was hard not to stare at the children's runny noses, at the flies dancing on their eyes. No wonder they look miserable, Archie thought. The stench of unwashed bodies too, but that could easily have been some of the passengers from the ship.

Then deep into the souk, the herd breaking up again, as smaller groups formed. Lured by expert sellers with their perfected, mock deference. The tourists lingered at leatherware stalls, at textile stalls, at stalls with gold and other precious metals.

Archie's eyes stayed fixed on her sunlit arm as she caressed the jade material. But he could see the boy too. Bare-footed, whippet-like, dark eyes swivelling subtly. His hand snaked into and out of her bag, almost too quick for the naked eye. She must have felt something, swung round and the boy was off, heading in Archie's direction.

'Stop him, he's got her purse!' The companion's voice, first time he's heard it, surprisingly high for such a tall man. Shopkeepers, fishmongers and tourists all stop what they're doing and turn to look. The boy ducks to Archie's right but he grabs his spindly forearm, wrenches the purse from the boy's hand. Archie holds him for a moment then lets him go. The boy stares at him for the briefest time and knits his brows. Then he turns, racing down an alley, quickly lost amongst the mass of carts, boxes, legs and bodies. Gathered in by his people.

The companion, half a head taller, arrived in front of Archie, his chest rising and falling. 'You let him go. I saw you.'

She got there a moment later. Her musky scent. Close, so close. Archie could have reached out and touched her arm, that sunlit arm. He looked up at the companion, tried not to tilt his head too much. 'He was a slippery little bugger.' Then he turned to her. 'Anyway, you've got your purse back, that's the main thing.' He held it out for her to take. A safe distance.

'Yes, you're right. Thank you. Thank you…' The faint trace of a Welsh accent.

'Archie. Archie Thomson,' he said in his best Queen's English.

She fiddled with the purse, didn't offer her hand. 'Thank you, Archie. And I'm Nesta.'

The companion cleared his throat. 'Yes, yes. Nesta. And I'm Carwyn.' He stuck out a long, pink, freckled hand and took a short step to his right, forcing Nesta to move back a little, away from Archie. 'Sorry. It just looked like you let the little runt go deliberately.'

Archie looked at him, gripped the man's hand briefly, hard like he was issuing a challenge. He wanted his silence to say something. Like, maybe I did let the boy go. And if I did, so what? I got the purse back. Isn't that what matters? What would happen next if I kept hold of the boy? The local police? Endless questions and statements in hot, airless rooms? The boy's already slim chances ruined. Or maybe not, maybe they release him after we've returned to the ship. In any case, letting the boy go was the best thing to do.

Carwyn broke the silence. 'Look, I think we owe you a drink at the very least. Hopefully, we'll see you in the bar this evening. I think I've seen you in there before? Sevenish? Meanwhile, I think we'll head back to the ship. It's all been a bit of a shock for Nesta.'

She rolled her eyes theatrically and smiled at Archie. 'Well, not a shock I can't handle. But, yes, maybe we should head back now.' Carwyn steered her away, his palm under her elbow. Was he gripping her? But she let his hand stay there.

After they left, the fabric shopkeeper walked over to Archie. 'I see, my friend. We all see what you do. Please, my friend. Please, you must take tea with us.'

Archie put his hand on the man's shoulder, thanked him but made an excuse, said he must get back to the ship too. And his eyes followed them, Nesta and Carwyn, as they made their way through the crowds.

He stood in a small square of shade on the quayside in front of the lighthouse, staring east across the water towards Port Faoud. To his left the jetty leading to the open waters of the Mediterranean; to his right the entrance to the Suez Canal. It was quiet here but, despite the patch of shade, still hot under the blazing sun. Space in front of his eyes. Room for his jumbled thoughts and sensations to tumble out of his head and carry out to sea or down the canal. Her voice, her sunlit arm, her smile. The scent of her floated out over the water, then drifted back, circling slowly round his head, lingering under his nose. He needed to think of something else.

A long, wailing voice started up from somewhere above and behind him. The call to prayer filled the air. I'm in Egypt, he thought, as if it had suddenly dawned on him. He started to laugh out loud, then stifled it into a cough. But nobody noticed him. He shook his head. His brother Bob had been in North Africa during the war. Retreated all the way east across the desert to Egypt with Montgomery; and then advanced all the way back to Morocco, chasing Rommel and his panzers off the continent of Africa.

Archie remembered watching the newsreels at the Palace. It was the first good news of the war. As a ten-year-old at the pictures, he found it hard to separate the newsreel images with their dusty, desert tanks and artillery, from the main feature which followed. Usually some hastily made British war film where they spoke with clipped, English accents and beat the filthy Hun hands down. For a young boy, the pictures on the screen were all about heroes a nd villains – whether real or imagined. But out in the Sahara, Bob must have known what was real, experienced it first-hand. Ten years, Archie thought. An age gap of ten years. The difference between being a schoolboy at the cinema and a young man fighting for his life in a brutal war.

And Bob was part of the reason why Archie was here in Egypt, on his way to Australia. Bob and his wife Jessie had headed out to Australia the year before with four children in tow, the eldest of them just turned seven. After the war, life was a struggle for them. Bob seemed to change jobs as often as Jessie gave birth. But while the children grew, the jobs fizzled out. When Jessie saw an advert in the *Evening News* for the Assisted Passage Scheme, they didn't hesitate. Just as well. The voyage from Liverpool to Sydney tested their patience, and their stomachs, over six long weeks. But after a month in internment camp on arrival, Bob got a job at the huge steelworks in Wollongong, south of Sydney.

Jessie wrote regularly to her parents and to Bob's too. Ma and Pa shared the letters with Archie and his sisters who still lived at home. They read about Bob and Jessie's new house, provided by the steel company. They read about the warm, dry weather; about Bob's steady job with good pay and not-too-long working hours. They read about the local social club with its bowling green and cheap beer; about how most people were friendly. And they read about how nobody asked what school you went to or what age you were when you left it or what your parents did for a living. Archie's sisters tried to read between the lines. They said they must be homesick. They said it must be hard for the older children going to a new school in a new country where everyone spoke funny. They said the heat and the flies must be unbearable. And whoever heard of a place called Wollongong anyway? But whatever Jessie may have left out from her letters didn't interest Archie at all. He was too busy peering at the atlas and placing his index finger under the strange place name, in tiny letters, a fraction of an inch below Sydney. He wished they had a bigger map. He lifted his head from the book and took in the double-page spread of Australia as if seeing the size and shape of the country for the first time.

And now here he was, in Egypt, standing at the entrance to the Suez Canal. Something else came into his mind. A black-and-white poster. What did it say? *See you in Australia*. A young couple running through the sea, water splashing up their legs. On the left, the woman is wearing a ruched, fussy-looking, one-piece swimming costume. Her dark hair is short, her eyes screwed up as she runs towards the sun and the camera. Her left hand is being held firmly by the man, his eyes screwed up too. He wears a pair of light, candy-striped trunks. There is sunshine, there are shadows. The couple are caught in a moment of pure ecstasy, the froth of the waves forever cooling them, tingling their legs. You can almost feel the salty, sandy heat on your skin as you stand there looking at the image in the window.

He remembered staring at it in Leith Provident, the big co-op on Great Junction Street. Had he seen himself in the poster, his future self? He can remember thinking about Wollongong, liking the sound of the name, trying to imagine the steelworks, the lack of snobbishness in the place. But the poster? Maybe that was the icing on the cake. Back in Leith, the fantasy in the picture was too much to imagine even vaguely, let alone try to will it into being. But here and now in Port Said, he wasn't so sure. If he allowed himself, he could summon up the image, replace the bland faces of the models with versions of himself and... he almost said the tooth fairy... Nesta.

The sun was overhead now, no wonder it was quiet on the quayside. He felt the burn on his scalp and forehead as he walked slowly northwards along the quay towards the *Fairsea*.

His sisters used to tease him about the girls he met at the Eldorado. It was the only dance hall in Leith. Even on nights when none of his sisters were there, they would get reports from friends or friends of friends. 'Are you an item?' they would ask. 'What's she like?' 'Do you like her hair like that?' He had met his fair share of girls at the dancing, stepped out with a few of them but never for long. Word went round that he was no fun. He was always talking about how he wanted to get out of Leith, how he wanted to see the world. 'Big plans for a butcher's apprentice,' they said.

Butcher's apprentice. 'I had no choice,' he told people. He was bright, did well at school and could have stayed on longer. Maybe a chance of a junior clerk's job up town in a bank or an insurance company. But when Archie was fifteen, Pa lost his left leg below the knee in an accident at work, his trouser leg caught in a machine just as it started turning. Pa was given a small pension, enough for him and Ma to get by on but not enough to feed Archie and his sisters. 'We're sorry son,' they told him, 'but you'll need to leave the school.'

He got a job with McKay the butcher through the kirk. Mr McKay was a church elder, Ma took the Sunday school class occasionally. McKay was looking for another apprentice after his latest recruit was called up for National Service. 'There's an opportunity for you for eighteen months at least,' Ma said, 'maybe longer if that other laddie gets posted to Palestine or the likes.' So Archie knuckled down and learned the butcher's trade. Six mornings a week he was out of the door before seven o'clock, cutting across Leith Links and up the Kirkgate to the shop on Tolbooth Wynd. He stuck at it for seven years until the itch appeared. Australia was making eyes at him.

*

On closer inspection, Carwyn looked younger than Archie thought when he'd first seen him. It was the Welshman's thinning, reddish hair that made him seem older; that and the dry, wrinkled look of his pink, freckled skin. Probably in his mid-thirties, certainly old enough to have served in the war. It was just him, Carwyn, when Archie arrived in the bar not long after seven o'clock. Carwyn said Nesta was sorting out some laundry and would be along in half an hour or so. He made a dismissive wave as if to say: you know what women are like. Plenty of time for men's talk. The older man thanked Archie again for what he'd done in the souk. 'Cheers,' he said, raising his gin and tonic while Archie supped a pint of ale.

The canal was busy, and with Egypt in charge now, paperwork was taking longer. Or so the crew said. In any case, the *Fairsea* was staying put on the west jetty for the night. When word got around early in the afternoon, passengers with money and a taste for adventure, but mostly money, hired guides and went off to Giza to see the pyramids and the Sphinx. They drifted back to the ship in the cool of early evening, their reddened faces backlit by the lowering sun.

Carwyn was first to ask questions. Where are you from? Where are you going? What are you going to do there? Why on earth are you going to Australia in the first place? The usual questions that everybody asked everybody else. The man had a strong Welsh accent, but he spoke slowly. Almost too slowly. For a moment Archie wondered if he was taking the rise but pushed the thought aside.

Archie was candid enough, he saw no need to hold anything back, saw no need for invention. He was keen to get his talking done as quickly as seemed decent. His questions for Carwyn were jostling for position in his mind; he was trying to rein them in, ready to release them smoothly.

Don't mention her, not yet, he thought. 'And yourself Carwyn, what takes you to Australia?'

The older man's pale lashes flickered briefly. He seemed to weigh the question. Archie glanced out of the window at the silhouette of a woman dragging two protesting children along the deck, her arms stretched out behind her.

Carwyn pursed his lips. 'That's a very good question, Archie. You see, on the face of it I'm going to Sydney to teach at the conservatorium. I'm a singing teacher. I mean, I teach singing.'

'But only on the face of it?'

'Well, I'm also accompanying Nesta on the voyage. She's going to the conservatorium too. On a music scholarship for the opera school. You see, my family knows her family in Cardiff. They were concerned about her travelling all this way on her own and they heard that I was going out to the same place. Only, I was due to travel in January this year. Anyway, I agreed with the conservatorium to postpone my starting date by a few months so that I could travel to Sydney with Nesta.'

Accompanying? The questions were ready to cut loose, ready to run amok. But Archie steadied himself. 'And how is the accompanying going?'

Carwyn cocked his head, leaned in and lowered his voice. 'You know, it's going rather better than I expected if you know what I mean.'

Archie thought he probably knew what Carwyn meant. The urge was mounting to grab him by the throat, to stick the glass in his face.

'I'm sorry, Carwyn. You'll have to spell it out for me.'

'Well, I know I might be a bit old for her, but we do seem to be getting along very well. It's a pity about these separate dorms for men and women. Still, we have to make do with what's available if you know what I mean?' He lifted his glass, raised his eyebrows and smiled as he looked at Archie.

Archie looked out of the window again, banging his knee up and down on the underside of the table. 'And you're sure the feeling is mutual, as it were? Sometimes you can't be sure.'

Carwyn hesitated. For a moment he looked as if he'd said too much. 'I'm sure,' he said, 'as sure as I can be.'

Archie grabbed hold of that last comment, stored it away. From what he'd seen of them dancing in the sun lounge and wandering the deck, Carwyn had every reason to be sure. But you never knew, appearances could be deceptive. Archie changed the subject, talked about Egypt and how things seemed to be moving quickly under Nasser. How the French and the British weren't happy about being forced to leave the Canal Zone. He liked to keep himself informed, and not just about Egypt because of their voyage through the Suez Canal. Back home, he read the two main reputable newspapers – the *Scotsman* and the *Herald* – soaking up information about anything he thought might be useful. You needed to know more than just the football league tables and the price of eggs, he thought. He felt able to talk a bit about business, stock markets and world affairs; about the way the French and the British tried to hold onto their empires as if they couldn't see what was happening.

Carwyn nodded and made encouraging noises but Archie could tell he wasn't interested. He checked his watch. They had been in the bar for half an hour.

Archie stood up when she walked in. She wore a white, sleeveless cotton dress and had a just-washed look. Her hair was not quite dry. He imagined running his hands through it, feeling the dampness. Nesta sat down next to Carwyn, facing Archie. He could smell her now, wanted to run his fingers along the line of her neck and shoulder. Carwyn raised his hand to a waiter who was polishing glasses at the bar. Just a lime cordial with water for Nesta, another gin and tonic for him. Archie put his hand over his half-empty pint glass and said he was fine. When the drinks arrived, they clinked glasses. Nesta said thanks again for rescuing her purse. She looked down and played with a ring on her right hand.

Archie's stomach lurched and the volume of his heartbeat increased. He steadied himself and breathed out through his nose. 'And congratulations to both of you.' He looked at Nesta. 'I hear you're an item.'

She swung round to face Carwyn, her bottom lip dropping open. Carwyn looked straight at Archie, eyes blazing. 'That's not what I said.'

Nesta's voice was like ice. 'So what *did* you say, Carwyn?' He ignored her, still staring at the younger man.

Archie stood up. 'Look, I'm sorry, maybe I got the wrong impression from what you said earlier, Carwyn. I think I'd better leave both of you to sort it out. But thanks for the drink anyway.'

He climbed up to the boat deck, taking the stairs two at a time. As he stood trembling at the rail, flies and moths busied themselves in the gathering gloom, settling on his nose, fluttering in his hair. He swiped at them forcefully.

The man in the khaki suit chuckled as he walked past. 'You're wasting your energy,' he said. 'You won't win, you know.'

6

Adelaide, 1997

He won't listen to her. It's like the man has a death wish. How can you carry on smoking twenty or thirty cigarettes a day and hope to survive cancer surgery?

She's surprised the latest diagnosis is only a recurrence of the skin cancer. Is that what gives him… the gall? or the confidence… to keep smoking. He told her he started when he was fifteen so he's been going strong for nearly fifty years. 'Why stop now?' he says, 'it won't make any difference.'

Last year, the consultant said he was hopeful they'd caught all of it after the mole on Archie's arm was removed. But that faint optimism seems pointless now. The latest check-up showed another mole reddening and spreading on his back. Surely Archie felt it changing? If he did, he kept it to himself. Which is what he usually does with most things. The biopsy was almost an anticlimax. Next is a trip to Sydney to see a leading specialist – the private medical insurance will pay for that. Still, at least it's all out in the open now. They can face it together, she thinks. Like they've faced so many challenges over the years. Although, God knows, they've brought some of them upon themselves.

She remembers the very early days. Archie living in Melbourne, her in Sydney at the conservatorium. She wrote every few days with news about her course, impressions of Sydney and what her digs were like. Some things she kept to herself. It was encouraging to get a letter from him at least once a week. You could never call them love letters, the ones he sent, but they had an intensity and a sense of purpose. He sent her progress reports: how much overtime he'd worked at the meat processing plant; how much he'd saved that week; what he'd learned at his night school class about business administration; how many jobs he'd applied for in Sydney.

When she looks back, it all feels so flimsy, as if it could have fallen apart in a moment. She could have written to him and said, *sorry Archie, I don't think this is going to work*. Or, *I feel differently now*. Except that after what happened on the ship, she felt bound to him and the binding held firm. So, while it may all feel flimsy from a distance of forty years, she doesn't remember ever questioning the pact they made out there in the middle of the Indian Ocean.

'Shall we tell the kids?' she asks him.

'After we've seen the specialist,' he says. She likes that he says *we*. They will be away in Sydney for a few days. Ewan and Hannah are bound to call during that time. She will try to have a quiet word with each of them one evening this week while Archie's at the golf club. Reassure them it's just a precaution at this stage. They do love Archie, for all his faults. Sometimes she feels a little resentful at the way the children make excuses for him these days. 'He was only trying to do his best for us,' they'll say. But if Archie can be forgiven, what about her? They've never told her that she was only doing her best too; perhaps they don't think she was. They may as well say, *Mum, you were too selfish to do your best for anyone but yourself*. Or is it simply her own guilty conscience reminding her that she's not blameless?

At the end of the letter from the clinic there's a small, black-and-white street map with the name of the hospital in Sydney highlighted in red. It's just north of the harbour bridge, off the Pacific Highway. 'We need to book flights and a hotel,' she says. 'I'll take care of it,' he says. He still has his business account with the company, being a trustee of the pension fund.

She checks the date for the appointment. Next Tuesday – a week today. It occurs to her that Jim will be in Sydney then. Where did she put that note of his itinerary he gave her? Perhaps they could meet for lunch or dinner. She feels like the time spent with Jim last weekend was more awkward than it should have been. She and Archie were distracted by the results from the biopsy which came on Friday, just before Jim arrived for the weekend. And that played into Archie taking it all out on Ross that evening. But let's be frank, Ross is a scruffy little bugger and he isn't family. He may as well have had a target painted on his back.

The trip to Victor Harbor on Saturday repaired some of the damage but not all of it, she thinks. Perhaps her little show of emotion on the bluff didn't help. Her nephew was very quiet that day. And timid, you might say. Something stirs in her mind. There's a story that Archie told her a long time ago but it's just beyond the edge of her consciousness and she can't quite grasp it. No point wasting energy trying to catch it. She lets it go. These things are happening more frequently, she decides. It's as if the past, *her* past, is a jigsaw, and individual pieces are disappearing. The rate at which they vanish is accelerating too. At first, it was just the odd piece that she could do without – some general bit of sky or sea or distant mountain. But now, more often, it will be an important piece, someone's hat or a flag waving or the steeple on a church or the sign above a shop.

She shakes her head as if snapping herself out of a dream. A quick look at the kitchen clock – ten forty-five. She needs to be at the museum for twelve. There's an Adelaide Festival Corporation board meeting and she promised Allie she would make it this time. How many meetings has she missed in the past twelve months – two? Three strikes and you're out, that's what the rules for trustees say. They wouldn't be quite so brutal, would they? Probably just a quiet word after the meeting. Still, she must make the effort. Being on the festival board is one of the few genuinely responsible activities she has left. And it's the best way of staying in touch with what's happening in the arts in this sleepy city.

She grabs her car keys and shouts a quick farewell through to Archie in the conservatory. Says she'll be back by five, she has a few errands to do while she's in town. Another little lie, but now is definitely not the time to tell Archie about the sessions with Louise. Which reminds her: try to stay in the moment, that's what her counsellor keeps telling her.

*

Jim was right about the bumps. She swerves to avoid another pothole and indicates right, off Belair Road. No sign of Archie's car on the drive. When she gets in she finds a note on the console table in the hall; it says he's gone to the club and he'll get something to eat there. She takes a moment to allow her feelings to separate and order themselves. Firstly, there is relief that she doesn't have to cook; and she doesn't have to tell him white lies about what errands she did, or rather didn't do, after the meeting. But there is something else – hurt perhaps? Possibly. Hurt that he's avoiding her even more than usual because of the cancer thing. But where is the evidence? There's nothing unusual about Archie spending an evening at the golf club, particularly while it's still light until nearly eight o'clock. Her right hand rests on the table, the other covers her mouth and nose like a mask, smothering her sobs before they surface. She would love the pair of them to sit down and talk honestly about what it all means. Whatever pain it causes both of them, she would love Archie to share his fears, to try and shape them into words. No, forget the words, she simply wants her husband to let her hold him. Archie's going to die soon, she thinks. He won't survive this.

She takes off her jacket and shoes, slips on her sandals and goes through to the kitchen. In the fridge there's a half-eaten tub of coleslaw from Grace's Deli and some celery sticks. She takes them out, pours a glass of white wine and sits on a wicker chair in the conservatory. At times like this it's easy to feel that life is coming apart. Louise calls it excessive consciousness. Too much awareness of the self. A tendency to step outside yourself and look at the hollowness within. She's not at all sure about Louise, or the letters after her name, for that matter. Still, the sessions do seem to help.

It was one of those chance meetings at a fundraising event for the festival. Wine and canapes, working the room, the sort of thing that even five years ago, she did without thinking. Enjoyed doing. But now she finds it tiring and would prefer to sit on the terrace with a magazine. Perhaps Louise saw inside her head that evening. Perhaps Louise is trained to see all that. Perhaps that's how Louise gets her clients. But that's unkind.

In the past three months they've had – what – ten sessions? In that time, she has told Louise about almost everything from the present right back to when she and Archie got married. At first, Louise wanted her to talk about her childhood, but she saw no point. 'I had a blissfully happy childhood and youth,' she told her, 'it was only when I set off for Australia that things became complicated.'

'So, let's start there,' Louise said.

'Oh no,' she said, 'I'm not ready for that. Let's work our way backwards, shall we?' She wonders if it was the prospect of forty dollars a session over several months, years even, that prompted Louise to agree to her suggestion a little too readily.

She dips a stick of celery into the coleslaw and carefully scoops it into her mouth. The crunch is satisfying, the combination of flavours delicious. There, simple things can still bring pleasure. Like that Huntsman spider and her beautiful web in the corner of the conservatory window. She gets up, checks the spider is on the outside.

Today, she told Louise about Archie's cancer diagnosis. Louise was empathetic in a well-practised kind of way but told her: 'You need to look after yourself first. There's no point trying to help others until you feel better, until you've understood how you arrived at this point.' But that sounds so self-indulgent and, anyway, she doesn't have the luxury of time. Which reminds her, in some odd way, to call Ewan and Hannah. The children knew about last year's treatment of course, but Archie has insisted on keeping quiet about this latest episode. She has no compunction about telling them behind his back, particularly with Archie and her going to Sydney for a couple of days next week. What would Ewan and Hannah think if they were to call and get the answer machine for two days? What if they drive all the way up to Belair and find the house empty? Of course, she could say they're just taking a short break. And – there's a thought – she could tell them they're just going to Sydney to spend more time with Jim. No, she decides, the children ought to know the truth about what's going on with their father so they can prepare themselves for what lies ahead.

She calls Hannah three times in quick succession but there's no reply. When she tries Ewan, he answers just before she hangs up. He sounds tired, says Carrie called him on Monday, said she was sick, and could he have Shane for a few days. She imagines the scene, Ewan driving home from work, a stale, sweaty smell in the ute. Stopping off at the after-school club to collect Shane, then another stop at a pizza place or maybe a drive-through. Still, it could be worse. At least Ewan and Carrie remain on good terms. You can't ask for more than that – you hear so many stories about ugly divorces these days.

'And have you got all his medicines?' she asks. Ewan says yes, he has it all sorted and tells her that Shane is pretty calm despite the change to his routine. She waits for her son to ask a favour. Such as, *Mum, can you take Shane to school and collect him, please?* But the request doesn't come, and she doesn't offer. It's not the best situation in which to break the news about Archie but she presses ahead, determined to get it done. She half expects Ewan to break down over the phone, but he sounds calm. 'Yeah, well, Dad pulled through last time and I guess he'll do it again,' he says. Silence. She leaves a gap which she hopes he will fill with questions about how she's bearing up, and if there's anything he can do to help. More silence, then Ewan asks if there's anything else. 'No, no,' she says, 'I'm fine, don't you worry about me.'

That's the trouble with children, she thinks, after hanging up: they never react the way you want them to. She can just picture Ewan when she went to bring him home after the year he spent with Bob and Jessie. He was old enough, she thought – three or four? – to have missed his mother and to have shown it. It was a Friday morning and she was feeling a bit rough after the end-of-tour party the night before. She drove out to Wollongong to collect him, wearing her best stage smile. When Jessie opened the door, there was Ewan standing at the back of the dark, narrow hall. But when she crouched and opened her arms wide, her son turned and ran screaming into the living room. It took four hours of tears and coaxing and promises that she would never leave him again before they loaded his bags into the car and headed for the airport.

Before she goes to bed, she makes a note to call Louise in the morning. Next week they will be in Sydney. She really ought to have another session with her counsellor before then.

7

Albury, 1997

Distracted by a saucer-sized spider in the corner of the window, I didn't hear the question.

'Sorry?' I said.

'How many sugars?' The spoon in Jessie's hand moved swiftly towards my cup.

'No. No sugar, thanks.' I reached forward and put my hand over the cup, felt a damp heat on my palm.

I had phoned the evening before to ask Jessie if I could visit them in the morning. 'Fine,' she said, 'make it ten o'clock; that gives your Uncle Bob time to get dressed and have his breakfast.'

Albury is not a big place, so it was easy enough to find the area on the edge of town. Sturt Gardens was just off the estate's main artery. Rows of wood-panelled bungalows with metal roofs stood on either side of the road. Lawns and driveways ran straight down to the roadside – there was no pavement. A raised wooden verandah ran across the front of their house. I half-expected to see Bob dozing in a rocking chair but there was nobody outside.

'Choccie biscuit?' Jessie lifted the plate and almost pressed it into my chest.

'I will, thank you.' A refusal would have been rude. I settled into the softness of the sofa with my cup of tea in one hand, biscuit in the other.

The living room was sparsely furnished in a crowded way. Two bulky armchairs and the matching sofa with drab, brown velveteen covers. Their tasselled skirts brushed the navy carpet whose silver flecks sparkled in sunlight filtered through net curtains. A wide sideboard stood against the wall behind Jessie's chair, its surface covered in seventy-fifth birthday cards. Oversized photographs seemed to use up every piece of wall space. It felt like a family portrait gallery. In the centre of the room we sat around a mahogany veneer coffee table where a flower-patterned teapot rested on a cork mat.

Bob sat upright in his armchair, his left hand gripping the handle of a walking stick. He reminded me of my late father: small, wiry, and now rather shrivelled. I imagined that since retirement, like so many working-class men of his generation, his muscles had withered after a life of manual labour. The stroke wouldn't have helped either – Bob had suffered a severe one the year before and his speech was still a little slurred. His accent was wholly Australian, Jessie's too. She did most of the talking but perhaps she always had done.

Jessie was keen to let me know about their family, three generations of it. Her hair was dyed a dark brown which seemed to enhance her sense of robustness. By comparison with her husband, she looked positively sprightly.

'We came out with four children,' she told me, 'and now there are twenty-seven children and grandchildren. And then there's our first great grandchild due next month. So, fingers crossed, including your Uncle Bob and me, that'll make a nice round thirty. For now.'

I found myself comparing them with Archie and Nesta. As far as I knew, they added up to five, all told. 'So, six times more than Archie and Nesta,' I said. I have no idea what possessed me to say that. I smiled at both of them, but I felt awkward, as if I was accusing them of breeding like rabbits and it was about time they stopped.

Jessie smiled gently. 'Yes,' she said, 'but we're a fair bit older than them and, as I said, we already had four kids when we came out here. So, we had a head start. Or four head starts! Archie and Nesta didn't even know each other when they set off.'

'But they met on the ship?' Christ, I was like Pavlov's dog.

Jessie lowered her eyes and fingered a loose thread on the arm of the sofa. 'I've not heard that one before.' She looked up and scanned the photographs on the walls, slowly, deliberately. 'Would you like to know who they all are?'

We spent several minutes walking around the room, with Jessie, like an experienced tour guide, stopping at each photograph to explain who was who. The various generations had clustered around Sydney and Melbourne, she said. I struggled to keep up with my aunt's running commentary, but I nodded regularly and tried to ask questions whenever she paused which wasn't often. The three eldest children had settled on the western outskirts of Sydney. The four youngest, all of them well into their thirties now, were dotted around Melbourne. Their youngest daughter had even married a Serb. 'Well, that would never have happened in our day,' Jessie said, 'but times have changed and mostly for the better.' And she was proud that her eldest granddaughter had been the first in the family to go to university and was now a solicitor. She worked with deprived families in some of Sydney's troubled western suburbs.

When Jessie finished the tour, we sat down again. Bob had nodded off and shook himself awake, his newspaper dropping from his lap to the floor.

'You must have seen a lot of changes over the years,' I said, raising my voice for Bob's sake.

Jessie cocked her head. 'You know, I wouldn't know where to begin. When we started off in Wollongong everything was a lot smaller and a lot quieter. Safer too. We used to let the kids roam free. In the holidays they would be off after breakfast and you'd never see them again till lunchtime. Well, you wouldn't do that now, I can tell you. Still, I expect it's the same back in Britain.' She looked at Bob. 'But we've never regretted it, have we? Never looked back. Bob was over thirty years at the steelworks. And when I think of all the jobs he had in Leith.' Jessie leaned across and grasped her husband's knee. 'I'm saying, you became a real steady Eddy, didn't you?'

'Aye, that's right,' he said, looking at her with a lopsided smile.

They had settled in Wollongong almost as soon as they arrived in Australia. But no one from their family still lived in the steel and mining city south of Sydney. This was why, Jessie explained, she and

Bob moved all the way to Albury after he retired from the steelworks. Albury was well-placed on the highway between the two main cities. 'Broadly speaking,' she said, 'half of the family live in Melbourne, half in Sydney.' I couldn't grasp the logic – why set yourselves down here when your family was four or five hours away in either direction? Perhaps it was to avoid favouring one group over the other. In which case, the result seemed to disadvantage both, equally.

Jessie insisted that things worked well for ten years or so until Bob had his stroke. For a while after that, Albury didn't seem like such a good idea. They were left even more isolated from their family groups while Bob recovered, relying on a rota of weekend visits, once a month, from their children. But Jessie was resourceful. At seventy-three she learned to drive. She nursed Bob back to reasonable health and kept up her social life which, for both of them, centred on the local RSL club.

'We spend most afternoons at the club,' Jessie said. 'We don't bowl so much as we used to but we do like to play the pokies.'

I could picture what she was talking about. On the face of it, the Returned and Services League is a support organisation for men and women who serve in the Australian Defence Force. But for a lot of Australians the initials are a byword for cheap food, beer and bowling greens. And increasingly, the clubs were known for their large gambling halls full of slot machines, Las Vegas style.

In Adelaide, one of the university staff had taken me to a local branch for lunch. The building was set into the side of a rugby league stadium. Or perhaps it was the other way round. Through the foyer on the ground floor was a room half the size of a rugby pitch. It was filled with rows and rows of one-armed bandits and fruit machines. From what I remembered, every machine had someone sitting in front of it on a high stool. On ledges beside them sat buckets of tokens which they fed into slots. The scale of it, the repetition of people's actions and their intense concentration made me think of a factory floor. But these people weren't making anything at all, and certainly not money. On my journey from Adelaide to Albury I got used to passing through small towns where, more often than not, the biggest, brightest building was the local RSL club.

I looked at Bob and Jessie's retirement bungalow, their three-piece suite, and their lurid carpet. I imagined their lives of bingo and occasional games of bowls and sitting with a bucket of tokens at a one-armed bandit. I thought, what a disappointment that they had simply transferred their undernourished lives in Edinburgh, for what? For slightly better nourished lives in Australia where the weather was warmer, and the spiders were bigger. Almost immediately I regretted my thoughts. Jessie leaned forward and asked if I was alright. I nodded. 'Thanks,' I said, 'just tired from all the travelling.'

In their own way, hadn't Bob and Jessie also grabbed life with both hands? Hadn't they done that simply by filling in the forms, by packing their bags and, with four small children in tow, boarding a ship bound for Australia? So why did I feel like they had missed an opportunity? Passed up on a chance to make more of their lives. I thought again of Archie, and for a moment I saw him as the material opposite of the man dozing off in the armchair next to me. Archie, who worked his way up from nothing to be a director in a large business; to be captain of his own golf club; to be father of two children – who from what I knew, were more than a little damaged by their upbringing – former boat owner; minor partner in a small vineyard; all-round Mr Achievement. So bloody what? What did any of it matter so long as you were content with your lot? I couldn't envy the smallness of Bob and Jessie's lives. But I did envy their having stuck at it, their evident sense of belonging.

Before I left them, I tried to turn the conversation back to my uncle and aunt in Adelaide, curious to find out what Bob and Jessie knew about how they'd met. Perhaps I felt guilty about snooping and was clumsy in how I went about it, but they pushed the subject away. Or rather, Jessie did. I'm not sure Bob even heard what I said. She was always keen to turn the talk back to their children and grandchildren, a seemingly bottomless pit of stories. And why not? If I wanted to learn more about Archie and Nesta, I would have to wait till I reached Canberra.

On the doorstep I hugged Jessie and shook Bob's leathery, sun-spotted hand. As I drove off, I stuck my arm out the window and waved. When I reached the junction at the end of their road, I saw them in the mirror. Jessie's hand was on her husband's elbow as they disappeared through the front door. I thought, we've only just met for the first time, and I'll probably never see them again. Part of my family.

All this way to the other side of the world and I had spent less than two hours with them. Yet, I had spent the whole weekend with Archie and Nesta. How come? Driving back to the motel, I tried to convince myself that starting off in Adelaide had been a practical decision; something to do with connecting flights and such like. But I soon stopped kidding myself and admitted the truth. It was because Archie was successful and well-off. I had imagined that he and Nesta led interesting lives. They also had a large house with a granny flat attached. And I was curious about them. They could show me around, do the whole host and hostess bit. As for a weekend with Bob and Jessie in Albury? Perhaps lunch out at their local RSL club and, if I was lucky, an afternoon sat in front of the pokies. All the same, I felt a deep sense of guilt by the time I parked up at the motel.

*

I wasn't hungry, so I skipped lunch, checked out and was back on the Hume highway well before one o'clock, heading for Canberra. It was a drive of two hundred miles and my guidebook told me that navigating the ring road of the country's capital could be notoriously difficult. The countryside was greener now, with rolling hills, grazing sheep and familiar-looking trees. It could have been somewhere in England except for the roadside flocks of dusty budgerigars and endless miles of straight, empty tarmac with that feeling of going nowhere fast. Time to kill and time to think.

Back home, I had looked forward to being in Canberra more than anything. The collections of the Australian National Library held most of the materials I wanted to look at. There were records of convict voyages and arrivals in Sydney; convicts being assigned masters; absconding and imprisonment; and eventually, for many of them, their tickets of leave, certificates of freedom and pardons. And so much rich, additional detail: ships' logs, surgeons' journals, convict diaries, transportation registers, indents, jail records, newspapers and so on.

The joy of being able to hold and scrutinise original documents; to see Walter Avery's name in ink; to smell the man through the mustiness of time. It felt like a once-in-a-lifetime chance, and with it, an opportunity to further my research.

My family were crowding my thoughts too; they shouted to be heard, urged me to search out their stories. They were all brave in different ways, I decided. But especially Archie, Bob and Jessie. From what I'd heard, none of them had jobs to go to in Australia. It seemed to me they took the plunge because there wasn't enough to hold them back. Not family ties or lifestyles or girlfriends or jobs or prospects. But most of all, they can't have had a strong sense of belonging in Edinburgh. I wondered what all of them felt on those long journeys more than forty years ago. How many times did they question what they were doing and what was waiting for them at the other side of the world? I thought I understood how Bob and Jessie might consider their prospects to be no better or worse in Australia than they were in Edinburgh. Bob was thirty-three and an unskilled labourer with a wife and four children. And he'd been through the war and survived it. How much had his experiences influenced the decision?

But Archie – I couldn't imagine he signed up with the intention of working as a butcher for the rest of his life. He was ten years younger than his brother and had no ties. Did he go out with a conviction that this new, relatively classless country, would give him opportunities that he would be denied in Britain? Or was it just an adventure, an opportunity not to be missed? Perhaps he felt cheated by being too young to fight in the war. Was this his chance to make up for it, to reap the rewards of the peace that millions had paid with their lives to achieve?

And then something came back to me. It was when Jessie talked about her granddaughter and her work as a solicitor with deprived families in Sydney. Her voice was full of pride, yes, but it wasn't only about family. There was civic pride too. We're giving something back, she seemed to say, after all this country has done for us.

So that left Nesta and she was a different matter. Music scholarship, she said up on the bluff. I knew she had been a singer, possibly an opera singer. I wasn't sure. Although she didn't really fit my stereotype of an opera diva. Perhaps she only sang minor parts or was simply a member of the chorus, if operas have choruses. But going out to Australia on a music scholarship must have been a different experience from the others. Excitement at the opportunity. She was going to university, after all, a university ten thousand miles from home.

I remembered how she made the distinction on the bluff. She said something like: 'I went out on a music scholarship, Archie went out on a wing and a prayer.' And she said he was brave. I thought of the lookout on Mount Buffalo, how I ran down the hill all the way to the car. I felt like the polar opposite of Archie. He grabbed life with both hands, I ran away from it as fast as I could. Ran away from responsibility, from relationships, from ambition. Fearful, that was me.

My first memory of running away from things was the bow and arrow incident. I think I must have been about seven, perhaps eight; at least I hope I was – it suits my purpose to imagine being as young as possible. In the small, territorial world of the council estate, we played close to home. Stray too far, say more than half a dozen houses or flats either side of your own, and you were crossing the border. The nearest play park was five minutes' walk from our house. It was no more than an open, grassy space the size of a football pitch with a small playground at one end. I passed it on my walk to and from school, but I would never dare to stop and play there.

It was a sunny, warm afternoon, as they often are in our memories of school holidays. For several days, our local gang had been making bows and arrows. Most of them used garden shears to cut switches from big bushes, ones that the council had planted at the bottom of all our gardens. The string was begged from parents or stolen from their sheds. Someone, probably an older boy, must have had a penknife which we used to make notches in the ends of the arrows so that they slotted into the string. But I remember my bow and arrows being cut from bamboo canes, for some reason, which made them better than the others. The bow was strong and flexible, and it arced slightly when I pulled the string back with the arrow. Someone suggested going round to the park and shooting our arrows there. We must have felt brave. I expect being armed made a difference.

We stopped at the edge of the play park and I remember it was very busy and noisy with children of all sizes. But most of them seemed to be about our ages. There were no grown-ups, of course, things were different back then. A group of smaller children – one of them was a girl – saw our bows and arrows and started goading us. 'Let's see you fire them then,' they were saying, 'bet you can't fire them right.' I must have been angry, so I fired an arrow and it hit the little girl in her eye. It was an accident. All I remember is running and running, harder and faster than I'd ever run, all the way home. And the voices behind me, shouting: 'Come back you coward, we know where you live.' I ran up our path, went round to the back of the house, dumped the bow and two remaining arrows in the shed, dashed in the back door and raced upstairs to my room. I lay on my bed panting for breath. When I regained it my heart was still pounding like it would burst out of my chest at any moment.

I knew I wouldn't get away with it. Just lay there waiting for the letter box to rattle. I kept making the sound of it in my mind, a kind of preparation. Nothing in me wanted to go downstairs and tell my mother what had happened. The chasing children must have seen me run up our path, memorised the house number and gone back to tell the girl's mother, because the letter box did rattle a while later. I heard a woman's raised voice followed by my mother's shocked tones. I clasped my hands over my ears, trying not to wet myself with fear.

The sound of the front door closing was followed by a long silence. Eventually, I heard my mother shouting at me to come downstairs this minute. When I reached the bottom of the stairs she slapped my legs, shouted at me and sent me back to my room. Her slaps and shouts were nothing, meant nothing compared to the fear I had felt running home and hiding in my room. When my father got home from work, I was called down again to the living room. My father was never comfortable with giving me a row, I think he saw that as my mother's job. He said a few words but he didn't shout and once more I was sent to my room. The punishment had been increased now – I was to have no tea and was ordered to stay in my room until morning. I'm sure there was something else about the whole incident, but I seem to have forgotten it now. In any case, what I remember is quite bad enough.

I like to think that the bow and arrow disaster hasn't had a lasting effect on me; that it didn't set me on a path of always running away, of always trying to hide from fear. I like to think that, but I'm not sure I really believe it.

As I turned onto the Canberra ring-road I gave myself a mental slap. You're here in Australia, driving into the centre of the capital city. That's bravery, I told myself, not fear.

In the event, the ring road proved easy enough to navigate and I reached my hotel just after four o'clock. Feeling restless, I checked the street map and headed straight to the National Archives. A brief pang of guilt about snooping into Archie and Nesta's lives, followed by a justification – up there on the bluff, hadn't my aunt almost encouraged me?

*

'Your access is limited to five files or one box of records in any single viewing.'

Her badge said Roz, but I decided against using her name for now. 'And is it just one viewing per day?'

Roz pressed her palms against the edge of the counter and gave a little smirk which revealed faint dimples. 'Thought you'd ask that. Look, there's no firm rule but we expect you to be reasonable. Fortunately, we're pretty quiet this afternoon. If you let me know what you're looking for I can probably help you find it quicker anyway… if we've got the records, of course.'

I leaned forward, rested my forearms on the counter and told her what I was interested in. She kept nodding as she scribbled on a pad and said okay several times, stretching out the vowels the way Australians do. She looked up from her notes. 'Have you used a microfiche reader before?' Roz paused. 'And what's so funny?' she said.

I loved her directness. 'Sorry, I didn't mean to laugh. Look, I'll be frank. I'm a history academic. I'm meant to be half a mile down the road in the National Library, poring over dirty old manuscripts and convict transportation records. But I'm not, I'm here in the National Archives because I want to find out more about my family.'

Roz smiled properly for the first time. Small, even teeth. 'So, you probably know how to use a microfiche reader, at least.' Was she making fun of me or just being playful? 'Let's have the details then,' she sighed. Roz confirmed they held microfiche copies of detailed passenger records for arrivals and departures at all Australian ports from 1924 onwards. The films were sorted by country of origin, year and voyage. That was it as far as indexation went. She turned and sat down at her computer to find out the number of films covering departures from Britain for the years 1954 to 1956. I tried not to stare but I couldn't help it. Short dark hair, neatly styled; small and slim but not boyish. The word elfin came to mind.

She stood up a couple of minutes later. 'Looks like twenty-four reels of film, one for each voyage. Each film contains a copy of the passenger list with port of debarkation. Since we're not busy, I'll let you have all the films at once. We'll call it a box.' She reached under the counter and pulled out a sheet of paper. 'You fill in the forms. I'll get the reels and we'll set you up on a reader.'

The room had cubicles set out in a grid like you find in an open-plan office. The place was quiet apart from the soothing hum of air conditioning. A man sat with his back to us, regularly turning a dial on the machine in front of him as he scrolled through a reel of film. I couldn't see anyone else. Roz walked to the end of the farthest row of cubicles and sat down at the reader. She spooled the first reel onto the machine and switched on the monitor. Then she stood up and prompted me to take a seat. I caught a scent of peaches from her hair when she leaned forward to turn the dial. Her bare arm was lightly tanned, and I longed to touch it.

Roz looked at the screen as she spoke. 'So, each film is a series of images of the passenger list which should be sorted in alphabetical order by port of debarkation. That means Fremantle passengers first, then Melbourne and finally Sydney. But hey, I guess you're familiar with passenger lists. Only, in your case, they're convicts, and the lists are handwritten?' She flashed me an impish grin.

My stomach fluttered, but I managed to nod stupidly. 'And you're okay for me to change the reels? I wouldn't want to disturb you every time I need to change the film.' She pursed her lips and made a slight droning noise. 'Okay,' she smiled, 'since it's you. Any problems, you know where to find me.' Her hand seemed to half-wave of its own accord as she turned and left the room.

I watched her all the way, hoping she would turn around just to check I was still there. But she disappeared from view without a backwards glance. I pushed the chair back on its castors, clasped my hands behind my neck and let out a long breath. My first thought was, how long can I find excuses to keep coming here? But I also fought hard to push Roz from my mind for all sorts of reasons. Because I needed to start working through the passenger lists; because I was only in Canberra for three days; because I only met Roz twenty minutes ago; because I had no idea what her situation was or whether she… whether she what? Felt the same way? *Hah, forget it Jim, it's not worth it. Life is so much easier now that it's just you. Let your emotions loose and it will only end in tears; and probably sooner than you think. Much sooner.*

The first reel contained fifty-seven images of a passenger list. Another tinge of guilt about what I was doing but a ripple of excitement too. Printed at the top of each sheet was the name of the ship, the *Georgic*, followed by the date at which it docked at each Australian port – it reached Fremantle on the twenty-third of February 1954. And where it had sailed from, in this case, Liverpool. Finally, the name of the ship's master, the medical officers and the shipping agents. Below the heading was a list of passengers in alphabetical order of their surnames, about fifty to a page. I did a quick calculation and was surprised at the numbers – nearly three thousand people on this voyage. In the column to the right of the surname was each person's first name followed by their destination address in Australia. It looked promising. First of all, I wanted to find Archie. I turned the dial quickly, scrolling through the images for Fremantle until I reached the records for Melbourne, where I knew he disembarked. The details had all been typed which made reading much easier than I was used to with handwritten convict lists. I scanned both pages of surnames starting with T but found nobody called Archibald Thomson. I checked again, more slowly, but he wasn't there. Next I went back and did the same for the Fremantle and Sydney debarkations, just in case. Again, I drew a blank.

Before I changed the reel, I glanced at my watch – ten past five and closing time was five-thirty. Time for one more film. With luck I might just find Archie today but Nesta was a wholly different problem. For a start, I had no idea what her surname was before they married. In spite of the warnings I had given myself, I felt a warm glow. I knew for sure that I would be back here tomorrow with a chance to see Roz again.

8

Aden, 1955

Billy sat on the bottom bunk and shook his head. 'No way, if Sinatra's in it. I can't stand that wee eyetie.'

Archie laughed and dropped down from the upper bunk. 'Just remember the crew are Italian, big man, so I'd watch what you're saying and who you're saying it to. Anyway, there's *The Lavender Hill Mob* tomorrow night if that suits you better.'

Billy swung his arm dismissively. 'Bloody English. I've got enough of them to deal with onboard without watching them at the pictures too.'

'Tell you what Billy, why don't I see if they've got *Whisky Galore!* and ask them to show it every night from here to Melbourne?'

Billy gave a concessionary laugh. 'Fair enough. Look, I'll maybe just take a stroll round the deck, then look in on the main lounge, see if anyone fancies a game of draughts or a hand of cards. This Red Sea is like a mill pond and that suits me just fine, so I may as well make the most of it.'

Archie thought about the film. He'd never seen *From Here to Eternity*, but he knew what it was about. For some reason, it attracted him in a way it would never have done back home. Maybe it was to do with being on a ship but, hopefully, the *Fairsea* wasn't about to be bombed by the Japanese. Part of him felt hesitant about going to the show, but his stronger side told him to get on with it. It was three days since the incident with Nesta and Carwyn in the bar and he hadn't caught sight of either of them since. If she's there, she's there, he couldn't go skulking around avoiding her for ever.

His gaze swept the room as he entered the fore lounge, its lights already half-dimmed. He spotted Nesta on the left side of the second row from the front. On her own, or no sign of Carwyn at least. Archie went to his right, to the end of the fifth row back, where the chair was angled slightly into the room. He could just see the screen and Nesta without needing to move his neck. She sat completely still, facing the white canvas as it flickered into life. It occurred to Archie that Carwyn could be here on his own somewhere. Maybe he was at the back of the lounge watching Archie.

'The film is two hours, give or take,' Luigi had said when Archie asked him earlier. 'And, yes, there is a ten-minute intermission halfway through. Just enough time for the bathroom and a quick smoke.' The lounge was almost full, and the noisy chatter faded to a murmur when the credits started to roll. The film was in black and white which surprised Archie. He thought all American films were in lurid colour these days. In a strange way the picture felt like it belonged to a distant past, a past he was sailing away from, day by day. Where Archie was going there would be no war and no obsession with all things American. Surely Australia had its own films, its own music, its own dances, didn't it? He hoped so. As for the Japanese? So many things had changed in the decade since those mushroom clouds ended the war in the Far East. He'd read that Japan was rebuilding fast, putting its energy into developing modern industries. And when you looked at an atlas, Australia was a lot closer to Japan than it was to America. Maybe the world was tilting on its axis a little, maybe he was heading for the right place.

Billy was spot on about Sinatra though. Great singer, but there was something about the guy that made you want to hit him – hard. Made you sympathise with Ernest Borgnine. Archie stuck it out until the intermission. When the lights went up, he stayed in his seat and waited for Nesta to make a move. She stood up, tucked her bag under her arm and joined the line of people leaving the room on the far side from Archie. If he timed his own move right, he could bump into her casually as they entered the foyer.

Say something. Quick, before the moment's lost. 'Are you enjoying the film?'

'Archie. I haven't seen you for a few days.' She stood facing him, her eyes locked on his eyes. He held his nerve and held her gaze.

'And I haven't seen you either, come to think of it. How are you?'

A bulky man squeezed past him, pushing Archie forward, closer to her. So close he had to raise his arms slightly. It was either that or touch her waist, her hips.

Nesta let out a short, nervous-sounding laugh. 'I think we're standing in the wrong place. Shall we take a quick stroll around the deck? It was so stuffy in the lounge.' She made her way out of the foyer, glancing round at him. 'And sorry, I didn't answer your question. I'm quite enjoying the film. It's a bit heavy on the melodrama but it's alright for a bit of light entertainment. I suppose it all helps to relieve the boredom.'

He murmured agreement but his mind was elsewhere. This was no time to hesitate, something had to be said before the moment was lost. 'Look, about the other evening. In the bar, I mean. With Carwyn. I'm sorry, I shouldn't have said what I did. It was just…'

'It was just, you wanted to know if what he'd been telling you was true. Is that it?' Her voice sounded playful but he heard something anxious in it too. Archie watched the corners of her mouth turn up, her eyes sparkle.

'Well, maybe. Alright, I did want to know. But I'm sorry if I made it difficult between you two.'

'To be honest, Archie, I think you did me a favour. It certainly helped to open my eyes. Let's just say that Carwyn and I had a frank discussion after you left the bar. Up to that point, I had no idea what he was up to.' She turned her head, looking out to sea, and her voice seemed to slow as if she were talking in her sleep. 'Call me naïve if you like, but honestly, I wasn't leading him on. That wasn't my intention.'

A bell rang, signalling the end of the intermission.

'We'd best be heading back,' she said.

Archie sighed. 'I think I'll give it a miss. Like you say, a bit heavy on the melodrama.'

He thought Nesta looked at him like she cared. 'But what will you do?'

'Probably take a stroll up on the boat deck. I do that most nights. I like to look at the stars, watch the ship making its way across the map. If that makes sense.'

She was silent for a moment. 'Yes, it makes sense. I think it's good to remind ourselves how long this journey is. Of course it makes sense. Look, I'm sorry but I need to go. Perhaps we'll have a chance to talk again.'

'I hope so.'

He stood and watched her join the noisy group of people making its way through the foyer and into the fore lounge. Part of him wanted to go back in too. But if he couldn't be with her to talk to, what was the point? As he climbed the stairs to the boat deck his legs felt heavy. He fished his cigarettes and lighter from his pocket, waited until he was standing by the rail and made sure the first drag was long and slow. Where to next? More strange feelings, like an aching loneliness. Like something being slightly out of reach, a train that's just left an empty station without you. No! No, he told himself, it's up to you to make it happen. For God's sake, don't have any regrets. Make bloody sure you have that chance to talk again.

The wind picked up a little from the east as the ship edged towards the open water of the Gulf of Aden. Archie stubbed out his cigarette and crossed the deck to the starboard side. Faint lights flickered from some distant land. Probably French Somaliland, he thought, there wasn't much else round here. Wherever it was, people were out there in the darkness, across the sea, cooking and eating and talking and laughing and crying.

'You were right about the stars.'

Archie's neck hairs tingled. He turned to face her. 'Yes, they seem to get bigger and clearer every night. It's like the ship's sailing upwards.' He heard his own voice and felt separated from the words he spoke. 'So what happened to the film?'

Nesta stepped forward and stood next to him, rested her hands on the rail. 'The lounge was so hot and stuffy. I thought of what you said about looking at the stars and decided, yes, that would be better than this.'

'I'm glad you did.'

He wanted to rush ahead, to empty his brimming heart. But he felt paralysed too, as if the words were stuck in his throat. 'Anyway, you were saying, before the bell went for the end of the intermission?'

'Was I?' She turned to face him, that faint smile on her lips again. And then it vanished. Did she see his seriousness? He hoped so, he didn't want her to play games.

'About Carwyn. How he got the wrong impression.'

Nesta lowered her head. 'I feel so stupid. At first, I felt safe. Because he was there, it gave me confidence to enjoy myself. I could walk into the restaurant, or take the dance floor, without feeling self-conscious or nervous. That's a good feeling.' She raised her head and looked at him. A kind of defiance. 'I don't suppose you can imagine what it might be like for a woman on her own, cooped up on a ship for five weeks or whatever it is.'

Archie looked over her head at the darkness then returned her gaze. 'No, I suppose I can't really imagine. It's just that, when Carwyn hinted that you were an item, I wasn't surprised. I remembered seeing the pair of you once or twice on board, and then in the souk at Port Said, of course. Anyone would have thought you were together. So, what I said in the bar, I didn't mean to cause problems between the pair of you.' He let the lie linger in the night air.

She smiled, warmly he thought. 'As I said, you helped open my eyes to what was going on.' She lowered her head again. 'I thought we were just friends, no more than that.'

Something occurred to Archie. 'So, tomorrow morning. You won't be going ashore when we dock in Aden. I mean, if you don't have... anyone to go with?'

'Well, I'm sure I could tag along with some group or other. I saw plenty of people doing that in Port Said. Or...'

Archie hesitated briefly. 'Or I could...' he thought of 'accompany' but rejected it, '...we could go ashore together, if you like?'

'Yes, I'd like that, Archie, I really would.'

He looked away from her, out to sea again. Billy, he thought, I really hope Billy's not feeling too good tomorrow.

*

The boy looked no more than five or six years old. Archie assumed the man in the too-short shorts and white plimsoles was the child's father. The man squatted in the piercing light of the square, squinting through the viewfinder of his camera. A couple of waves of his hand told the boy to move a little to the right. The mother stood by the cameraman and shouted encouragement in educated west of Scotland tones. And then it was done. Captured for posterity, young Ronald wearing his kilt, clan tartan no doubt, standing in ninety degrees of scalding, midday heat by the clock tower in Aden.

Nesta was smiling, Billy had a stupid grin on his face. Archie looked grim. There was something about the scene that made him want to scream. And no amount of Nesta, her scent, the freshness of her pink cotton dress, could stop his feelings about these... these bloody tourists. Maybe Billy's presence also tilted Archie's mood that way.

More likely he'd simply had enough of the endless stream of comments from the crowd of passengers after they all disembarked at Prince of Wales' quay. Men, young and old, mouthing off about how smart the local policemen looked in their khaki shorts and shirts, their black belts with brass buckles, black sandals, all topped off with a black fez. 'That's the empire for you. Very smart compared with the Egyptians in Port Said,' they said. 'All those thugs of Nasser with their Luger automatics and lazy sneers.'

The groups of passengers crowded along the road from the quay and caught sight of the RAF base across the bay at Khormaksar. Archie remarked loudly, 'If I had ten bob for every time I've heard the words "empire" and "colony" in the last two minutes, I'd be a bloody rich man.' So, when they arrived at the clock tower, the so-called Big Ben of the East, and saw the boy in his kilt, Archie was ready to explode.

Nesta touched his arm lightly. 'I'd like to go to the market.'

Archie turned to face her, felt his anger begin to drain away. He looked at Billy and raised his eyebrows. 'Fancy it, Billy? You missed out on the souk in Egypt. And remember, it's a British market here. You might even get a cup of tea and a scone if you're lucky.'

Billy stuck his hands in his pockets and said he didn't fancy it, no offence. He'd had enough of stuffy, smelly places, having been laid up in his bunk with a sick bucket for most of the past few weeks. If it was all the same with them, he was going to find a shady café by the sea. Somewhere with a breeze and a view and an ice-cold beer. Archie was torn. Of course, he wanted to be alone with Nesta but he didn't want to push Billy away. This was the first time they'd been on dry land together since they left Liverpool. But Billy was adamant.

The pair of them pressed on up the hill of the Crescent into the Tawahi district, jagged rock walls of the Crater towering above the buildings. The *Fairsea* crew said there was no souk here. Streets with shops and some market stalls, yes, they said. But Aden is an English city, so no Arab souk. At the top of the Crescent, Nesta turned right into a narrow street. Shops selling leather goods were busy with tourists; busy with local men shouting to each other in their own language, shouting to tourists in English. She slipped her arm through Archie's, clasped her hand on his forearm. He smiled at her, tried to hide the thumping of his heart.

She stopped to look at stalls of bags, purses and wallets, shoes and slippers. 'I like these,' she said, picking up a pair of embroidered slippers. The toes narrowed to a point which then curled up and back like a cobra. Archie thought they were too small for anyone to wear. A baby, possibly, but babies didn't wear slippers, or not ones like that.

'They're so small, must be an ornament. Which reminds me,' he said, 'I need to send something home. They'll be expecting me to.'

Nesta held the tiny pair of shoes in the palm of her hand. 'How about these? They're quite exotic, don't you think? And sweet. I'd like to send something to my family too. I didn't manage it in Port Said what with the... the incident. Perhaps we could each buy a pair? Bargain for them?'

That was just fine with Archie, so they haggled with the shop owner but not for too long. Just for the fun of it really. The man wrapped each pair of slippers ready for mailing and gave them directions to the main post office, back towards the quay. They stopped in the square by the clock tower again and looked across the water. From here, halfway up the hill, they could take in the scale of the bay. Nesta started counting the number of ships out loud but gave up at thirty-something. On the north bank of the bay, beyond all the shipping, stood the British Petroleum oil refinery; its towers glinted in the sun. Archie felt his stomach rumble and suggested stopping for lunch. They found a restaurant near the square, grateful for the shade and a breeze off the sea. The menu was British. Makes a pleasant change after all that pasta on board, they agreed.

While they waited for the food to arrive, Nesta talked about her impressions of Aden. How hot it was; the tarry smell in the air, a dryness in her throat; how many ships there were in the bay; how it all felt very strange, so many reminders of home out here on the edge of the Arabian desert. Archie lit a cigarette, listened to the quiet lilt of her voice.

'You know, it's the second busiest port in the world, after New York,' he said.

'Really. But how do you know that?' She looked at him squarely, like she was interested to hear his answer.

Her hand waved the smoke away so he stubbed out the cigarette and cleared his throat. 'It says so in the leaflet. There was a pile of them on a table outside the restaurant this morning. I took one and read it from cover to cover. Aden's all about the oil refinery. And its location too, at the bottom of the Arabian peninsula. Most of the ships bring crude oil from all over the area to be refined here and shipped onwards to Europe and beyond. But it won't last forever.' He nodded towards the bay. 'There are rebels out there in the desert, beyond the refinery. This place wants independence just like all the other colonies. Sorry, I didn't mean to go on.'

Nesta leaned back in her chair as the waiter set down a plate of lamb cutlets. 'No, don't say sorry. It's interesting, really. Perhaps I'll look out for these leaflets before we go ashore again.'

'Well, I think you've missed your chance, I'm afraid.' Archie laughed as he cut his shepherd's pie through the middle, watching the steam rise. 'We don't dock again until we get to Fremantle. Then Melbourne and Sydney. You're going to Sydney, right?' His hands shook a little when he asked the question.

Nesta talked about her music scholarship. The conservatorium was right in the centre of the city, next to the botanic gardens. Her digs were already arranged in a boarding house close by, sharing a room with another girl; Canadian, she thought.

Archie's mood darkened a little. His pie lost whatever flavour it had. The hot breeze brushed a few papery leaves across their table. Nesta going to Sydney was hardly news, Carwyn had told him as much in the bar. But hearing the words from her lips felt like a slap in the face. He let the sting subside. Don't give up before you've even started.

'Sorry, I didn't catch that?' he said.

She repeated the question. 'And what about you – where are you going?'

Had Carwyn not passed on to her all that Archie had told him? Maybe they didn't get beyond talking about their own issues after he left them in the bar on the ship that evening.

'I'm going to Melbourne,' he said. 'No job to go to though. I'm a butcher by trade but I reckon I can find something better out there. I don't plan to spend the rest of my life hacking carcasses and serving in a shop.' He wondered if he sounded aggressive or defensive or a bit of both.

Maybe Nesta thought so too because she changed the subject and asked about his family, where he came from. He told her about life in Leith. It felt strange, talking to someone about where he lived, his ma and pa, his brothers and sisters, his job. Had he never done this before? Maybe a bit, with girls he'd stepped out with. But all of them lived in Leith anyway, knew the area and probably knew some of his brothers and sisters as well. No, this was different, as if he was standing back and watching his whole life to date from a distance. It felt like a kind of reckoning for everything that had brought him to this point. He thought it didn't add up to much.

Archie finished chewing a mouthful of pie before asking Nesta the same questions. She said she was from Cardiff, effectively an only child. Two older brothers had died before she turned ten; the first from tuberculosis, the second was killed at Tobruk. When she was fourteen her voice began to stabilise. 'Mezzo-soprano,' she said. Archie had no idea what she meant but nodded anyway. With their sons both dead, her parents wanted to invest everything in her singing talent. She had graduated last summer from Cardiff University and now here she was, on her way to Australia.

Archie thought it was odd that she would go off to the other side of the world, leaving behind her parents who had already lost so much. He felt a chasm open between himself and Nesta. Sydney and opera, Melbourne and butchers' knives. They were travelling on the same ship, but with different destinations, different prospects.

They split the bill and walked down to the post office with their pairs of slippers. A British Army jeep with two officers revved its way up the Crescent. Nesta turned, shaded her eyes and watched it sweep around a corner and out of sight.

'It's a funny old place but I wish I could stay a bit longer,' she said. 'Someone said there's a bathing club over the other side of the hill. Sounds like fun.'

Archie said nothing and kept on walking. The brown paper of his parcel started to feel damp. He shifted his grip and held it tightly by the string, allowing it to cut into his fingers.

They stood a couple of yards apart in separate queues at the post office, reached the counters at the same time, each handing over their East African shillings. Archie's parcel was handled more quickly than hers. He waited outside under the canopy, grateful for some shade but his head still throbbed in the relentless heat.

Was that it then? he wondered. Was that as close as they were ever going to get – her arm in his, shopping for souvenirs to send back home?

They walked in silence along the quay towards the *Fairsea*. Half way along, Archie looked up and saw Carwyn on the promenade deck. He appeared to be watching people closely as they went on board across the gangplank. Like counting sheep into a pen. Then he scanned the quayside, caught sight of the pair of them. Archie watched Carwyn stare for a moment, then turn abruptly and disappear inside.

'I think we've been spotted,' Nesta said. Archie sensed a hint of amusement in her tone but there was a tremor there too.

'Does it matter?' He heard the snap in his voice.

'No, not really, I suppose.'

Archie watched lines appear on her forehead.

'He'll probably be feeling jealous,' she said. Almost a whisper.

'And does he have reason to be?' He wished he hadn't said that.

Nesta pursed her lips but Archie thought he saw laughter in her eyes. He hated her at that moment. She kept on walking and said nothing. He snatched a look, convinced he saw amusement still etched on her face. God, this was all wrong, it wasn't meant to feel like this. Back on board, when they reached the foyer, Archie muttered a few words – even he wasn't sure what they were – and ran downstairs, the soles of his shoes rattling on the metal steps.

9

Adelaide, 1997

It is a warm, late summer morning. Birdsong twangs and echoes through the garden's thick foliage. She closes her eyes, hears an orchestra tuning up, the rising murmur of an audience. And then Habanera from Carmen comes into her head. Tentatively, she sings the first two lines but her voice is thin and reedy. Love is a rebellious bird, indeed. But all of that is long gone. And it's far too early for daydreaming, she needs to concentrate on the here and now.

She sets her mug of coffee down on the mosaic tabletop and flips open her spiral-bound diary. The entries have been made with a green felt-tip pen. Her hand is highly individual and attractive; the sort of script marketing people use to advertise stylish pens. Louise at ten-thirty, so she will need to leave the house by ten. Later this afternoon she has to call in at the Indigo gallery to collect a tapestry. But before all that, there's Archie to see to. Unusually, he's not up and about yet and it's past eight o'clock. Then she hears a creak and looks up at the bathroom window being pushed open, followed by the sound of running water. Good. Now there's time to call Jim at his hotel in Canberra. Perhaps she'll catch him before he goes down for breakfast.

Often, she pictures cities by their opera houses and concert halls. With Canberra, however, she struggles. There's no worthy building that she can single out and hold in her mind's eye. Her head is full of wide streets, of trees, grass verges and smooth, white buildings which seem rather pleased with themselves. And that silly lake in the middle of it all, splitting the city apart, making it feel bigger than it is, really. She has never liked the place. Planned. Soulless and clinical. Still, it's a long time since she visited. Perhaps it has changed for the better, but she doubts it. You shouldn't design and build cities from scratch, she thinks. They're not like pieces of furniture to be assembled and used in their instant completeness. She lifts her empty coffee cup, holds it to her lips. No, cities ought to grow like people; they ought to allow for the passage of time and the effects of different experiences to leave their marks; for mistakes to leave imprints and blemishes which become part of their character. Accidental. Soulful and emotional.

Jim answers on the third ring, says he was about to go down for breakfast when he heard the phone. She tells him that she and Archie will be in Sydney next week. He sounds pleased but you can never tell. It's so much easier when you can see the whites of their eyes. And he's smart enough to make an oblique enquiry about the purpose of their trip. 'Don't feel obliged to meet up just because you'll be in Sydney,' he says, 'I'm sure you must have a busy schedule.' She's not falling for it though and ignores her nephew's comments completely. But there's something else. She asks him how his research is going at the National Library. It strikes her how long a pause can last on the phone. Eventually, Jim tells her he's been distracted by a visit to the National Archives. She almost senses his cheeks reddening. Something flashes through her mind: her tears on the bluff. After a moment, she says 'That sounds interesting and you can tell me all about it next week.'

They make arrangements to meet on Tuesday afternoon, a few hours after Archie's appointment at the clinic.

*

Have I seen her in that suit before? she wonders, feels sure she would have remembered it. A warm, reddish brown – burnt sienna comes to mind. It's off the peg, but the cut's too good for a chain store. The trousers are creased like a blade and they complement Louise's long, willowy shape. She likes that her counsellor dresses smartly for their sessions. Looks professional. None of that new age stuff with scarves the size of tablecloths and yoga pants covered with cat hairs. Or, God forbid, crystals. Although, there is a noticeable scent in the air, possibly of bergamot.

The room resembles something like her bank manager's office, without the desk. Mid-grey carpet tiles have been laid neatly. The walls, bare apart from a clock and a print of some limpid lagoon, have been painted pale blue. She sits opposite Louise. Matching navy armchairs with high backs and visible, ornate legs. Oxford or Cambridge? She can't remember. But she does recall where they left off at their session on Tuesday, two days ago. Louise had encouraged her to talk more about her marriage, her career and her children. A kind of eternal triangle in which Nesta's guilt is making up for lost time. It has been starved, held at bay over so many years, and now the beast is feasting. Not that her guilt overwhelms her. More that it rises up when she's least expecting it, like an enormous belch. And then she returns to her usual state, her perfected external self. Until the next time.

Louise picks up her cup of coffee from the low, oak veneer table between them and asks about Archie. Nesta tells her about the trip to Sydney next week to see the specialist. For some unknown reason, she also mentions that her nephew, Jim, from Archie's side of the family, will be in Sydney at the same time; that she has arranged to meet up with him again.

Louise seems curious. Perhaps she takes the reference to family as a route into the past. A way of unlocking Nesta's secrets. A portal – is that what they call it? Louise asks about Archie's family, something they've never discussed. Where are they from? Has Nesta ever met them? It feels like a whole new subject, one which reaches deeper inside her than she had realised. She tells her counsellor about the Thomsons, how many of them there are, or were. She talks about their pasty complexions which seem to blend in with the little grey council houses in which they live. She talks about their presbyterian dullness and their small-mindedness. She talks about the pathetic way they tried to look down their noses at her on the two occasions she has had the misfortune to be in their company. And she tells Louise all the other opinions she usually keeps to herself. When eventually she stops talking, Nesta closes her eyes, lets out a long breath and rests her head on the back of her chair.

Louise appears to take the hint, gives her a moment or two, then leans forward. 'I take it Archie's not like that,' she says, 'but what attracted you to him in the first place?'

Silence. Where does she start? She has never told anyone the truth about how they met. Not even her children, although they've never shown much interest. She draws deep from her well of memory, tells Louise about the voyage, mentions Carwyn, and describes the incident with Archie in Port Said when the boy stole her purse. That piques her counsellor's interest. 'Archie sounds very gallant,' Louise says, pronouncing the word in a garbled Australian-French accent.

Nesta places her hands on the arms of her chair, as if she's about to get up. 'You know, I've never told anyone this before. I think Archie let the boy go deliberately. He seemed to send me a signal. Look, this is how heroic I am. How fair-minded I can be. And I fell for it. At the time, it seemed like fate.'

'You've never asked Archie about it?'

'No, never. By the time we got to know each other better, the moment had passed. There were more important matters to deal with.'

Louise frowns and curls a strand of hair behind her ear. 'But surely you've had forty years to find time to ask him.'

Nesta hears a ripple of laughter in her counsellor's voice. God, I can do without the mocking tone, she thinks. I'm not paying her to laugh at me.

'Look, Louise, there's no point in latching onto the first piece of the jigsaw.' Latching on? An image of feeding Ewan with a bottle of formula flits through her mind. 'What I mean is, that might seem incredible as an isolated piece of information. But you need to look at it again, once you know the whole story. Once the jigsaw is complete, if you like.' Some missing pieces float into view but she bats them away.

Louise lets her arms rest on her lap, turns her palms upwards. 'So, can we try to fill in the missing jigsaw pieces? For example, can you tell me about these "more important matters" you had to deal with?'

Some of the missing pieces, she thinks. Nesta mirrors Louise's body language and hopes it's noticed. She talks about meeting with Carwyn and Archie in the ship's bar, and the consequences of their encounter. She mentions seeing Archie at the film show and going ashore in Aden with him. Louise probably thinks she's not answering the question but that's just tough; she will do it when she's good and ready.

'You know, for the first time on the voyage, I felt free. At the beginning, I was content to feel safe with Carwyn. He helped me find my sea legs, if you like. But after the big falling-out, there was a release. I suppose I wanted to have fun, to explore my feelings. And Archie was a way of doing that without being trapped or constrained in some way.' Nesta knows she's improvising but the words feel right, convincing. She warms to the task.

'Can you say more about the feelings you explored?'

Nesta rocks forward, clasps her knees. 'You have to realise that up to the point when I boarded the ship in Liverpool, I had been a very dutiful daughter. After what happened to my brothers, Mum and Dad invested everything in me. And I don't mean just money. I did everything they expected of me. Studied hard, practised my singing, did the right things to look after my voice. And avoided boys. Well, mostly. But I was twenty-two by the time I left for Australia. There was a grown-up me desperate to get out and show itself. That's what I mean by exploring my feelings.' A brief pause while her mind skips forward.

'And then that dreadful meeting in the ship's bar changed everything with Carwyn. It made me think about how I had behaved until then. Had I led him on? I was sure I hadn't but, all the same, he got the wrong impression and that's what counted. God knows how, but when I met Archie accidentally, at the film show, it never occurred to me to be cautious about how I acted. I do remember feeling a little thrill when we stood on deck watching the stars. Archie was nervous, I could tell that from his voice, the way he kept clearing his throat. And he fidgeted a lot. It gave me control, that's what I realised. It was such a different… such a new feeling for me. I sensed that this man wanted me. I quite liked that. And I liked him too, from what I'd seen so far. But I wasn't about to go swooning and falling into his arms.' She nods rapidly. 'No, as I say, I felt in control and that was a good place to be.'

She watches Louise glance at the wall. 'How are we doing for time?' she asks. Louise smiles and says, 'Don't worry, we're doing just fine.' Then she asks Nesta to talk about Aden. Did she still feel in control when they went ashore?

Nesta sits upright again, rests her hands on the arms of the chair like some queen from centuries past. 'Completely. I learned a little more about Archie. Some good things, some not so good. For instance, he was quick to get angry. I got the impression that he hated most of the people from the ship. Tourists, he called them. According to him, they all thought the British Empire still ruled half the bloody world, including Australia. He reckoned they were in for a shock when they got here. And Aden was a strange place. A little piece of empire on the edge of Arabia and it provided plenty of ammunition for Archie. We'd only been off the ship for ten minutes and his mood began to annoy me.'

'So, I dragged him off shopping for souvenirs. I couldn't have walked around those streets on my own. I felt safe there. Archie made me feel safe. He was what we used to call solicitous, but he never gave the impression that he was after something in return, if you know what I mean.' Nesta looks at the floor, breathes deeply then meets Louise's gaze again. 'After that, we stopped for lunch somewhere. We sat in the shade. The heat is a killer there, it's like Alice Springs in the middle of summer. Well, not quite, but you get the picture. I remember dry leaves from a tree falling on the table and scuttling off in the breeze like cockroaches. Anyway, Archie was rather quiet as we walked along the quayside on our way back to the ship. As soon as we got on deck, he just muttered something and stomped off down to the dormitories. God, what have I done now? I thought.'

'And what did you think you'd done? It sounds like Archie was upset.'

'Now this we have talked about at least once in the past forty years. I'm not sure I thought I'd done anything wrong. But ages later, it was when we were arguing about something else, Archie said that in Aden I was just toying with him. That I was just using him as a chaperone so I could go ashore and explore the city. He said I had no feelings for him, that we would never have got together if it hadn't been for what happened later.'

'And is that true?'

Nesta hugs her knees again, lifts her feet off the floor. 'You know, I've never been able to answer that question. Things happened and they changed everything. I often tell myself it was a matter of chance. But I do know it wasn't as simple as that. So few things in life are just a matter of chance, don't you think?'

10

Canberra, 1997

I was about to go down for breakfast when the room phone rang. That sort of thing always makes me jump and, instantly, I expected bad news. Maybe something's happened to Mum, I thought, but that was ridiculous. My family didn't even know where I was staying. It turned out to be Nesta. She told me that she and Archie were flying to Sydney for a couple of days next week, at the same time I was due to be there. Could we arrange to meet up? she asked. I tried to sound pleased, but I was suspicious too. They hadn't mentioned this trip when I left them in Adelaide last Sunday. Why not? Had they arranged it in the meantime? God forbid, they were doing it for my benefit.

I made some comment about not wanting them to go out of their way just to see me. Said I was sure they must have a busy schedule. But Nesta brushed that aside without telling me why they'd be in Sydney. She insisted on seeing me, so we arranged to meet the following Tuesday afternoon at some café they knew down in the Rocks area. Before we hung up, Nesta asked how my research was going. For a moment, I felt confused, that she was asking me about my snooping into her past, her and Archie's past. I wish I'd kept my mouth shut. But, somehow, I couldn't help myself and told her how I'd been distracted by some of the information in the National Archives. She sounded interested, said that she would look forward to hearing all about it, but it's so hard to tell when someone's on the other end of a phone line. All the same, I can almost hear my voice now – like I'd told her I had just uncovered some dark, family secret.

My body felt light and loose as I walked from the hotel to the archives. It was a ten-minute stroll along the flat, manicured avenues of central Canberra. Cars and buses hummed and purred. Cyclists and pedestrians made their way along wide paths towards parliament and the embassy district beyond. Everyone seemed to have a purpose, including me. Yesterday I had made a start on my research. Not my academic research on Walter Avery, which is what I should have been doing. No, my research into Archie and Nesta's voyage to Australia. And I met Roz, someone I was drawn to – that rare thing, for me at least, where you experience something way beyond words and ordinary feelings. Stupid or not, I told myself I was ready to go wherever these feelings led. In the gentle warmth of a late summer morning, I was confident that Roz would be waiting for me at the service counter when I arrived.

Alright, I'll be honest. When I walked up to the desk and there was no sign of Roz, my spirits dropped and pooled in a mess on the floor. I scanned the island of desks beyond the counter, but she wasn't there either. How brittle my moods were, back then. How stupid of me to stake my whole ability to function on a woman I didn't even know. Someone I had spoken to for no more than twenty minutes the day before. I backed away from the counter, went back to the foyer and stood there, pretending to pick through a rack of tourist leaflets. I was thinking hard. A day off, perhaps? Or she's sick. Or maybe she only works part-time. Whatever the reason, I had to find out.

Stella or Shelly – I can't remember exactly – was at the counter. I told her I'd been here yesterday and what materials I was researching. 'Roz, I think her name was,' I said, she'd been very helpful. 'Oh Roz,' she said, 'she'll be in late morning. Dentist appointment, I believe. Anyway, I can set you up with what you want,' she said.

Two hours I spent in the research room. Two bloody hours in front of a microfiche reader, pretending to look at images of passenger lists. My eyes scanned the names, but they may as well have been ingredients for a cake recipe for all I cared. Most of the time I was glancing at the door, looking at my watch, staring into space. I hated the effect Roz was having on me. Eventually, I decided I'd had enough and went in search of a coffee.

Everything in the café was white. The ceiling, walls, tables, chairs and lighting – all of them were white. Even the floorboards were a patchy white. I stared out of the large, bare window at silver green trees and sun-bleached grass. Watched the traffic cruising along Kings Avenue. When I turned back to drink my coffee, I saw Roz through the archway, pushing a tray along the counter. She swivelled her neck and laughed at the tall man behind her. He leaned forward, briefly held her upper arm. A whisper, then they broke free from each other. Their laughing eyes met. At that moment, I felt I could have hit the guy. But at least she was here, at last.

I kept a close watch on Roz and the man. When they carried their trays through to the seating area, I shielded the side of my head with my hand and looked out of the window again. I saw a pair of ghostly reflections drift by. There was only a handful of customers and little noise, but I didn't hear her voice. They must have sat at a distant table, somewhere behind me.

I needed to get out of there so I left the archives and took the short walk over to the National Library. This is where I should have been. I had given myself the morning off to search through the films for signs of Archie and Nesta. But only on condition that I spend the rest of my time in Canberra at the library, doing my academic research. I checked in at the research centre and confirmed I would be there first thing tomorrow morning. After that, I went down to the lake shore and followed the path round towards Lotus Bay. There was a faint breeze and shallow waves oscillated across the surface of the water. Something to break up the endless flatness, at least. For a while, I sat on a bench in Lennox Gardens and ate a sandwich I'd bought at a lakeside kiosk. I tried to dig myself out of this emotional hole. *Just remember, here you are in Australia. Australia, for God's sake!* Maybe it was my mood or maybe it was Canberra, but it didn't even begin to work. This city could be anywhere. Fabricated, featureless. A postcard from Canberra – of what? Where was its Harbour Bridge or its Flinders Street Station?

As I walked back slowly to the archives, I chided myself. 'Stop giving the city a hard time,' I said, 'it may yet come good.'

*

When I got back, I saw Roz standing at the counter. I stopped at the edge of the foyer and searched for a bottle of water in my backpack. I took a long drink and listened to my heartbeat ringing in my ear. As I approached the counter, opening lines ran through my head. *How was the dentist?* Or, *I saw you in the café earlier.* No, neither of them would do at all.

She looked up. 'I missed you this morning.' A sparkling look in her eyes.

'Yes, your colleague said you'd be in later. I mean, I only mentioned your name because you were really helpful yesterday. I just thought it would be easier…' *Stop right there. Stop digging.*

'That's okay. I'm glad you thought I was helpful,' she said. 'So, you want the same films you had out this morning?'

I nodded and Roz went off to retrieve the reels from the fire cabinet. When she came back, she handed me the stack of boxes and got me to sign a chit.

'Still searching, then?' she said. 'I know it can be tedious but if you find what you want in the end… well that makes it worth the while, doesn't it? Seek and ye shall find, and all that.'

'Of course. You don't get anywhere without giving things a go, do you? Anyway, thanks for these. I'd better get on, there's still a lot to go through.'

She smiled. 'You just let me know if I can help at all. You know where I am.'

The room with the microfiche readers was busier than it had been in the morning, not that I'd taken much notice. I found a spare desk near the door and settled down. Roz was still occupying my mind, so I went over our conversation several times. I felt we were back to where we left off yesterday and that was good enough. For now.

This morning had been a wash-out, so I scrolled through the two or three films I thought I had gone over earlier, in my distracted state.

I looked at them in date order, earliest voyages first. There was nothing on the first one but then on the next, I had some success. Proof that my mind had been elsewhere earlier. Like yesterday, I turned the dial forward, looking first at the names of those who got off the ship in Melbourne. Then, I turned backwards for Fremantle and forward again for Sydney. And there they were, in the Sydney section. Six entries for Thomson, all with the same destination address: Dept of Immigration, York St, Sydney. Bob and Jessie and their four children. Arrived in Sydney on 1 August 1954. I tried to picture them walking down the gangway of the *New Caledonian*, about to set foot in Australia, a chill wind snapping in from the ocean. Wrapped up tight in their well-worn winter coats. Making a fresh start. I stared at the names for a long time, a tingle in my cheeks and a faint tremor in my chest. Before I changed the reel, I made a note of the film and sheet references, sure I would be able to get a printout for a small fee.

Four more films drew blanks. Thousands of migrants in less than a year, arriving at the other side of the world from where they'd come. And the more I looked, the more I thought I glimpsed some of the people behind the names. The Barkers, all eight of them stepping off the *Georgic* in Fremantle on their way to the remote mining town of Kalgoorlie. Or Aidan Wainwright, getting off in Melbourne – on his own perhaps – and heading for Castle Forbes Bay, Tasmania. Aidan still had a long way to go.

An hour later, I had my second success. Archibald Thomson disembarked the *Fairsea* at Melbourne on 15 May 1955. His destination address said: Department of Immigration, 8 Elizabeth Street, Melbourne. I knew what that meant. He had no sponsor so, initially, he was going to an internment camp. It might be a hostel somewhere not too far from the city centre. But it could also mean an old army barracks with wooden huts, communal showers and toilets. If he was lucky and found a job quickly, he might be able to afford digs somewhere in town. I tried to picture Archie, looking full of purpose as he took in his new surroundings. But, somehow, I couldn't quite see him. Again, I made a note of the references for the film and the sheet.

So that left Nesta. My initial task was to check if she was on the *Fairsea* too. But I had two problems. First, I didn't know her surname before she married Archie. Second, I had no idea if Nesta was her given name or if it was short for something else. I pushed the chair back, folded my arms and looked up at the ceiling. So, what *did* I know? I knew she was Welsh, and she was known as Nesta.

'How are you doing?'

I must have jumped a little. Roz perched on the edge of the table and looked down at me.

'Sorry, you look like you're deep in thought,' she said. 'I didn't mean to startle you. I was just passing and thought I'd see how it was going.'

I met her gaze, determined to hold it. 'No, it's fine. I was miles away. Actually, do you mind if I ask you something? About names.'

'Fire away,' she said, so I asked her about the name Nesta, but she'd never heard of it. Struggled to suggest what it might be short for, if anything. I talked a little about what I was looking for and why.

'You mean you haven't asked them?' Roz said, a challenge in her voice.

I didn't want her to think I was snooping so I explained how Archie told me that Nesta was the family historian. And how my aunt had reacted when I spoke to her on the bluff. Roz nodded like she believed me. There was an intimacy about sharing the information. It felt like our secret.

'Yes. Families,' she said. I waited for her to say more but she just made a little grimace and looked away. A moment later she pushed herself off the table and said, 'Anyway, I must be getting back. Look, let me know how you get on with Nesta. I mean it.'

At first, I considered searching the *Fairsea* film by using common Welsh surnames. It was easy to list the obvious ones: Davies, Edwards, Stevens, Thomas, Williams and so on. Like naming the Welsh rugby team back in those days. But even if I did that, I would still be looking for someone with a first name of Nesta. On the other hand, I could just run my eye, very slowly, down the column of first names on each of the fifty-two sheets. After thinking about the merits of each, I chose the latter approach.

The names were easy enough to read but the letters had an inky thickness which made them appear slightly blurred. I rested my eyes for a few moments after each sheet. There was nothing under Fremantle which didn't surprise me. Nothing under Melbourne either which was disappointing. My eyes throbbed and my head hurt. I was starting to lose concentration with a few sheets to go when I saw it in the Sydney section.

Williams Nesta   Sydney Conservatorium of Music, NSW

I took a deep breath and looked again. The Welsh surname was perfect. And although Sydney was a surprise, the first name and the address made me feel certain I'd found her. So it was true, they *did* travel on the same ship but they got off at different ports. I couldn't be sure that they'd met on board but it seemed likely, even though the *Fairsea* had thousands of people on board. For a moment I saw Nesta on the bluff, dabbing her eyes with a tissue. Had something happened on the voyage, perhaps?

From what I'd discovered so far only one thing was certain: Archie and Nesta travelled to Australia on the same voyage. Anything else was speculation.

I was making a note of the sheet reference when something caught my eye. On the same page, several rows down from Nesta's name was an entry which had been scored out. I thought it must have been done with a pencil because the typed first name and surname were partially visible underneath. It wasn't possible to make out the names, but I scanned across to the destination address which hadn't been touched. It said: Sydney Conservatorium of Music, NSW. I looked at the list of surnames again. There were seven rows between Nesta's entry and the scored-out name. The surname in all seven rows was also Williams. The first row below the scored-out name said Williams too. Then I looked at the destination addresses for the others: Parramatta, Katoomba, Hurstville, Brisbane. Just the two of them for the conservatorium – Nesta and her scored-out namesake. They could be siblings or cousins. Or were they married? Despite a growing sense of guilt, I felt drawn in more deeply.

Back at the counter, I returned the boxes of film to Roz, all except the two from which I wanted copies made. She loaded the films onto a reader.

'So, a successful session?' she said, handing over three sheets of paper still warm from the printer.

'Very, thanks. In fact, there's something I hope you might be able to help with.' I showed her the copy of Nesta's sheet and pointed to the scored-out name. 'Any idea what this might mean? Not that it matters. I'm just curious because the destination address is the same as my aunt's and I reckon they share the same surname.'

Roz put on a pair of glasses and peered at the list. 'I've not come across this before. Could be this person never sailed from Liverpool in the first place. Or maybe they got off the ship earlier – Suez or Colombo or wherever they stopped back in those days. Or they might have died, I guess. Look, we're kind of busy right now but I should have a chance to look at this later this afternoon.' She looked at me over the top of her narrow-framed glasses. 'How are you fixed for the rest of the day?'

I hesitated but nothing in me wanted to lie. 'I'm pretty much done for the day. I guess I might do some sightseeing.'

'So, you'll be free in an hour or so.' She smiled, leaned across the counter and whispered, 'But, hey, don't tell the locals I said that. No, seriously, if you can come back around a quarter past five?'

'You close at five-thirty though. I don't want to put you out at all.'

'No worries. If we run over time, you'll just have to buy me a drink.'

Was I grinning stupidly? Possibly. More likely, I just looked shocked. I took a deep breath and said, 'Or dinner. I'd really like to buy you dinner.'

'Okay,' Roz said, 'see you later.'

I walked back to the hotel replaying the conversation in my head. Did I really say, buy you dinner? Should I have said take you out to dinner? But what did it matter – she said yes.

*

Roz placed her knife and fork neatly on the plate and pushed it away from her. 'God, that was good. You probably think I haven't eaten for days. Like you're feeding some poor homeless person you've picked up off the streets.'

'I'm glad you enjoyed it. And thanks for choosing the restaurant. I wouldn't have had a clue.' I looked at her, as if to confirm she was really there. A voice in my head told me to be careful but I slapped it away. Part of me hated this situation. All I really wanted was to race ahead and feel comfortable in Roz's company. For it all to be so natural that neither of us had to try. I knew that took time, but I didn't have time to spare.

I had arrived at the archives just after twenty past five, a few minutes late. Roz pointed to a waiting area in the foyer where cushioned stools were set around a low table covered with tourist leaflets. Five minutes later she joined me. She wore a short denim jacket over a cotton dress, and a brown leather bag hung from her shoulder. The archives would be closing shortly, she said, but we could stay in the foyer longer. Security would let us out when we were ready.

Roz produced a sheet of paper from her bag and unfolded it. She had checked all the records for the *Fairsea* voyage that Archie and Nesta took in 1955. There were no recorded deaths on the voyage; nor was there any information about passengers leaving the ship permanently before it docked in Fremantle. 'The passenger list,' she said, 'was typed up after the ship left Liverpool; it was a record of people who had boarded there and which port they were destined for in Australia.' Roz had also talked to some colleagues about the mystery of the scored-out name but none of them could explain it. So, none the wiser, we left the archives and walked to a lakeside fish restaurant. 'It's not expensive,' she promised. But I really didn't mind.

A waiter cleared the table and asked if we would like to see the dessert menus. I looked at Roz. She shook her head, smiled and patted her stomach. We ordered two coffees.

It seemed an age and a whole world away since I had noticed her in the café earlier. The man I saw her with turned out to be her flatmate's boyfriend. Not that I'd asked. She mentioned it when talking about something else – he was part of a team working on a long-term project to put most of the archive's records onto the World Wide Web.

'In time, I expect they'll do the same with the convict transportation records,' I said. 'And then there'll be no need for people like me to travel all the way to Australia. We'll be able to sit in our offices and look at everything with a few clicks of a mouse.' I felt a wave of sadness pass through me. *Change the subject.*

'Are you from Canberra?'

Roz laughed and reached for the salt cellar. She turned it round a few times. 'No. I grew up in a little town called Rockhampton. Bet you don't know where that is.'

'Somewhere north of Brisbane?'

She looked up, surprised. 'Yep, you're right. Only, in this case somewhere means six hundred kilometres.'

'So how on earth did you end up in Canberra? Sorry, I don't mean to pry.' We leaned sideways in opposite directions to let the waiter set our coffees down.

'No worries,' she said. 'It's a long story but I'll give you the short version, for now.'

Roz spent most of the next ten minutes or so addressing the salt cellar but when she finished, she put it down firmly on the table and turned to me. 'So what do you think?'

It's funny. I often feel like nothing surprises me. Whatever people tell me about their lives, or the lives of others, I'm never shocked. It has nothing to do with personal experience. God knows, my life has been endlessly unremarkable. Perhaps it happens because I read and research a lot about harsh experiences, and that gives me a kind of vicarious worldliness.

So, when Roz told me about her life, I didn't feel shocked at all. But I did feel privileged. Why would this stranger, who I so wanted to get to know, tell me such personal details? She seemed to be laying bare who she was and doing it deliberately.

Roz told me she was an only child. Her father worked in tourism. From Rockhampton he arranged trips to the nearby Keppel Islands on the Great Barrier Reef. Fishing and diving trips mainly. He was away from home a lot of the time, particularly in high season. Her mother 'kept house', she said, never worked for a living. Roz went to the local school and had no particular hang-ups, just the usual stuff. One day, when she was twelve, she came home from school and found the house empty. Her father was guiding a fishing trip out on the reef and wouldn't be back for another week or so. There was no sign of her mother. No note to say she'd gone shopping or whatever. And the car had gone. Roz tried the neighbours, but they knew nothing and had seen nothing.

In the end, the woman next door phoned the police who, in turn, got in touch with Roz's dad. The neighbour took Roz in for the night while her father made his way back from the Keppels. When Roz woke the following morning, she expected her mother to push the door open and tell her it was time to get up. 'And it's been like that every morning for the past twenty years,' she said. Every morning she goes through the same waking up routine, but it never happens. She wonders where her mother has been all this time and what she's been doing.

I scraped some froth from the bottom of my cup. 'And you feel sure she's still alive?'

'Not sure, no. But I tell myself stories about her. They've never found her... alive or whatever... so what else have I got? I may as well make something up, invent a life for her.'

'And your dad – what does he say?'

Roz stared at me. 'About three weeks after Mum went missing, I was still bursting into tears several times a day. At first, Dad was okay about it. Not warm but not angry, either. And then one day, when I was crying in the kitchen, he turned to me. He said, "You won't get by on tears, Roz." And then he went off to work.'

I wanted to reach out for her hand. Or more than that – to wrap my arms around her; tell her everything would be alright. Whatever that meant. But part of me also took it as a warning. As if she was saying, so I took my father's advice and that's how I've got through the past twenty years, by toughening up. By growing a shell so hard that no one can break through it. Perhaps I wasn't thinking straight. After all, there was also her waking up routine and the stories she made up about her mother. Roz was complicated, that was all I could come up with, for now.

II

Indian Ocean, 1955

He was desperate for a cigarette. And fresh air. That combination would make everything a lot better. But Walmsley, the First Officer, was still writing on the ruled sheets of foolscap. Sitting opposite him across the formica table, Archie couldn't make out the words, but he followed the slow, cursive script with its long loops and curlicues across the page. They had been cooped up in the small, stuffy office in the deck house for more than four hours. Archie almost asked if they could open a window before he remembered there were no windows. Just a dirty old desk fan whose wisps of air died before they reached the end of the table. The guy may as well blow me a kiss, Archie thought, it would have more puff in it.

Walmsley looked up. 'Please bear with me, Mr Thomson, I won't detain you much longer. Hopefully.'

The man's clipped tones and thin moustache made Archie think of wartime films. And come to think of it, the First Officer did have a look of John Mills about him: small and wiry, his dark eyes full of concern; or was he just a good actor?

'What I would like you to do now, if you don't mind, is to read over the account I've written and let me know if there's anything you think I may have got wrong. Then, when we're both happy with it, you just sign on the dotted line and off you can jolly well go!'

Archie took the sheets and counted – there were twelve of them. The cigarette and fresh air would have to wait. He looked at the First Officer's neat but flamboyant script which covered both sides of the paper. His father's hand came to mind; there was nothing showy about Pa's writing, but it was readable and solid. He pictured him, pipe in hand, at the gate-legged table which dominated the living room. What would he be writing? Probably checking the deductions from his wage packet then setting out where the money would go: there would be so much to Ma for food and other groceries; a regular amount to the bank for bills that would fall due; and, if there had been overtime that week, something to the post office account for Christmas and birthdays and maybe a week at a cottage in the Borders if they were lucky. There would be a pittance left for Pa but he didn't seem to mind. He had his bible and his vegetable patch, he said, and that was all he needed for recreation. And what would Pa say if he could see his youngest son now? Archie thought he would tell him to play fair, to tell the truth and to make sure that truth was written down accurately. God sees everything, he would say. Archie began to read.

*

Three days had passed since the *Fairsea* left the sheltered waters of the port of Aden and steered a south-eastwards course for Fremantle. Two weeks the itinerary said, two more weeks at sea and then Australia, at last. When the ship entered the fringes of the Indian Ocean the waters were calm, and nobody complained. For many passengers, memories of crossing the Bay of Biscay were still fresh, even if the stale smell of sick below decks was long gone. On the second day out of Aden, a north-easterly picked up, rocking the ship like a baby's cradle, but no one was lulled to sleep. The restaurant and bar both stayed open; there were daytime games on deck and dancing in the evening, but numbers were low.

During those two days, Archie saw nothing of Nesta. He wasn't avoiding her, but he did wonder if she was avoiding him. The cooling-off period suited him, he decided. It gave him time to think, to bring his feelings up to date after what went on in Aden. The more he thought about it, the more he recognised his problem. He liked Nesta a lot. No, it was more than that, but he wasn't ready to use the word love yet to describe how he felt. A strong attraction. A very strong attraction – that would do for now. The issue was how she made Archie feel. She made him feel inferior. He examined the words closely and knew they were wrong. He felt inferior, yes, but wasn't he the one doing that to himself? Did Nesta really treat him as if he was some kind of amusement or plaything? He wanted to think not but his heart said otherwise and that was the essence of the problem. How could he get her to take him seriously? In Aden he told her he didn't plan to spend the rest of his life as a butcher. Did he say it to impress her? Hardly. But he wanted her to know that he was ambitious. Archie Thomson was going to Australia to make a name for himself.

*

Billy lay on the bottom bunk. He closed his eyes as the packed dormitory slowly tilted sideways, taking Billy's head and stomach with it. 'At least I had Aden,' he managed to say.

Archie stood splay-footed, his hands holding onto the frame of the upper bunk. He looked distant. 'Aye, you'll always have Aden, Billy. Maybe that was as good as it gets. You and me both.'

The big man raised himself on his elbow. 'Christ, you're full of the joys of spring, Archie. What's got into you? Have you been reading the bible or something?'

'Wash your mouth out, young man. And may the Lord strike you down and send you straight to Hell!' Archie leaned down and made to punch Billy lightly in the stomach, but his friend turned away from him, mumbling about feeling sick again.

Archie stood up and gripped the bunk a little more tightly. 'Well, I'll leave you to commune with your bucket. I'm off for a smoke and a stroll. May as well make the most of it while I can. You heard the crew earlier, this weather's going to get worse. A lot worse.'

The promenade deck was deserted apart from a couple of hands mopping the stairs. Archie nodded to them and held his nose as a sour odour of sick wafted past him. He stopped to look at the Order of the Day board. Someone had scrawled *cancelled* in thick red pen across the notice for tonight's film show. Probably just as well. *20,000 Leagues Under the Sea* would have been rubbing salt in the wound. But the bingo session and dancing in the sun lounge were going ahead, it seemed. Archie imagined the bar would be quiet. He glanced at his watch – just gone seven. Darkness crept across the rolling ocean like a fog. Through the window of the bar he watched Carlo, the barman, take glasses from their racks and store them in wooden crates on the counter. In a dark corner to the side of the bar a solitary customer sat, facing the wall. The man's shoulders were hunched as he dipped his head to drink from a tumbler. Archie saw no one else but thought there must be more people in other dark corners.

All stairs to the boat deck were roped off so he walked towards the bough on the starboard side. The wind whistled through the ship, making canvas flap angrily and legs of steamer chairs scrape the deck. And then a lull as the *Fairsea* pitched forwards steeply. Archie gripped the guard rail and braced himself. The sensation reminded him of a fairground ride where the floor suddenly collapses, and your stomach seems to appear in your mouth. He couldn't remember what it was called. Some moments of calm followed, long enough to pick a cigarette from his packet and cradle the lighter, his back to the wind. He drew in long and deep and watched the ember burn fast in the ocean air. Purple clouds, smudges against the night sky, hurried southwards across the empty sea. After a few quick draws, Archie flicked his cigarette overboard, a brief glow before it disappeared from view, carried away by the wind.

His thoughts turned to Australia. They were on the last leg of the voyage now; yes, it was a long last leg and it would feel longer still if the weather worsened. But they would get there. He knew he had to find a job using his trade as a butcher. He had no desire to work in a shop though. Why swap a butcher's shop in Leith for another one in Australia? According to the leaflet from the Assisted Passage Scheme, there were opportunities in the meat processing industry around Melbourne. That would do for starters. And whatever the conditions were like in the hostel he was assigned to, he would stick it out there as long as possible; it should be an easy way to save money. He had no concerns about dormitories and communal toilets. After all, he'd got lucky when he broke his wrist at work last year and missed his National Service call-up. It was only right that he should suffer a bit.

So far so good with the initial plan. Then there was the question of night school. Something to set him on a new path. Melbourne was a big city and there were bound to be openings in other trades. No, not trades, he reminded himself. A profession – that's what Archie thought he wanted. Wearing a shirt and tie every day, maybe even an office of his own with a telephone on his desk. Stop fantasising, he told himself, be practical. Yes, night school, but for what? Something commercial maybe. He was good at selling, or so Mr McKay often told him when Archie persuaded a customer to buy a few more ounces of silverside or such like. 'Go on, you and your man deserve it,' he'd say, 'after all those years of rationing.'

The *Fairsea* pitched sideways, pressing him forward, his ribs hard against the rail. Archie held on tight and braced his neck to stop his head from pulling him downwards into the ocean. Everything slowed as he stared at the hungry sea before the ship see-sawed back to port. Still, he clung to the rail, but his right hand was wrenched free, forcing his whole body to swing round like he was about to make a theatrical bow. At that moment he saw the man come rushing towards him, heard his primal grunt above the roaring wind and sea. Archie ducked and sat down, wedged against the rail, when the ship tilted downwards again, as if emptying itself into the ocean. He looked up, and for a moment he saw the man above him, his reddish hair sticking straight up like a flame; his pink face frozen in surprise, before he somersaulted overboard. Archie sat there, his whole body shaking. His breathing quickened and his heart pounded like a drum roll. He gripped the rail so tightly that the flaking paint stuck to his palms and the rusty iron beneath would take days to wash off.

*

When the two deck hands found him, he was still sitting, both hands gripping the guard rail. It couldn't have been long after the man went overboard; a few minutes at most, he reckoned, but he wasn't sure.

Archie told the hands what happened, and he saw one of the men rush up the stairs towards the boat deck. The other man helped him to his feet and guided him along the swaying deck to the main lounge. The place was deserted, it looked like there wouldn't be many takers for bingo or dancing this evening. It can't have been much longer before the First Officer arrived. Archie was drinking hot, sweet tea which made him want to gag. But the sugar rush worked and he told the officer he was fine. He wanted no fuss. A few minutes later he was sitting opposite the First Officer in a cramped room in the deck house; they had been there ever since.

As Archie recounted events, Walmsley made notes. He interrupted Archie frequently. 'Let me just get this straight', he said, or 'So, what you're telling me is…' It occurred to Archie that things would be easier if he said it was an accident; that the man was thrown hard against the rail and tumbled overboard as the ship pitched downwards. That he tried to grab him, but he was gone in an instant. But Archie was thinking on his feet. There would be other questions. Did you recognise the man? Did you know him? If he denied it, he thought it would look worse later on, when the lost man was identified through a process of elimination. Other people would come forward and say they'd seen them together; that it may well have been an accident but wasn't there more to this story than Archie was letting on? Better to play it straight and tell the truth. Face up to the consequences although his conscience was clear – he had done nothing wrong.

Archie placed the tenth sheet of foolscap neatly on top of the others. The account was accurate enough so far. He could have asked for minor changes but decided against it; they weren't important. No, he needed to concentrate on the last two sheets, the ones that attempted to provide a reason for the attack, as Archie described it. Or rather, a motive for the attack, because that's how Archie viewed it. He finished reading the First Officer's transcript. There were a few things Archie wanted to be changed.

'All good?'

Walmsley was a little too cheerful for Archie's liking. 'Good's not a word I would use. And anyway, there are a few things you've got wrong.'

'Such as?'

Archie spent several minutes explaining again that he didn't know the man. He went over, once more, the incident in the souk at Port Said and the drink in the *Fairsea*'s bar that followed. How he had never spoken to the man since that meeting, over a week ago.

The officer stared at Archie. 'Of course, all of this is subject to confirming the man's identity but let's assume you've got it right. If he was grateful to you for rescuing his... his friend's purse, why on earth would he want to attack you? Unless, of course, there's something you're not telling me?' He leaned back in his chair and folded his arms. 'The woman, for instance. You say that you never spoke to the man after the meeting in the bar but what about the woman?'

'I've already told you that I accompanied her when we went ashore in Aden.' Archie shivered suddenly. The effect of the tea was wearing off.

'But why you? Why not the unfortunate Carwyn? Unless you had usurped him in some way. Is that how it was?'

Archie knew he was being wound up. He took his time before answering. 'She asked me if I would accompany her in Aden. I didn't ask why she wasn't going ashore with Carwyn. That's all.'

'Very well. Let's make these minor changes and get this report signed off. Of course, we may need to speak to you again... once we've talked to other interested parties.'

After the changes were made, they both signed and dated each page of the report. Walmsley shuffled the papers. 'And you should see the Medical Officer first thing tomorrow morning. Get yourself checked over. You've had a bit of a shock, you know.'

Archie looked at his watch – just past midnight. The wind had dropped but the night air was heavy and moist. He felt in his pocket for his cigarettes. Walmsley was a bastard and Archie pictured himself banging the man's head against a lifeboat. Pictured the man crawling on his knees, begging forgiveness. He was going to Australia to get away from entitled little shits like him with their fancy educations and their condescension. And then his well-earned rant was interrupted. He saw his face again – Carwyn's face – and that look of surprise when he knew he was going overboard. What did he think in that moment?

He must have known he was about to die but what were his final thoughts? Archie sat down on the edge of a steamer chair, put his head in his hands and wept.

*

It looked like Billy hadn't stirred in his bunk. He was probably grateful to have survived the wind-ravaged night and was now drifting unconsciously in calmer waters. Despite his lack of sleep, Archie slid from the top bunk, showered while it was quiet and sat down for breakfast in the restaurant at seven-thirty on the dot. He was keen to tune into the rumour mill as early as possible. Had word got around about a man going overboard? And if it had, what were people saying? More than anything, he wanted to see Nesta. The rational part of him knew it was best to avoid her, something he'd managed for the past three days without even trying. She was bound to be contacted by Walmsley this morning, with the Medical Officer to hand, no doubt. They would break the bad news and perhaps interview her for the record. After all that was over, then would be the time to try to see her.

But despite the risks – because for all he knew, he was being watched – Archie wanted to speak to Nesta first, before the officers had their say. He wasn't sure what he would tell her. Probably give her his version of what happened. And then what? Would she fall into his arms? Would she stop laughing at him and start to take him seriously?

He found a table, ordered coffee then picked up a tray and joined the queue at the refectory. The smell of cooking fat made his stomach lurch, but Archie was determined to stick it out. He listened in to various conversations, even joined in one or two, but they were all about the wind and how awful the night had been. There was no mention of anyone going overboard. Back at the table, the waiter poured coffee from a large pot. The man just nodded and smiled when Archie asked him if the crew had had a busy night. Archie's hand shook when he lifted the cup; carefully, he put it back down in the saucer. Maybe he should go and see the Medical Officer after all.

In a wide corridor off the main lounge was a room which was used as a surgery. Most of the time it was occupied by the Nursing Sister, who did her best to deal with the worst cases of seasickness and the effects of minor accidents. A hand-written notice, threaded with string, hung on the door. *Engaged.* Archie flipped it over briefly and read *Please knock.* He looked round to see if there was a queue of patients, but the area was deserted at this hour. The general noticeboard was on the opposite wall across the corridor and he pretended to study it while keeping an eye on the door of the surgery. Fee rates for the ship's surgeon; the location and opening hours of the laundry; a statement that national dried food for infants was not available to purchase on board. Archie read the notices several times, but took nothing in. He swung round when the handle on the surgery door creaked.

Nesta came out, closing the door carefully. She stood there right outside the room, staring at nothing. Gone was the amused smile. Her face looked worn, her hair tousled, like she had just got up. Maybe she has, he thought. Maybe they had woken her in the dormitory and brought her here to break the news, with the nurse on hand to provide support.

Archie walked across to her. 'Nesta.' His voice was a hoarse whisper.

She turned her head towards him. 'My God, what have we done?'

Archie felt she was looking through him at something distant, something he couldn't see. 'Let's get away from here.' He cupped her elbow with his hand and guided her towards the doors to the promenade deck. They walked briskly to the stern and sat on a slatted, wooden bench. The grey morning sky had a tired look and the wind seemed to have spent itself, for now.

'So, they've told you?'

Nesta nodded.

'Look, I don't know what they've said. But you have to believe me, it was an accident. I mean, I had nothing to do with it. He just came rushing at me. And then, the ship...'

She rested her hand on his forearm. 'But you did have something to do with it, Archie. We both did.' Nesta took her hand away and looked out across the ocean. 'Whatever he did, he didn't deserve this. I can't believe he's out there somewhere. But he is. Carwyn is out there.'

Yes, but I'm here, he wanted to say. *What about the living?* Instead, he put his arm around her shoulder. 'I know. I'll never forget his face.

He looked so... so shocked. I just wish I could have stopped him somehow.'

Nesta rested her cheek on his shoulder. He nuzzled the top of her head, smelled her unwashed, wispy hair. Such a longing came over him, so strong he had to fight to push it away. Did she feel it too? He hoped so. They stayed there, barely moving, while the ship ploughed on, deeper into the future, leaving Carwyn further and further behind somewhere far below in the endless ocean.

In a few days, the Welshman's body would float to the surface in the warm waters of the Indian Ocean and the process of putrefaction begin. Even this far from land, seabirds would start to pick at the bloated corpse. Other scavenging creatures would join them until, in a week or two, all that remained was for Carwyn's bones to sink slowly to the ocean floor where they could rest at last.

Archie didn't want to let her go. The longer they sat there, the more he felt their bodies glue themselves to each other. He was too tired to move, too comfortable. But part of him also wanted to shake himself free of her, before he became stuck fast. He wanted time to think. And space, too. Whatever he needed to ponder, he had to do it alone.

Nesta lifted her head from his shoulder. 'We need to talk,' she said.

'I know we do. But, please, not yet. They said I should see the doctor or the nurse. Get myself checked out. You know, blood pressure and that kind of thing. All of this has worn me out.' Archie stood up and faced her, balled fists hanging by his side. 'Look, maybe you want me to act the big strong man. To tell you I'm fine. But that's not how I feel. I've never seen someone die before. Can you understand that?'

'Shhhh.' Nesta reached for his hand but he pulled it away. 'Of course, I understand, Archie. You have to do what you feel is right for you. We both have to do that. But we still need to talk. So, let's just promise we'll do that.'

He gave her a thin smile and reached for both her hands, holding them lightly. 'I'll see you back here at two o'clock,' he said.

12

Adelaide, 1997

She looks at Hannah's scarlet nails; it's hard to ignore them. Still, at least her daughter has polished them since she last saw her. It's an improvement, she decides, a sign that the girl is looking after herself, outwardly, at least.

The young woman at the counter shouts, 'two flat whites.' Hannah gets up and squeezes past another table on her way to collect their drinks. Her mother's eyes follow her, looking her up and down. Looks like she's eating okay. Perhaps a bit too much, actually. Or just too much of the wrong thing. That's the problem for young people these days. It's all out there. Too much temptation. And they believe they're invincible; that they can just have whatever they want: food, alcohol, sex, drugs, you name it. And because they're young, they have no idea what the consequences might be until later on when they find themselves in trouble or unhappy. You reap what you sow, that's what Nesta's mother drilled into her.

She tells Hannah about Archie's diagnosis and the trip to Sydney next week to see a specialist. Her daughter wipes a flake of Danish pastry from the side of her mouth with a paper napkin. 'Yes, Mum,' she says, 'Ewan rang me last night to talk about it.' Nesta is surprised her son had the time to call his sister, what with him having to look after Shane for a few days. But she says nothing. She's annoyed at him too – telling Hannah about Archie's cancer is *her* role. God knows, she can do without her children interfering. I wonder how much they talk about us? I wonder what they say about me? she thinks.

Nesta holds the cup to her lips, speaks over the rim. 'You've got another piece of pastry on your mouth.' Then, putting her cup down, she says sharply, 'No. Other side. That's it.'

Hannah lowers her head and gives her mother a hurt look.

'I'm sorry, sweetheart, I didn't mean to snap. I'm just worried about your father. It feels different this time. Perhaps because it's so soon after last year's treatment.'

'Yes, but Dad's a fighter. I'm sure he'll pull through again.'

'Funny, that's what your brother said when I told him.'

They talk about arrangements for the trip to Sydney for a while. Hannah looks at her watch, finishes her coffee and grabs her bag from the floor. 'Look, sorry Mum, I need to be getting back to the office. One of the other girls is off sick so it's kind of full-on.' She stands up, kisses her mother on one cheek and tells her she'll call her soon. 'And give my love to Dad,' she says over her shoulder. 'Tell him I'm rooting for him.'

Nesta finishes the dregs of her coffee. The children seem remarkably calm with the news about their father. They're either taking it in their strides or they're hiding their emotions. Probably the latter. After all, they've been well trained by parents who are experts at burying everything, particularly the past. Recently, she's begun to think it's a pity that neither Ewan nor Hannah ever bring up issues about their childhoods. The bad things, she means. Like, 'Mum, why did you send me away to live with Uncle Bob and Aunt Jessie?' If they did, at least it would give her an opportunity to hold her hands up and admit her failures. Ask for their forgiveness, even. Would she do it, though? And ask forgiveness for what, come to think of it? She's seen worse mothers.

It's far too early to go home and the coffee has given her quite a kick. On impulse, she cuts through the university and crosses the footbridge to the north bank of the Torrens. Karrawirra Pari, she reminds herself. It sounds so much better. Timeless.

She stops to watch a pelican sitting on the brown, grassy bank. Such strange-looking creatures, all out of proportion. Last week she read an article in the *Advertiser* about the birds attacking people and taking their lunches. It went on to say that the increase in the number of attacks was probably a consequence of people feeding bits of their sandwiches to the pelicans in the first place. Well, what do they expect, then? The birds are just like men. Give them a bit of encouragement and they'll want more. Won't stop till they're satisfied. You reap what you sow, that's what her mother always told her. She feels sure that particular thought has crossed her mind already today, but she can't recall when or where.

Or was it during the session with Louise yesterday? They certainly talked about actions and consequences. In fact, now she remembers it. They talked about cause and effect too.

'Try to think of it in terms of consciousness,' Louise had said. 'Cause and effect implies that you've weighed up the possible effect of your action before you've actually taken it.'

Nesta stares across the river at the city and repeats the sentence slowly in her head.

Then Louise had gone on. 'On the other hand, we know that actions always have consequences, but we don't necessarily consider that at the time.'

Yes, that was it. Nesta regarded it as a kind of recklessness. And then she recalls saying to Louise, 'So I didn't stop to think what effect my actions might have on Carwyn.'

She walks down the sloping bank, past the curious pelican, to the river's edge. The water is dark, much darker than she has ever noticed before. Plants wave lazily just under the surface and then she sees a shape move at speed beneath them. Her heart leaps and she lets out a gasp but it's only a duck emerging from the depths. Water runs off its back so quickly and easily she barely notices it. She catches her breath, walks back up the slope to the path and continues along the riverside.

Louise hadn't liked her use of the word recklessness. 'It implies a couldn't-care-less attitude,' her counsellor said. 'A kind of defiance.' Louise crouched in front of her at that point, put her hand over Nesta's and spoke quietly. 'That's not how you've described it to me,' she said. 'You told me Carwyn admitted boasting to Archie about his chances with you, didn't he? You had every right to be angry with him. And you had every right to go ashore in Aden with Archie too. So, there was no recklessness on your part as far as I can see. Unless, unless there's something you're not telling me?' Nesta sat motionless. Louise took her hand away and sat back in her chair.

She waits for a young woman to speed past on rollerblades, then crosses the path to a wooden bench under a scribbly gum. More than forty years have passed since the voyage. Some memories of it are so clear she can almost touch them. Like when she left the film show and found Archie on deck, gazing at the stars. Or lunch with him in Aden when dry leaves scuttled across the table. But other things are more difficult to remember. Her mind is not blank, rather it's a series of flashing images. No sooner does one image appear than it's gone again, to be replaced by others. She wants to grab them, pin them down and look at them, to study them like paintings or photographs; to search for hidden meanings or simply admire the quality of the light.

The sessions with Louise have helped, she's sure of that. And her counsellor is right, so far as she knows – Nesta wasn't reckless. But she does feel like she got away with it, although she's not sure what *it* is. Got off, scot free. Ever since then, part of her has always been waiting for a knock at the door. Does that explain why she seemed to guzzle life down, particularly in the early years? Was she trying to get her fill before someone grabbed her and said, 'we've got you – the game's up now?'

She never thinks that Archie got away with it, though. Because there was nothing for him to get away with, was there? For Nesta, he is always blameless, always the victim. Never has she questioned his version of what happened. And why should she?

Poor Archie. She looks at her watch. Time to go home. By way of the central market, she decides. I'll get him a nice steak. Filet, that's what Archie likes best.

*

He has eaten most of it, says it was delicious, but he doesn't have the hearty appetite she remembers. She sneaks a look at him while he refolds his napkin. Her husband is wasting away, shrinking before her eyes. Archie has always been wiry and sinuous, his face creased and wrinkled even in his younger days. Over time, more little crevices have appeared in his cheeks, his neck and forehead, as if eroded by the elements. Australia does that to men with Archie's features.

'Worry always ruins your appetite,' she says. She notices a deep sadness in his eyes.

'I wish that's all it was,' he says. 'I can cope with worry.' His hands start to shake and he clasps them tightly under his chin, elbows on the table. But then his arms are shaking too, and his head.

At first, she doesn't know what to do. This is not normal behaviour from her husband. He doesn't like a fuss when he's upset. 'But it's what you wanted,' she hisses to herself. And then she's up and round the table. Standing behind him, she has to bend down awkwardly to get an arm around his shoulder. He puts his hand on her hand.

'Stand up, Archie. Stand up and let me hold you.' He's not much taller than her and she wraps her arms under his armpits, feels the sharpness of his shoulder blades through the slack, baggy skin. There must be words, she thinks, but instead the only sounds are his sobs and the heaviness of their breathing.

Later, they lie in her bed. Something they haven't done for a long time, not since Archie's snoring got too loud and his night-time peeing became too frequent. But none of that matters now. He has been asleep on his back for a while and she watches him, her eyes adjusting to the darkening night. Then, carefully, she slips her arm across his chest, lets her hand rest lightly on his bony shoulder.

When was the last time they slept together? she wonders. It takes her a few moments. Last August, their fortieth wedding anniversary. Ruby. More than six months ago already.

Archie wasn't fussed about going away. A family meal out would do him, he said. Ever the romantic, her husband. Or was it a reflection of how he felt about the occasion? In any case, Nesta had put her foot down. God knows, there should have been no need for her to do so. But Archie's indifference prompted an extreme reaction – the less *you* want, the more *I* want. So she insisted on a trip overseas and settled for five nights in Bali at a luxury resort on the edge of the rainforest. They stayed in a secluded villa with an outside shower and its own swimming pool overlooking the ocean. The floorspace wasn't much smaller than their own home. Nesta loved it. The cool, cream-coloured walls were hung with vibrant batik tapestries. She can still smell the gorgeous, dark hardwood furniture; how she ran her palms across its smooth surfaces and clean lines. She raises her head from the pillow, checks her husband is still asleep.

In the mornings she took meditation or yoga classes. When she came back to the villa, feeling cleansed and serene, Archie would be standing in the lounge with the remote, switching between business channels on the television. She had forbidden him to bring his golf clubs. Perhaps that was a mistake. Most afternoons they went on some tour or other – cookery, local arts and crafts, that sort of thing. It helped pass the time, she realises in hindsight.

On the evening of their anniversary, they dined privately under a pergola on the terrace of their villa. While they ate, the waiter stood several paces away, statue-like. She remembers trying to talk lightheartedly to Archie about their wedding day. 'Well, the weather's certainly different,' she said. They had got married on a cold, windy winter morning at the Sydney registry office in Regent Street, opposite Central Station. But she was warm enough in her knitted red twinset and black swing skirt. A dress was an unaffordable luxury. Archie had offered to buy her one – he was making good money after he moved to Sydney – but she refused. 'We've got enough things to buy as it is,' she said. There was no rush to get married, no shotgun wedding. They did it because it was expected. And that was that.

So, forty years later, she made sure she was going to enjoy herself in Bali, no expense spared. Archie tried to play along but she could tell his heart wasn't in it. Perhaps it was the effects of his first round of chemotherapy.

She raises her head again to look at the bedside clock. Nearly midnight. Now, she pulls the cover up over both of them and tries to let her mind empty itself ready for sleep. She is sure there won't be many more nights like this.

13

Canberra, 1997

My research was a struggle that morning. Probably not helped by the National Library building. Frankly, it has a Stalinist look about it. You approach the place on wide, empty, concrete pavements and climb too many unnecessary steps to reach the entrance. At which point you might lean your head back expecting to see some brutalist sculpture looking down at you. I've visited more welcoming libraries.

After more than a week in Australia, I was finally ready to get down to some proper work. Walter Avery had been kicking his heels in the vaults of the library, waiting for my arrival. 'I'm here now, Walter,' I told him.

But I was distracted and couldn't settle. My family's story was pushing Walter aside. I thought about what I had discovered just along the road in the National Archives. Surely, I would ask Archie and Nesta about it when I saw them in Sydney next week? There was a problem, though. I had poked my nose into their business. How would I feel if someone did that to me? We're all entitled to our privacy, entitled to our secrets. Perhaps I wouldn't broach the subject with them at all.

In truth, Archie and Nesta were a mere sideshow at that point. Roz occupied most of my thoughts.

Last night, we had carried on talking in the restaurant for another hour or so. The place wasn't busy so nobody was pushing us to leave. Somehow, we moved on from Roz's tale about her mother's disappearance twenty years earlier. Roz told me how hard she had worked at school and managed to get a place at Sydney to study Australian history. After graduating, she worked part-time in the state archives which led to her doing fieldwork in Papua New Guinea and the Torres Straits islands for a year. She loved learning more about the history of indigenous peoples, she said. But the academic life wasn't for her, so she ended up in the National Archives. I kept waiting for her to talk more about her personal life, but perhaps she felt she had told me enough about that for now.

And then she asked about me. I liked that Roz didn't mention the Scottish thing; there were no questions about kilts or clans or comments about how beautiful it must be, as if everyone lived by the shores of some idyllic loch. All the same, I think I was tempted to reach for the salt cellar, just as Roz had done, but I tried to keep my body language relaxed and to meet her eyes regularly. It sounds a bit forced but that's the way it was for me back then.

What do you say when someone asks: what's your story? Where do you start? How much do you miss out and how much do you lie? It wasn't a job interview, but I did want to give a good account of myself. I must have skimmed over my background and settled pretty quickly on the safe ground of history, and Australian history in particular. After all, that's why I was here. We could have spent the rest of the evening talking shop about convict transports and primary sources and so on. But something in me was shouting to be let out. My heart beat more rapidly, and my breathing quickened too. At the same time, another voice was telling me to keep quiet. But before I knew it, I was saying that I felt this trip to Australia was about so much more than academic research. I said something about it feeling more personal than that, more important. Like some crucial point in your life when you want or need something to happen, to show you the path to take. And that was it. Roz just looked at me. I guess she was waiting for more. The trouble was, I didn't really know what I was trying to say but whatever it was just fizzled out. In the end, I remember being hunched over the table, turning the salt cellar round and round.

Roz made encouraging noises, but I felt embarrassed. She had told me an intensely private story about her life, and in return, I made some clumsy, self-centred remarks. I paid the bill. With the lights of the city shining on the water, we walked back along the lakeside path to the archives. In the car park, I told Roz I would be in the National Library the following day.

'Well, if you want some company at lunch time,' she said, 'you know where I'll be.'

At that moment, every part of me wanted to kiss her. 'I'd love that,' I said. And then I did kiss her, but only on her cheek. I told her how much I had enjoyed the evening and she said, 'Me too.' When she drove off, I felt an intense loneliness.

So, yes, sitting in a research room at the library that morning, I was distracted. My mind raced in all directions. For instance, I allowed myself to imagine a future with Roz in which I saw us the way you see actors in a television advert trying to sell a perfect lifestyle – clinking glasses in a smart restaurant or walking along a deserted beach at sunset. Little cameos which, even if they happen, make up a tiny fraction of people's lives. I knew these imaginings were silly, but they kept coming. Perhaps I just needed to let them pass on through.

Eventually, my head emptied and I began to concentrate on work. Walter Avery always raised my spirits. I could have any relationship I wanted with him. He never threatened me or caused me harm and, in turn, I had no expectations of him. I switched him on and off just as I liked. So when things got too much, I often turned to Walter simply for the fun of it, for the escape, for the safety of his company.

Walter Avery was a young solicitor's clerk from Gloucester. In eighteen thirty-three he was transported for fourteen years to the penal colony of New South Wales. His crime was writing menacing letters to the owner of a local flour mill. He wrote the letters anonymously but failed to disguise his handwriting. And he was also careless enough to boast about his scribblings to some drinking chums in the local tavern.

Walter pleaded not guilty despite the evidence. If only he had held his hands up and confessed to the crime he would have probably got off with a couple of years in prison. But Walter just couldn't help lying. You reap what you sow I guess, and Walter would have the rest of his life to reflect on his choices.

Decades later, his memoir was published as *Reflections of a Condemned Man*. Increasingly, it has been ignored because of its proven lies and gross exaggerations. But I still had faith in Walter. Yes, he was his own worst enemy but he didn't make up *all* of it. And there lay the fascination for me: how can we ever be sure about what really happened? Unless you were there, you can never be certain.

Of course, we could refuse to be fascinated in the first place. Stay well clear, it's not worth the trouble. So many people I knew scoffed at history altogether – it was dead and harmless and no amount of words, pictures, ruins and memories could bring it back to life. 'Better to use your energy dealing with the here and now,' they said.

'Thanks a lot,' I said, 'you're just rubbishing my job, my whole career.' I loved burying myself in the past. Occasionally, at some party or other when I'd had too much to drink, I would quote Cicero at the rest of them: *to be ignorant of what occurred before you were born is to remain always a child*. I don't remember anyone ever hitting me when I said that but perhaps they weren't those kinds of parties.

When I was younger I had aunts and uncles who berated me for showing no interest in my own country's past. But I shuddered at the popular imagery of Scottish history. 'Walter Scott has a lot to answer for,' I said. When I think about it now, I squirm at my youthful stridency, my dismissive tone, my plain ignorance. Sometimes I tried to see past the kilts and shortbread tins but my reading never lasted long. Always, my attention shifted elsewhere. I wanted exotic adventures and exploration. I wanted exile and a search for belonging.

So, I allowed myself to be fascinated with the penal colony of New South Wales. According to his memoir, poor Walter was packed off to join a convict gang improving the road to Bathurst through the Blue Mountains in the middle of winter. He complained of being robbed of his miserable food rations; of freezing in a flimsy tent with a thin, threadbare blanket; of his fear of being whiplashed for minor indiscretions; and, most of all, his fear of being buggered by the overseers or his fellow convicts. If even half of what he wrote was true, I could barely imagine surviving in those conditions. But imagining it was all I needed to do – history's vicarious fear was as close as I got and that suited me fine.

I still remember what a mess my thoughts were on that morning in the library. First, there was Walter Avery with his almost picaresque memoir, and his manic will to survive. And then there were Archie and Nesta with their own journeys to Australia, wholly different from Walter's. They chose to go there. It must have felt like an adventure of sorts but it was one with return tickets for home if they wanted to use them. They were free to choose either way. And whether they met on the voyage, or later in Sydney or Melbourne, it appeared to me they had gambled something. Gambled with the possibilities of life, avoided taking the safe path. I don't think I kidded myself that their lives had been one long upward-curve of achievement and fulfilment, but they did seem to have reaped what they sowed. Which somehow led back to me, here and now in Canberra, on my own Australian journey. It also led back to Roz, of course.

Relationships had been scarce and brief since my marriage ended five years earlier. I always blamed our eventual break-up on Ann and I getting together for the wrong reasons. We met during our first term at university in Glasgow, magnetised by our mutual innocence. Which is all very well if, in time, you grow together or even better, grow separately. But when, at eighteen, you both stop growing emotionally and cling to each other then, eventually, something has to give.

My watch bleeped – rather too loudly for a research room in a library. Twelve-fifteen. Time to walk over to the archives and meet Roz. I hurried through the drab gardens surrounding Old Parliament House. All around me was flat, empty space. I crossed deserted lawns and pavements which seemed to extend with every step I took. When I arrived at the archives Roz was waiting in the foyer.

'I've already eaten,' she said, smiling. 'Shall we just go for a walk? Unless you're hungry, of course.' She wore the same denim jacket from yesterday. It helped me feel some kind of continuity.

'A walk sounds good,' I said. I wanted to kiss her cheek again but maybe not here in the foyer. We wandered down to the lakeside path but it was busy with walkers, joggers and cyclists so we cut back into Telopea, Canberra's oldest park. Some of the trees were turning brown already. European trees, I thought, though the cockatoos didn't seem to mind. We made small talk about work. I gave Roz my views on the architecture of the National Library.

'Yes,' she said, 'a lot of the buildings around here can appear pretty brutal. And some of the parks and public areas are kind of soulless. But, hey, at least you don't have to go far to find a bit of space. Capital city but not many people. It has its advantages.' She laughed and waved her arm at the surroundings.

'So, you're quite settled here?'

We sat on a bench in the shade, not far from one of the footbridges which cross the storm drain running through the park.

Roz glanced up at me, then scanned the view. 'I suppose I've grown to like this strange city. But not so much that I wouldn't be happy to move on. In the right circumstances, I mean.' Pressing her palms on the bench, she swivelled to face me. 'So, you're off to Sydney tomorrow?'

God, this was hard. I glanced at her then looked away. 'I am. For five or six days. Then I have to go to Port Macquarie for the weekend. After that it's back to Sydney and the flight home.'

'That's a pity. If you had more time, maybe you could've taken a trip into the outback. Sydney's got the wow factor, of course, but I think this country's really about the outback. Spend some time out there and the memories will really stay with you.'

A wave of sadness washed over me. I so wanted to do all of that with Roz. But all I could see was me boarding a plane heading back to the old world.

Roz put her hand on my arm, leaned her face towards me. 'What's up? Have I said something wrong?' Her voice was soft like a caress.

'No, no.' I stared at the ground. 'Look, I... this will sound really stupid so I'll apologise before I even say it.' I took a deep breath and faced her. 'I know we've only just met but already I like you a lot. I feel that I want to get to know you. Want to spend time with you. But we don't have time. I'm sorry.'

Roz slipped her hand in mine and squeezed. 'Don't be sorry. And it's not stupid. I'm glad you said that. I wouldn't be here if I didn't feel something too. Of course it's not easy. We could be like ships that pass in the night. Well, maybe not pass. Bump into each other slightly.' She gave a little hiccupy laugh and nudged my arm.

I managed a brief laugh too. 'Bump into each other a lot.'

Her tone became serious, her voice lower. 'Look, I'm not an easy person to get close to,' she said. 'You know, what I told you about Mum and all that.'

I put my arm round her and told her I understood. She rested her head on my shoulder and I sniffed her soft hair. It smelled of peaches. 'But I want the chance to get to know you,' I said, 'difficult or not. I can't just head off to Sydney and feel like I'll never see you again.'

A cockatoo rummaged in a flower bed not far from us. Roz sat up and twisted to face me, the flicker of a smile. 'I know, Jim. But it's all very quick. I do like you. I like you a lot but... I'm not sure about risking my feelings. You know, Mum walked out and never came back. The whole rejection thing. And you live on the other side of the world. I don't know if I could cope with it.' She lowered her head and stared at the ground.

What was I supposed to say? I wanted to tell Roz that I would never leave her; that she could trust me completely. But another part of me was grabbing my arm, pulling me back. You've only known her for five minutes. In fact, you don't really know her at all. Don't go making rash promises you might not be able to keep. We sat there for an age. The cockatoo flew off to the other side of the bridge. I followed its flight and watched it strut confidently, digging with its beak for seeds and berries amongst fallen leaves. The bird's yellow crest waved in the freshening breeze.

My head ached. One of us had to say something.

'I've got a suggestion,' I said, trying to sound brighter than I felt. 'Tomorrow I head for Sydney and I'll be there until a week today. That's when I need to go to Port Macquarie for the weekend. Why don't we give ourselves a week and see how each of us feels about everything. I could call you next Thursday.' I gave her a pleading look.

'And the rest of today?' she said.

'That's up to you, I think.'

Roz took my hand again. She looked me in the eye. 'Jim, I want to spend time with you and get to know you. I really do. But I want it to feel right. Like we're in the same place, wanting the same things. I know it's hard but does that make sense?'

It did make sense and I told Roz so. But I hated the implications of not speaking to her for a week.

*

I expected the rest of the day to be a wash-out. But perhaps the meeting with Roz helped clear my head. At least I had told her how I felt. At least we talked. And there was still a chance of seeing her again.

Whatever it was, I spent the whole afternoon in the library deeply engaged with Walter. The man could read and write which made all the difference to his prospects. He was given a job as clerk to the storekeeper at the Sydney barracks. But could he stay out of trouble? Sadly not. The storekeeper was charged with defrauding prisoners of their full rations and appropriating them for his own use. And who was responsible for keeping the stock records? Walter Avery, of course. He was found guilty of colluding with the storekeeper which was how he ended up in a road-building gang in the Blue Mountains.

It was gone five when I left the library. I headed down to the lakeside and took a long walk back to my hotel. I thought about cutting through Telopea Park but I spotted a pair of cockatoos and changed my mind; those birds knew too much about me already. So I strode along the pavements, past streams of cars and buses carrying thousands of government workers north over the lake, back to their homes and their families.

The evening was busy and I was glad of that. I reviewed my notes from the library and packed most of my things, ready for an early start in the morning. It was only a three-hour drive to Sydney but I wanted to stop along the way. Anywhere to pass the time, really. The next week stretched out before me like a prison sentence.

Before I went to bed I checked my wallet for the slip of paper with Roz's phone number on it.

14

Indian Ocean, 1955

'Leave it, Billy. What did I say about not making things worse? People are bound to talk and stare. Christ, they're only too happy to have something to relieve the boredom. We'd be doing the same in their position, you know.'

His friend grunted, turned round in his seat and dunked a piece of toast in the remains of his egg yolk. 'Aye, fair enough. The thing is though, who's been telling them in the first place? That's what I want to know.'

'Who do you think? The crew, of course. Not that I'm blaming them. And anyway, there's nothing I can do about it. If anyone wants to ask me what happened, I'll tell them. I've got nothing to hide.' Archie rocked back in his chair and folded his arms tight across his chest.

Billy placed his knife and fork neatly on his plate and pushed it to one side. 'So how was Nesta when you saw her last night?'

'Distant. No, I take that back. Preoccupied. Her mind's full of stuff. How to contact Carwyn's mother. What her own parents will think. And when they'll all find out. Mr bloody First Officer says they've already radioed ahead to Fremantle. "Got to go through the proper channels," he says. You know how these people speak.'

Billy had no idea how those people spoke but nodded anyway. He pushed his chair back and told Archie he was off to join a game of deck quoits.

Archie strolled to the stern and sat on a shaded starboard bench. He had barely touched a thing at breakfast. But he drank three cups of coffee which he reckoned would keep him going for the rest of the morning. In the two days since Carwyn went overboard, Archie had only managed to doze fitfully during the long, sticky nights below deck. He was surprised by what kept him awake. Carwyn barely crossed his mind. It was the consequences of the Welshman's death which stopped him from sleeping.

Archie thought of himself as a victim. He hadn't invited the attack, had he? And he told the truth to Walmsley. Well most of it. He hadn't mentioned part of the conversation with Carwyn in the ship's bar back in Port Said, about how he dropped him in it with Nesta. Nor had he said anything about his feelings for her. It was none of anyone's business. And if people saw the pair of them walking the decks or sitting on a bench, so what? They had something in common now, plenty of reasons to spend time together. Nobody knew what they were saying to each other. If that was all he had to worry about, then fine. He could handle it, handle it all the way to bloody Melbourne.

But there was more. The unknown. He'd made his statement and signed it off with a clear conscience. But where was all of that going to lead? Official reports? Inquests? More questioning? And who was in charge of all these things? Sometimes he imagined himself being marched off the ship in Fremantle, handcuffed between two policemen. The crowds, ten deep on the decks, shouting, 'Murderer, hang him!'

'Rum do. Still, you look like you're bearing up.'

Archie recognised the fruity voice and looked up at the man in the khaki suit. 'What's a rum do?' The words came out like they left a bad taste in his mouth.

'Chap going overboard the other night. Welshie, so we hear. Word is, he had a go at you.'

'Is that right?'

The man leaned forward and offered Archie his hand. 'Name's Somerville by the way. As in the college.'

'Eh? What college?' Archie didn't get up but shook the man's hand firmly.

'Never mind. Thing is, I saw the poor chap just before it happened. Didn't realise at the time, of course. But put two and two together after a chat with one of the crew. Welshie came out of the bar, almost knocked me over. Stonking, he was. Could barely walk. Wind didn't help but nonetheless. Absolutely sozzled. Shouted at him to get below decks before he did himself an injury but just ignored me. Went stomping off along the prom deck. Mentioned it to the First Officer. Offered to give him a statement. Funny chap, that one. Bit smarmy in my view. But there we are. What's done is done. Just wanted to let you know. Not your fault. I'm spreading the word.'

Archie stood up. 'Right. Well, thanks for letting me know, Mr Somerville. I… I need to… I've got an appointment now.'

Somerville chuckled. 'That's the ticket,' he said, 'keep your spirits up.'

Something registered with Archie. He didn't stop and try to make sense of it at that moment. But later, he thought about his anger. Anger towards people he assumed were privileged, people who had it easy in his view. People for whom doors opened and who never had to work too hard to get what they wanted. He had no problem about judging people on first sight or when hearing their accents. But simply being angry and pushing them away might not be best for Archie Thomson and that's what mattered. Maybe he needed to keep his powder dry, to consider if some of these people could be useful to him. He needed all the help he could get, after all.

And where did all this anger stem from? He supposed it came from a frustration with the whole system, the whole problem of bloody class-ridden Britain.

He remembered a conversation with Mr Semple, a science teacher and the careers master at his old school. It took place not long before Pa's accident. Semple had a musty smell like an old coat left in a cupboard for too long. His thatched, grey hair was piled up in a corrugated swirl. Archie could smell the man's sour breath from the other side of the desk.

'Now then, Archibald Thomson. I'm looking at your grades and they're well above average, I'm pleased to say. Particularly in History and Geography. As you know, you'll be sitting the school leaving examination in a few months. Have you had any thoughts about what you want to do when you leave school?'

Archie clasped his hands between his legs. 'If possible, sir…'

'Speak up, boy.'

'If possible, sir I'd like to stay on. I'm wondering if there would be a chance, a possibility I mean, of going to the university. I mean if I work hard enough.'

Even now on the ship, Archie could see Semple's face breaking into a mean smile, grey hairs sprouting from his flared nostrils. 'Well that's admirable. Admirrrrable.' He leaned across the desk, almost whispering. 'But let me tell you, laddie. University's not for the likes of you. I'm not saying you're not bright enough. Far from it. But you come from a large family. I should know, I've taught many of your brothers and sisters over the years. A lot of mouths to feed. I'm sure your parents will be glad to have another one of you earning. Can't be easy.' He leaned back again and looked at Archie squarely. 'Think about it, Thomson. There's plenty of work out there for those who are willing to do it.'

A few months later, Pa lost his leg in the accident at work. Archie wondered if Semple had engineered the whole thing just to prove his point.

When he got back to the dormitory, a young lad in uniform was hanging around the entrance. He told Archie the First Officer would like to see him in his office at four o'clock if that was convenient. Archie bit his tongue and said 'Yes, that's fine.' He glanced at his watch. It was almost time to meet Nesta in the main lounge. 'We've nothing to hide,' she said, 'so let's meet where we can be seen.'

The lounge was quiet. Voices from a whist drive in the corner echoed in the large, open room but there were only a few other groups dotted around the place in murmured conversation. When they could find it, people liked to guard their space. Most families were on deck, joining in organised games, enjoying the cloudless sky; grateful for the calm of the endless, blue ocean. An older crowd would be in the sun lounge, eyeing the clock in readiness for Aperitif Time at eleven o'clock.

Nesta sat on a mock-leather chair leafing through a magazine when Archie arrived. She looks haggard, he thought, but said nothing. No hugs, no kisses, just a quick smile and a 'how are you?' 'Bearing up,' she said and asked him about his morning so far. He remembered Somerville and told her what the man had said.

'Carwyn liked a drink,' she said, putting the magazine down on a side table. 'Always gin and tonic. Mother's ruin they say. Carwyn's too, it seems.'

'Well, let's not jump to conclusions. And another thing. Walmsley wants to see me again this afternoon.' Archie leaned forward in his chair, elbows on knees. He ran his hands through his thick, dark hair then sat up again.

'Perhaps he wants to clear things up,' Nesta said. 'I mean, if this Mr Somerville has spoken to him. And surely the barman must have said something.' She took an emery board from her bag and examined her thumb. 'It's funny, really. One day, your life is sailing along quite happily – sorry, didn't mean to pun – and the next it's…'

'Thrown overboard?' Archie heard the harshness in his voice.

'Sorry, I didn't mean to sound insensitive.' She put the emery board back, clicked her bag shut. 'Look, Archie. I don't mind admitting that I'm struggling to cope with all of this. Perhaps I just need to concentrate on the practicalities. Like people usually do when someone dies. Make arrangements for the funeral, dig out the insurance policies, contact relatives. That sort of thing. Only in my case it's about writing to Carwyn's mother and writing to my own parents. And, no doubt, I'll have to contact the conservatorium too as soon as we get to Sydney. And then there's dealing with Mr Slimy Walmsley. You know he's asked me about Carwyn's luggage and his personal effects. What does he think? We were travelling companions, for God's sake. I barely knew the man.'

Archie looked at her and raised his eyebrows. 'Let's go for a walk,' he said, 'the fresh air will do you good.'

*

Archie was a few minutes early for the appointment so he stopped to read the noticeboard.

Grand Equatorial Ceremony
Hear Ye! Hear Ye!
All loyal subjects of His most Serene Majesty King Neptune are
requested to come to the Sun Deck at 4pm tomorrow and bow in
submission to their Liege Lord.

He had read about this in the leaflet for the voyage which arrived through the post in early April. Sitting at home, a thick haar hanging over the Firth of Forth. A typical spring day. He remembered trying to imagine what it would be like out here in the middle of the Indian Ocean. Nothing like this.

Walmsley had acquired a new fan, one that worked. Just as well. The afternoon heat was baking. Archie silently chanted his new catechism. Be polite. Don't get angry. Don't be defensive.

The First Officer sat upright at a small table, opposite Archie. 'Thank you so much for coming, Mr Thomson. Nearly there. Just want to bring you up to date with matters and clear up one or two loose ends if we can.'

'No problem. I'm happy to help.'

'Good. And how's your health, first of all? Did you manage to see the MO?'

'I saw the nurse. She took my blood pressure, checked me over. Everything seems fine. Physically, I mean.'

'Well, I must say, that's a relief after what you've been through. Now, as you can imagine, we've been carrying out an investigation, as it were. Trying to establish Mr Williams' movements on the day of the accident. The thing is, we've spoken to several crew members who said they saw Mr Williams drinking heavily throughout the day. In fact, the barman...' he glanced at his notes, '...Carlo, confirmed that he saw him leaving the bar rather the worse for wear just after seven thirty. And, quite a stroke of luck, a passenger offered us the same information earlier today. Said the man had almost knocked him over he was so drunk. So, my question for you, Mr Thomson, is this: did Mr Williams appear to have been drinking when you saw him?'

Archie paused before answering. 'No. As I put in my statement, all I saw was a man rushing at me. He was sort of... roaring. He sounded angry. That's all, I'm afraid.'

Walmsley smiled. 'Very well. The main thing is that we have evidence about his physical condition, as it were. As for his mental state and his motive for, as you put it, rushing at you – well, we may never find out. Perhaps that's gone to the bottom of the sea with Mr Williams.'

If the man wanted Archie to respond, he was going to be disappointed. Archie just nodded.

They stared at each other until Archie's eyes ached. Eventually, Walmsley blinked. 'Now, just one more thing. About the practicalities. You see, when something like this occurs we need to follow procedures, as it were. According to what you told the crew when they found you, Mr Williams had gone overboard several minutes earlier. Given the time lapse and the weather conditions, the captain decided not to ready a lifeboat. Nor did he decide to turn the ship. Difficult decisions but eminently sensible in my opinion. We did radio for help but the nearest ship was six hours away. It's a bloody big ocean. We've not heard a squeak from any other vessel, let alone any of the islands. Maldives, Seychelles, even the Chagos – they're all still ours of course. Just.'

Archie's eyes never left Walmsley who talked mostly to the ceiling.

The First Officer went on. 'In any case, when we dock in Fremantle we will need to go through the standard notification process with our consulate in Perth. And with the Australian police too. I don't foresee you being required to step ashore. However, I must inform you that you may need to assist with further enquiries at a later date. And there may be an inquest but that's up to the Aussies.'

Walmsley put his elbows on the table, made a steeple with his hands. 'All clear?'

Archie nodded, resisted an urge to blow out his cheeks. He breathed through his nose a couple of times. 'All clear, yes. Is that it?'

'Yes, that's it.' Walmsley shuffled his papers and slipped them into a manilla folder. 'You're heading for Melbourne, I see. Any plans?'

'Find work. Meat processing, probably. For now.' Don't be defensive. 'I'd like to make something of myself. Climb the ladder, if you like.'

Walmsley smiled. 'Good. That's what the Aussies want. People with a bit of go in them. Bright young Scotchman like you should do well.'

Archie didn't pick Walmsley up on his use of the English term. But later, he told Billy just to get it off his chest. 'Typical,' the big man said, 'they can't even get our nationality right.' Archie agreed but he knew they would have to get used to it, and worse. Probably a lot worse. There was no point in being too touchy, not where they were going.

*

During the next few days, Archie tried to balance his time between Billy and Nesta. Every morning, he took breakfast with his friend and joined in occasional games of cards or deck quoits. But he also recognised that Billy was finding his own way, at last. The big man made friends easily with some of the younger crowd and Archie began to see the old Billy surface again. His way of not taking life too seriously went down well. And so Archie spent less and less time with Billy until they barely saw each other from breakfast until bedtime in the dormitory. Sometimes Archie envied his friend's freedom. But not much. He had Nesta, or so he began to believe. And isn't that what he wanted?

The meeting with Walmsley had cleared his mind of dark imaginings. There was space in his head now which he started to fill with future plans. Instinctively, he didn't trust the First Officer, of course, but he was willing to take the man at his word for now. If there was an inquest later, so be it. Play fair and tell the truth as Pa would have said. And that's what he had done.

So Archie saw Nesta more often. They met for coffee at eleven o'clock every morning and spent the rest of the day walking, eating and lounging on the sun deck. Once, they tried to play deck tennis but Nesta was hopeless so they gave up after half an hour of missed shots and frustrated yelps. Most evenings they went to the film show or danced to Bastoni's Quartet in the bar or the sun lounge. Archie's dancing was as bad as Nesta's tennis but he tried to treat her laughter lightly. Tried hard to learn the steps. 'No! Left foot first, silly,' she admonished him. When he looked at her smiling eyes, he saw affection in them.

When Nesta suggested they go to the Mad Hatter's Dance, he was sorely tempted to draw the line. Fancy dress, masquerade, whatever it was, it wasn't his sort of thing. 'How do you know if you don't try?' she said. 'Come on, it'll be fun.' He hated the word, hated the whole notion of fun, as if it somehow cheapened life itself. But he wanted this woman, wanted a future with her whatever it took. And right then it took him dressing up as Tweedledum, courtesy of the *Fairsea's* costume hire service. Nesta, a demure Alice, laughed and laughed. 'Never again,' he said. And he kept his word.

There were things they never talked about. They were silent about the accident, silent about what would happen when they got to Fremantle. And they were silent about their futures, too. Archie felt the pressure increase daily. He didn't want this time to end but they would reach Fremantle in two more days, Melbourne in a week. They needed to talk. Later in the evening would be best, he decided. It would give Nesta time to think over what he had to say.

They went to the late film show, *Happy Ever After*, a comedy with David Niven and Yvonne de Carlo. Archie didn't fancy it but Nesta was keen. She said if David Niven was the lead it was bound to be light and harmless. Just what they needed. So Archie gave in. Maybe the film's title was a sign of good luck. In any case, Nesta's assumption was right. The film was so light it could have floated away on the ocean breeze.

Afterwards, they climbed the stairs to the boat deck. The night was moonless and the ship rocked gently through the swell. Above the drone of the engines they could just hear waves brush against the hull. They came up here towards the end of most evenings. Usually they talked about the film they'd seen or who caught their attention on the dance floor. And sometimes, but not always, they kissed in the deep shadows of the lifeboats. Nesta often seemed nervous but he put it down to caution. It was all very well being seen around the ship together but there were limits to what they were willing to put on display. Occasionally, mid kiss, they heard a loud cough and pulled away from each other, their heads turning this way and that. Probably a deckhand they told themselves. Once or twice Archie thought it might be Carwyn rising from the deep, come to have his revenge. He never shared these thoughts with Nesta.

Archie's seriousness gripped him tightly. He didn't reckon on kissing tonight. He started by telling Nesta, as if she didn't know, that they would reach Fremantle the day after tomorrow.

'So we need to start thinking about what will happen after that,' he said.

'You mean about an inquest?'

'No, I mean about us.' He saw a faint look of shock on her face, like she'd just received bad news.

Archie carried on regardless. More determined even. 'Look, it's hardly news, is it? It's not as if the past couple of weeks have all been a result of what happened to Carwyn. Not for me, anyway.'

'No, of course not,' she said. And then she sighed, let her shoulders sag. 'You're right, Archie. We do need to talk about us.'

Archie took this as his cue to do the talking, to make his proposal. There was no preamble, no scene setting. He told her about his plans for when he got to Melbourne. How he would find a job in a meat processing factory. How he would stay in the hostel to save money, whatever the conditions. How he was going to sign up for a course in business management at night school. How, whatever it took, he was going to make something of himself there, in Australia. And finally, how he wanted her to be a part of it all.

He looked at Nesta then. Searched her eyes for a sign. He willed her to say, *That's great, Archie, and I want to be with you too, come what may.*

'And I'm going to Sydney,' she said. 'I'm going to spend a year learning to be a better singer. And then... and then, I don't know what will happen. I want to be good enough to sing opera, to join a company. And if I do, I don't know where that will be.'

'So you're saying we don't have a future together.'

She leaned forward and hugged him. He kept his arms by his side. 'No, of course I'm not saying that, Archie.' She pulled back again and smiled at him. 'We can try to have a future together. I'd like that. I'd really like to try. But it won't be easy.'

Later, lying on his top bunk, Archie went over what he thought she'd said. What did he expect? Couldn't he see that coming? But she did say she wanted to try. It felt like a consolation prize when his heart was set on winning. On the other hand, she hadn't rejected him. No, the door to a future with Nesta was still open. Slightly. He just had to push hard. Push with all his might.

15

Adelaide, 1997

She never watches daytime television. Rarely watches television at all. Archie must have left it on when he'd finished with the business news. Two presenters sit on the edge of a red, L-shaped sofa. Behind them is a vast window with a sunny, elevated view of the opera house, the harbour bridge and the rest of downtown Sydney. It's not really a window, of course. She knows that, everyone knows that; or she hopes they do. The female presenter wears a two-piece suit which looks almost canary yellow but perhaps that's just the television. The woman's dark brown hair is far too big. Her male colleague wears a beige jacket with a lime green tie; his hair looks as if it's been surgically attached to his head. Nesta wonders if daytime television looks like this in every country or is it only Australia? The whole thing feels like a parody.

'It's just gone eleven-thirty and time for our final guest this morning,' the big-haired woman says. The camera has closed in so that her head and torso fill the screen. 'A man who I'm sure is very familiar to a lot of viewers. And he's here to talk about an exciting new production which opens at the opera house this evening. Gavin Whistler, good morning and welcome to Brunch in Sydney.'

Nesta gawps as a tanned bald head with a carefully groomed grey beard fills the screen. The smile is slightly lopsided and he nods to acknowledge some half-hearted applause. From whom? she wonders. The floor crew?

Gavin Whistler. Good God, he must be what – seventy? She hasn't seen him for years. The Octopus, they used to call him. Or Gavin the Groper; the terms were interchangeable and richly deserved.

She had toured with Gavin Whistler many times in the sixties and early seventies. Never gave in to his oily charm and wandering hands though. Her lesson had been learned long before then. She shudders. Sometimes she muses why she never took up with a musician or another singer. So many did, it was almost expected. A kind of hothousing for classical music genes. But she always found the atmosphere suffocating in rehearsals, and during performance seasons, without getting involved with some narcissus too. It was a relief to go home and escape all the precious, needy personalities.

Right from the start Archie was never needy. And when his career took off too, he was often away with work elsewhere in Australia or in Japan. Their different lives suited each of them very well until Ewan came along. Poor Ewan, he should have been more wanted. But at thirty-three she was never going to give up her career, settle down to change nappies and attend coffee mornings for new mothers.

'Christ, is that Gavin Whistler?'

Nesta glances round as Archie walks in with two identical suitcases and sets them down on the floor.

'Pity that poor woman presenter,' she says. 'I hope she's been warned.'

Archie snorts. 'It's not like it's a secret. The whole bloody country's known about him for years.'

'Yes,' Nesta says, 'but it's not the sort of thing people talk about.' She grabs the remote and mutes the television. 'Anyway, more important things. How are you feeling?'

'Never mind *how* I'm feeling,' he says, 'it's *what* I'm feeling that bothers me.' He lifts Nesta's case, tests the weight of it. 'Two nights,' he says, 'two bloody nights.'

This happens every time. She has explained it to him so often but he doesn't understand. He simply can't grasp the notion of choice, a woman's need for it. Next, he takes his own case and holds one in each hand. He raises and lowers his own bag like a yo-yo, grips Nesta's like a deadweight. 'See,' he says, 'feel the difference.'

In normal times she plays along with it. 'Well, it's easy for men,' she'll say. 'Look at you, two pairs of slacks and three shirts.' Slacks. She hates the word but Archie uses it. Golfing slacks. He says that's what the Japanese call them. Japanese business English. She's often told him he should write a manual for aspiring entrepreneurs. Japanese business etiquette for Australians? 'I haven't got the time or the energy,' he says. Instead, he gives occasional lectures at the Adelaide Business School.

She went along to one of them a couple of years ago. 'Why not?' she said. 'You used to come and watch me perform.' Sometimes. It was held in a small lecture theatre full of twenty-somethings. All eyes were on her husband. He was far enough away, she hoped, so they didn't get a whiff of peppermints and stale cigarette smoke. Some of them looked sceptical when they flicked through the handouts. Archie can't use a computer. The notes for his presentation were typed up, photocopied, stapled and handed out at the door. All courtesy of the university.

Archie talked for over an hour. Not once did Nesta see him refer to his notes. Not once did he hesitate. She remembers her growing sense of incredulity. This man up there, leaning casually against the table, was her husband of forty years. She had never seen him at work. Of course, over the years she had sat with him at business dinners and stood with him at cocktail parties. But those were intimate and inclusive. Nothing like this where Archie was the centre of attention.

He talked about established markets for Australian canned food in Japan and South Korea; about opportunities in emerging economies like Malaysia and Indonesia. He explained about regulations, food standards and trade deals. Her eyes began to close. But then he reached his long finale about Japanese culture and etiquette. Some of this she knew but Nesta's interest was still piqued. Her husband emphasised the importance of the Seven Gods of Fortune; in particular the gods of business and prosperity, Daikokuten and Ebisu. The latter, he said, was more important as his origins were truly Japanese. 'Many other deities,' he explained, 'have their origins in Hinduism.' By this time, Nesta wondered if she was dreaming.

And then came the questions. Hands shot up. She watched Archie scan the room, a king and his audience. Whatever the question, he took time before answering. Looked at the ceiling, steepled his hands under his chin. 'What about China?'

'Good question,' he said and laughed. 'How long have you got?' He had all the tricks. Twenty minutes later it was over. Nesta sat and listened to the young people's noisy chatter as they filed out of the theatre. The man's a performer, she thought, just like me.

But he is still the same man chuntering about Qantas weight limits for hold and cabin bags. He can go on as much as he likes but it won't change a thing. Her bag is packed.

She lets him grumble on. Ignore him and eventually, like a child, he will run out of steam. But part of her cautions the usual approach. This is different. A few nights ago, Archie cried in her arms. And for the first time in months, they shared the same bed. In the days since, they haven't spoken about it. Nesta would like to talk but she won't push her luck. He cried, they slept together – what more does she wish for? It is tempting to be greedy; to wish for Archie's recovery, for this cancer to be killed once and for all. But does she really want that? Would it be better for her in the long run if he didn't recover? The thought is there before she can snuff it out. She tries to think of something else. What's for lunch? What's the code for the burglar alarm? But the demon thought is still there, waving at her, insisting on being heard. 'I hear you,' she tells it. 'I see you and hear you but you will have to wait.'

Archie shouts her name. 'Have you been listening to a word I've said?' Nesta makes excuses, says she was thinking about what to do for lunch. 'That's what I was telling you,' he says, 'I'm off to the club for a couple of hours. We don't need to leave for the airport till well after two.'

She is glad to have some time to herself. After Archie's recent tears and their physical closeness, her feelings of hurt have faded. Let him spend time at the club with his friends. There's some leftover rice salad in the fridge. She leaves it in the tub, adds a few generous spoonfuls of cashews and raisins and a slurp of olive oil, then settles down at the bistro table on the terrace. The liver-coloured tiles warm the soles of her feet like underfloor heating. The old possum is asleep on the roof of next door's shed, curled into a neat, furry ball.

Check the fridge, empty the bin, make sure the windows are closed and locked. Set the alarm. Is there more? Her mental holiday checklist feels a bit rusty.

She scrapes the last of her rice salad from the tub and walks through to the kitchen still chewing. Dishwasher, she thinks, glancing at the clock on the wall. Just enough time for the quick programme to finish before they leave for the airport. From the corner of her eye she spots demon thought waving furiously at her. 'I see you,' she says, 'and I haven't forgotten you.'

*

As usual, they arrive at the airport a little early. She walks beside Archie as he wheels the luggage trolley into the departures hall. A middle-aged Aboriginal woman in a yellow floral dress sits behind a trestle table on which bright, printed leaflets are spread out like a fan. Nesta knows this woman.

'I'll just be a minute, Archie. We've got bags of time.' She touches her husband's arm and walks over to the table.

The woman looks up and her smile fills the space between them. 'Nesta. What a lovely surprise. You off on holiday?'

'Sort of. Sorry, Winnie, I've only got a minute.'

They talk briefly about the family support group which Winnie runs. 'Good news,' Winnie says, 'I heard yesterday that we got the grant for the cultural links programme.'

'That's great,' Nesta says, and takes Winnie's hands in hers across the table. She hears Archie's rasping cough behind her. And again.

'I've got to go, Winnie but I'll call into the centre next week when I'm back from Sydney. Great news about the grant. There's so much we can do.'

'You go, Nesta. Have a nice time with your fella.' Nesta sees Winnie wink at Archie. Her husband's face is stony.

Nesta slips her arm through Archie's. 'Come on then,' she laughs, 'we haven't got all day.'

'Who was that?' he asks while they're queuing for the check-in desk.

'Winnie McMahon,' she says. 'An elder of the Kaurna people. You know, Archie, the people who were living in the Adelaide Plains tens of thousands of years before our lot invaded.' She says it with a smile and squeezes his arm.

'Look, they're calling us,' he says and pushes the trolley up to the check-in desk.

*

Twenty minutes after take-off, Archie opens today's edition of *The Australian* at the business section. He has a copy of *The Economist* tucked in the seat-back pocket. They have both folded down their tables. Archie has a coffee on his, Nesta an orange juice on hers. The flight isn't much more than a couple of hours but it's an opportunity to rest a while. Nesta scans the cabin from her aisle seat. Half-full, she reckons, and no screaming kids so far. She's feeling good today. Facing forward, facing the future. So much more energising than all this time spent raking over the past.

She nuzzles into the corner of the headrest. It's there again, hanging out of her seat-back pocket, tongue lolling. Demon thought. Alright, I'm ready for you now, she thinks. It feels a bit risqué, with Archie sitting next to her. She hopes he can't read her mind.

Her head is clear, remarkably so. She starts by considering how much she has already invested emotionally in the prospect of Archie's death. Nesta thinks about the future a lot, always has done. So much of her professional life was preparation. Her daily voice practice, or weeks in rehearsal ahead of opening nights. Time spent preparing for rewarding moments further down the track – next month or next week or tomorrow. She knows what it takes to get ready for an event.

But why is she preparing for Archie's death? They're on their way to see a skin cancer specialist, one of the best in the country. Why bother if there's no hope? She has to be more honest with herself. Does the prospect of life without her husband seem attractive in some ways? It would be better, she admits, than life with a shrivelled, diminished

Archie. She imagines driving him to the golf club. Parking up and helping him from the passenger seat into his wheelchair. Do they have a ramp there? She shudders.

How much better her life could be depends on her own appetite for the future, her willingness to believe that there are things worth getting out of bed for. It's not as if she's in perfect shape these days. There have been some recent memory lapses, she knows that. And the sessions with Louise have become increasingly troublesome and tiring.

In the end she settles for compromise. She will continue to play the role of supportive wife, of course she will. But she will also cut herself some slack to think about what life might be like without Archie. Don't get too far ahead of yourself though, she thinks. Be careful what you wish for. Something stirs in the deep waters of memory.

'Should be starting the descent soon,' Archie says, folding his newspaper. 'You must have dozed off.'

'Yes,' she says, 'I was miles away,' and squeezes his hand.

16

Sydney, 1997

'Move closer together,' he yelled at them. The two younger girls squeezed in on either side of the eldest one. All three leaned against the railing, the rocky outcrops behind them making the perfect backcloth. A few clicks later and they were done.

The man turned to me. 'Three sisters at the Three Sisters. You gotta love it, mate.' I laughed and said what I thought he wanted me to say.

When the family moved off I took their place at the railing and looked out across the wide gorge. Sandstone cliffs and edges stretched away to the blue horizon, their walls shot through with ochre in the strengthening sun. The early morning haze had lifted from the sea of eucalyptus trees, leaving a strong scent hanging in the air.

I wondered what Walter Avery would have made of it. I had driven west out of Sydney, across the Nepean River on a smooth asphalt road right up to Katoomba, in the heart of the Blue Mountains. The town was all car parks, cafés and signposts pointing to lookout platforms and neatly kept hiking trails. It was a far cry from Walter and the convict gang cutting and improving the road through to Bathurst well over a hundred years ago. And a much further cry still, from the indigenous people who had lived here for thousands of years before the British invaded. Perhaps Walter would have approved of these changes imposed by humankind but I wasn't so sure. 'What on earth is it all for?' I thought I heard him whisper.

Sunday wasn't the best day to visit but I was feeding my need for distraction. On the drive from Canberra to Sydney I had spent the whole time thinking about Roz. Going over and over the same things: *just call her when you get to the hotel; no, don't call her, you made an agreement so stick to it.* Speculating about the phone call next Thursday, whether she'd say yes or no. In the end, I was worn out with the endless loop of thoughts. 'For God's sake, you're nearly in Sydney,' I shouted. 'Make the most of it.' So that's what I was trying to do.

When I arrived in the city on Friday, I dumped my stuff at the downtown hotel and rushed across to Darling Harbour. I bought a ferry ticket for Circular Quay and waited at the jetty while the yellow and green boat docked. It looked comical somehow, like a giant bath toy. On board I headed straight for the bow. Faint ribbons of cloud streamed across a pale blue sky in the warmth of mid-afternoon sun. A breeze picked up as we rounded Millers Point and the harbour bridge came into view. The back of my neck tingled as we sailed under it, then goosebumps spread down my arms when we approached Circular Quay with the opera house on my left. I desperately wanted to share the moment with someone – another tourist, another first-timer. But the only other person near me was a grey-haired man in a suit. He leant back against the rail studying a magazine. So I kept it all in, my silent whooping, my dry-eyed tears. Sydney has the wow factor, Roz had said. And she was right. I wished she was there with me.

Katoomba certainly didn't have the wow factor, not for me. But despite the noisy crowds milling around, the cliffs and gorges still stretched out in front of me as far as I could see. Out there I was sure there were quiet places where I could lose myself if only I could find them. I made a mental note to come back in a few days. If you have time, I reminded myself.

A sharp scream made me jump. I turned round to see a small boy, no more than three or four, staring at an ice cream splattered on the ground. Then he began a little dance, all the time pointing at the ice cream and yelping in a trance-like way. A woman appeared, crouched down and put both her arms around him. 'Don't worry, sweetie, we'll get you another one,' she said. Only, she was shouting too, making herself heard above the toddler's yelps. It was my signal to move on. Nothing needs to be that loud.

I drove north, further into the mountains. The drone of the engine soothed me and I wound down the window to let in the scent of eucalyptus. It was tempting just to keep on driving but it had taken two hours already to reach Katoomba. In the small town of Mount Victoria I stopped at the general store to buy sandwiches and water and to check the map. The highway would take me right through to Bathurst. Or I could head north-east to Bell and then cut across all the way back to Sydney. It never occurred to me to turn round and go back the way I'd come.

From Bell the road was flanked by eucalyptus trees, rocky embankments and was almost empty of traffic. I sensed there was more beyond the trees. Something beckoned me. Round the next bend I pulled over on a scrubby patch at the side of the road. Grabbing my backpack from the boot of the car I headed through a wood as if late for an appointment. The trees soon thinned out but their scent lingered. On across flat, low scrub until I reached a vast rock formation. It whorled upwards in layers like something on a potter's wheel. There was a way through the bottom layer by staying close in to the wall. I thought of snakes and spiders, especially snakes, so I slowed my pace and kept my eyes down.

And then I stopped suddenly. My knees went weak as if the ground might collapse. Miles away, across a vast sea of eucalyptus, sandstone cliffs blazed in the midday sun. It took me a moment to realise that I was standing on the edge of a cliff too, and below me the wide gorge had been scooped out of the land like a huge linocut.

I took a couple of steps and laid down on my stomach. Then I crawled forward until my body was flat on the rock with my head over the edge of the precipice, facing the trees in the gorge below. I don't know how far down the treetops were. And it doesn't really matter. They were a long, long way down.

After a few minutes my back ached and my stomach rumbled so I pulled myself up and sat on a rock to eat the sandwiches. And I listened to the silence. Only a few days ago I had scared myself on

Mount Buffalo. This felt different. For so long I had thought that life was somewhere else. That wherever I found myself, there was always another place I had to search for. But here felt right. I had no desire to move, no feeling of restlessness. Here, in the Blue Mountains I had a sense of arrival. Perhaps this was a way to live, quietly, without obligations. Why risk falling when you can avoid the possibility in the first place?

Later, I looked at my map and worked out that those sandstone cliffs far away across the gorge were at Katoomba. So I *had* found somewhere else but I hadn't lost myself, far from it. Seek and ye shall find. Hadn't Roz said that?

*

The New South Wales state archives were housed in a series of buildings out in the western suburbs, thirty miles from downtown Sydney. From the approach road the whole place looked like one of those distribution warehouses you see along the edge of motorways these days. But the buildings weren't new; they dated back to the seventies when Sydney started to spread seriously westwards into the bush. It took me a while to find my way into the vast compound and park up.

I was back on the trail of Walter Avery. He survived his experiences with the road gang in the Blue Mountains and was returned to Sydney. There, he managed to get himself a job as clerk to the Superintendent of Convicts. Walter's reading and writing skills would always open doors for him. He painted himself as the innocent victim in everything that went wrong in his convict life. But in the archives I discovered some pieces of the jigsaw that Walter left out of his story. Was it deliberate or a lapse of memory? Don't we all choose to forget things sometimes? And they remain buried, dormant until one day they erupt and spill into our consciousness.

In Walter's case I discovered he had been charged with disrespecting the superintendent by failing to doff his cap to him. Walter had my sympathy on that one. And a few weeks later he was charged again, this time for returning to the barracks drunk and disorderly in the early hours of the morning. Seven days in solitary confinement seemed to have made no difference. The man was incorrigible.

After these omissions, Walter tells us how he was 'most cruelly and falsely' implicated in a scam to forge tickets of leave for two notorious convicts in irons. Predictably, he blamed the senior clerk and protested his innocence. But it was to no avail. He was convicted at the next Quarterly Sessions. They'd had enough of Walter Avery in Sydney and he was packed off on a steamer, heading up the Pacific coast to the penal colony at Port Macquarie.

It was time for a break. I headed through to the readers' lounge and poured a mug of coffee. This was the first chance I'd had to think properly about the note. When I dropped my room key off after breakfast the receptionist handed me a piece of paper. She said someone had tried to call me. The note said *please call Roz* followed by a number. Not her home number, so I guessed it must be work. 'Was it urgent?' I asked the receptionist. She shrugged.

There was no time to call before I left the hotel. I was already late setting off for the archives and I needed to get there in time for my pre-booked slot in the reading room. Sitting nose to tail on a slip road for the western motorway, I went through the possibilities. Why would Roz want me to call her now? Perhaps her mother had turned up after all these years but that seemed unlikely. And then it dawned on me. You idiot. She wanted me to call her at work because she could keep it short and impersonal. I've been thinking, Jim, and I don't want to see you again. Sitting in the traffic I blasted the horn in frustration and looked straight ahead.

I put my mug down on the low table and pulled the note from my pocket. I stared at the hotel headed paper, at the words and digits, willing them to tell me what it was all about but they stared right back. Surely Roz would have said if it was urgent. Anyway, for all she knew, I had already gone out for the day. It would have to wait.

*

The roads were relatively quiet when I headed back into the city mid-afternoon. Walking from the car park to the hotel I looked up at the deep blue sky, scarred with vapour trails. They reminded me that Archie and Nesta would be flying in from Adelaide today. She had given me the number for their hotel. 'It's just north of the harbour bridge,' she said but didn't name it. I couldn't think why – I only had to call the number to find out.

My back was stiff after sitting in the car and at the archives. After deciding to stretch my legs and get some fresh air I crossed the city centre and walked down Macquarie Street, thick with traffic, and into the botanic gardens. The place was busy on such a glorious late summer afternoon. Most people sat on the lawns or benches enjoying the sunshine. A few joggers sweated past, casting envious looks at gliding rollerbladers. I took a narrow path which disappeared around a corner into a deeply shaded avenue of tall bamboos. The canes were thick like drainpipes and I understood how these plants were used for fences and bridges and houses. More than mere garden canes. Much more than a small boy's bow and arrow.

When I emerged into sunlight I stopped to stare at a structure across the expanse of lawn, like a strange kind of castle. A high wall with several round towers and crenelated battlements ran along the front of a building. From this distance it looked like the pale wall and towers had been rendered or made from precast concrete. And inside the compound was a building seemingly too large for the space it occupied. It had a wide, latticed roof with gently sloping eaves in a Japanese style. At each end of the roof stood a stunted pagoda and in the centre a windowed turret, topped with a witch's hat.

I took out my tourist map and worked out where I was. The map showed a red circle with a black number fourteen. I looked at the key and found the name: Sydney Conservatorium of Music. This was where Nesta had come when she arrived here all those years ago.

The building beckoned, seemed to crook a finger towards me. Surely, they must allow visitors. I crossed several paths to the corner of the castle wall which continued round the edge of the building. More towers and battlements rose above deep shrubbery. And then the sound of engines rumbling and straining followed by a loud clattering like stones falling down a chute. I stopped to look through a gap in the shrubbery. Beyond the wall, this side of the building was clad with several storeys of scaffolding. The noise of drilling and warning alarms from reversing trucks throbbed in my temples. I carried on along the path and eventually out of the gardens through iron gates which led to the entrance for the conservatorium. A red-and-white metal chain was strung between two posts in front of arched, black double doors. On the chain hung a laminated sign: *Conservatorium closed for major refurbishment.*

I had a sudden urge to make that call to Roz. On the other side of Macquarie Street stood a bank of phone booths, the open kind with a plastic bubble hood. I hated these things but it would have to do. The traffic noise was muffled but I was distracted by fragments of conversations as people walked past a few feet away.

I dialled the number. Someone picked up and said hello tentatively.

'I'd like to speak to Roz please.'

'Jim, is that you?'

'Yes. Look, I just got your note and thought I'd better call. It sounded urgent.' I drummed my heel on the pavement. *Get it over with, please.* There was a pause like you get on a long-distance call.

'Not urgent, really,' she said. 'But, you remember that scored-out name? The one on the same passenger list as your aunt?'

'Yes, of course.' I wondered if she heard the relief in my voice.

'Well, I did some more asking around. Turns out there are some records that haven't been microfilmed yet. Confidential, for some reason. Anyway, I've found something. Mister Scored-Out has a name. Carwyn Williams. He went overboard somewhere in the Indian Ocean.'

'What?'

Roz's voice became a whisper. 'Jim, I'm sorry. My boss has just walked in.'

I said I understood and asked a few questions about how she'd been. She answered with yes and no and okay. Then, finally she thanked me for my call and hung up. I hooked the phone and stood there for an age. It wasn't the conversation I would have liked to have. Nor was it the conversation I feared. It would do. And, anyway, I could always call Roz at home later.

I crossed the street and walked back through the botanic gardens until I stood in the same spot as earlier, when I'd first seen the conservatorium. The place looked different now after the news from Roz. Forty years ago Nesta arrived here safely but not Carwyn Williams. Same surname as Nesta, same destination, only he didn't make it. Went overboard, Roz said. Poor Carwyn. Did Nesta know him? I felt sure she must have. The more I knew, the more uncomfortable I felt. Like the only real guilty secret was mine for sticking my nose into their past. And yet, there was intrigue here too – I couldn't deny it.

It was late afternoon and time to head back to the hotel. I had screeds of notes to write up from my research on Walter Avery at the archives. And then there was tomorrow's meeting with Archie and Nesta. What, if anything, was I going to say to them about what I'd found out?

I took a last look at the strange building. It felt like the castle walls were protecting its secrets. For a moment, I thought I saw Archie and Nesta quite clearly on the battlements, waving to me. And then they seemed to turn away, laughing at some private joke.

17

Melbourne, 1955

It was fish and chips but nothing like back home. Most Fridays, Ma coated the haddock fillets in flour and dipped them in a beaten egg. Then she pressed each side of fish onto a layer of breadcrumbs spread out on greaseproof paper. This was different. The thick, greasy batter smelled of empty beer bottles and the fish was tasteless and pulpy. Still, it was his choice, as he kept reminding himself. And stop comparing things with home. Home? This place was to be his home from now on – Australia, not this grubby hostel.

He thought he had prepared himself for the conditions. The sleeping and washing arrangements couldn't be worse than the ship, could they? On the whole, they weren't. When the woman showed him his room with a bed settee, table and one chair he thought, fair enough, better than a top bunk in an open dormitory. It was cold though, with the corrugated iron roof and being on the gable end. Archie reckoned the coming winter would be chilly in this barren hut. And noisy too – only a badly fitted hardboard wall separated him from the Tomlinson family next door. Already, he was sick of their twin boys running riot around the hut. The communal toilets and washing blocks were just as filthy as those on the *Fairsea*; he could cope with that. It was when the woman gave him his cutlery, mug and toilet roll that Archie's defences were tested. For all its faults, the *Fairsea* never felt like a prison.

When they had stepped off the ship three weeks earlier, Archie and Billy separated. Billy had digs down in Dandenong arranged by his sponsor, a construction firm with contracts to build houses in the fast-expanding suburbs. While Archie searched for work, Billy was already busy fitting kitchens and bathrooms six days a week. They had only seen each other once. The pair of them managed an hour of fast drinking after Billy finished work and before the pubs closed at six o'clock. Billy was full of it, couldn't stop talking about the work, the pay, his new mates. 'We'll stay in touch, big man,' Billy said, but Archie doubted it. Leith seemed a million miles away.

Archie found it easy to let himself feel abandoned. Billy with his instant job and comfortable digs twenty miles further south and Nesta... Nesta hundreds of miles away at the university in Sydney and all the images that conjured up. And where was he? Stuck in a bloody Nissen hut in Preston hostel. Sometimes, like now in the dining hall, he wished they were still on the ship despite all the trauma of the voyage. At least we were together, he thought, and all of this – the here and now – was ahead of me. Maybe this was his punishment for what happened to Carwyn. But these dismal thoughts never lasted long and he let himself indulge them when they came calling. Better to face the facts and then crack on.

He scraped the slops from his fish and chips into the bin and left the plate outside the hatch. Then he walked up to the washing block and rinsed his knife and fork under a tap. If he was quick, there was time to post his letter to Nesta before the last collection.

Archie began looking for work as soon as he arrived. There was no shortage of jobs for unskilled labour if he fancied it. Melbourne, like the other big cities, was booming and had been more or less since the end of the war. That was the whole point of the Assisted Passage Scheme. Populate or perish, the Australian government had said. The country's population was too small for such a vast continent. During the war, if the Japanese had been serious about invading, they could have rolled their tanks all the way from Darwin to Melbourne in no time.

And it wasn't only the British who were migrating. Displaced people from Europe – Greeks, Italians, Serbs, Croats and many more – had been heading ashore for several years, herded straight from the ships into migrant camps out in the bush. Already, Archie had heard tales about the riots a few years back at Bonegilla camp up near Albury. They said it was caused by anger about poor conditions and lack of paid work. He didn't think there would be a riot at Preston hostel, things weren't that bad. There were plenty of moaners around the place but they acted like they were resigned to their lot. Many of them admitted they were counting the days until their two years were up and they could return to Britain on another subsidised passage. Whingeing Poms, the Aussies liked to call them and Archie got the impression that Pom meant English. He thought the Celts, or at least the Scots, might be exempt from the locals' jeering mockery. He took it all in, preparing himself for the time when he found a job.

He could have got work the day after he arrived. Plenty of single men headed for labouring jobs on the Snowy Mountains project, building hydroelectric power stations and dams for water supplies. And there was so much construction going on in the city, he could have turned up on any number of sites and started straight away. Biggest of all was the Olympic village being built for next year's games. But Archie stuck to his plan – find a job in Melbourne using his butcher's skills and enrol in evening classes for something in business. Every day he checked the *Argus* and the *Herald*, walked to the local labour exchange and talked with the few men in the hostel he thought were worth the trouble. He had enough money to tide him over for a month or so if he was careful.

One morning the week before, he was sitting on his doorstep, smoking and catching a little warmth from the milky sun. Bob Manners came out from the hut opposite, followed by his wife, Elsie, who was on her way to work; she'd been taken on as a conductress on the trams. 'Love it,' she said, 'absolutely love it.'

'Good for you,' Archie said. He could just see her going down a storm at rush hour with her Marilyn Monroe looks.

Bob looked quite a few years older than Elsie. He was a beefy man with drooping cheeks and his hair slicked back to conceal a bald patch.

Archie walked over and opened his cigarette packet. He breathed in through his mouth to avoid the stench from Bob's armpits.

'Don't mind if I do. Thanks, young man,' Bob said.

They had spoken a few times, just to exchange names and say 'how are you doing.' Archie didn't quite catch the accent. Yorkshire maybe. 'Good try,' Bob said. He was from Worksop just over the border in Nottinghamshire. A fitter and welder by trade, he'd just fixed himself up with a temporary packing job up the road at Hawkins canned foods. Word had it, they were hiring all the time but never advertised. No need, they said, with people knocking on the door every day.

Archie dropped his cigarette butt on the cinder path and stamped on it. 'Sounds promising. So where is this place exactly?'

After Bob gave him directions Archie was off. He picked up his indentures from the hut and headed up the road in search of the factory. It didn't take long to find it, the smell of raw meat and sawdust wafting down the street to welcome him.

*

They could use some of these cuts at the hostel, he thought. After yesterday's porkless pork chops, Archie was so hungry he'd walked down to the bakers for a Four'n Twenty pie. Right now, he was busy preparing brisket, ready to be salted and cured for tinned corned beef. This was Hawkins' biggest seller and the butchers spent a lot of time with these cuts. Some days Archie got to work with chuck for meatballs and pies or round cuts for sausages. But mostly it was brisket. The work was monotonous, unlike in the back of Mr McKay's shop in Leith. Still, at least he was being paid to use his skills. He was sticking to the plan.

'You want to slow down a bit, mate. If you go any faster those bastards'll be cutting our rates.'

Archie stopped, steak knife in hand, and turned to face weasel-faced Brandon Hopper at the next table. 'Is that right?' He heard the threat in his own voice, tried to cover it. 'Aye, fair enough. I just like to relieve the boredom sometimes. See how fast I can work.'

'It might be boring, mate, but the pay's good so let's keep it that way. Alright?' Hopper laughed but Archie suspected he wasn't trying to be funny. The man was the local shop steward and so far he hadn't joked with Archie about anything.

Archie turned back and started to work more slowly but Hopper wasn't finished.

'Anyway, you lot ought to consider yourselves lucky.'

'What lot?'

'You Pommies. And don't give me the "I'm not a Pommie 'cause I'm Scotch" routine. You're all the bloody same to us.'

'Scots or Scottish. Scotch is what some people call whisky.'

Hopper ignored him and carried on, waving his knife for emphasis. 'You get your fares paid and a roof over your head when you get here. You get fed. And you get your pick of the jobs. Not like the poor bastards from Greece and the likes. They have to do whatever work's handed out by the government for two years. 'Cause if they don't, they get deported.'

'Save your breath, mate,' Archie said, 'I know the rules.' He slid his knife slowly through the brisket, admiring how neatly the blade parted the flesh.

It was a closed shop at Hawkins which had surprised Archie. He wasn't sure why. Maybe it was an image he had of Australia as a frontier country where selling your labour was a kind of free for all. He who works hardest wins the game. Something like that. In any case, he was sorely disappointed. The union at Hawkins had things sewn up. Them and us. But being part of a closed shop didn't mean having a closed mind and that provided Archie with opportunities, if he was careful. He'd been working there for over a month, long enough to see the sort of things that went on. Hopper and most of the others justified their regular breaks, the cleaning up time and their slow and steady approach, on safety grounds. Archie knew all about safety in the butchers' trade but that wasn't his point; it was the constant chatter and the way they broke off from cutting the meat to tell a story or a joke. Safety first, they laughed, you can't tell a joke and wield a knife at the same time. The management must have no idea what went on because if they did, surely they would have stamped it out. So why did Archie hesitate?

A week or so later he started an evening class in business administration at Preston Technical School up the road from the hostel. He wasn't hopeful when he first looked at the list of courses; it was all plumbing, joinery, gas fitting and other trades. But on the last page of the prospectus he found the only business course they offered. Tuesday evenings, starting next week. *NEW for this year!* the brochure said.

The classroom was modern with windows running the whole width of the room and formica-topped desks spaced out neatly. Nothing like his grim old secondary in Leith and just as well – he didn't want to feel like he was going back to school. Whatever the place was called, Archie preferred to think of it as a college.

On the first evening he counted the heads in the room, twelve of them including his own. All men, mostly older-looking than him. Some of them wore jackets and ties, like they'd come straight from work. When the lecturer walked in carrying a sheaf of papers, Archie thought he recognised him but wasn't sure. Tall and thin with wavy grey hair. Probably in his fifties and he reeked of pipe tobacco. The man said his name was Barry Hunter. And Archie knew where he'd seen it – in a list of senior staff on the noticeboard at Hawkins. Barry Hunter was the Production Director. After a brief introduction about himself and the course, Barry went round the room asking people for their names and why they'd chosen this class. Archie looked round at the others and listened intently when they spoke. Most of them were office clerks looking for a qualification to help them get a promotion or the prospect of a better job elsewhere. When it was his turn, Archie looked at Barry Hunter steadily, told him he was a butcher by trade, worked at Hawkins and was ambitious to make a career for himself in business.

Barry grinned, showing brown-streaked teeth, and said, 'We'll need to have a chat about that sometime.' Archie nodded and said, 'Whenever you like.'

The course was exactly what Archie wanted. He lapped up information about product design, production control, sales, marketing and distribution. Under the naked ceiling light in his cramped, miserable room at the hostel, he pored over textbooks borrowed from the local library. He did exercises and wrote essays. In the first few weeks his assignment marks were excellent.

At the end of the fourth class, as the men filed out of the room, Barry called to Archie. 'Have you got a minute?'

'Sure.' Archie tucked his folders under his arm and sat on the edge of a desk.

Barry took a duster to the blackboard and got straight to the point. Over his shoulder, he asked Archie how he liked working at Hawkins. This was Archie's moment, one he'd been thinking about ever since Barry Hunter introduced himself to the class. He didn't want to fluff his lines.

'The working conditions and the pay are good. I've no complaints on that score.'

The older man finished cleaning the blackboard and walked towards Archie, wiping chalk from his hands. He stopped, folded his arms and leant back against the table. A powerful smell of tobacco thickened the air between them.

'So what *do* you have complaints about?'

'I'm not saying I have complaints. Some things are just different from what I'm used to, I suppose.'

'Go on.'

Archie had rehearsed this bit so many times. He was word perfect back in the hut whenever he tried it out. But he hesitated – he knew this could go either way. Stuff it, what did he have to lose?

'Maybe it's just me but I get the impression that people don't really care about the work. About doing a good job. It's like they're laughing at you behind your back – all of you, I mean. The management. It's not how I've been brought up. But then I'm not an Australian so what do I know?'

Later, much later, whenever he replayed the scene, Archie would laugh privately. He hadn't said any of the things he'd rehearsed but it worked anyway, just not in the way he'd intended.

'I'm no fool,' Barry Hunter said. And he wasn't having a jumped-up young Scotch bastard, two minutes off the ship, telling him what he already knew. Like it was news to him that most of the workforce did as little as they could get away with; that they name-called management day in day out. Did Archie think Barry was born yesterday?

'But all the same,' Barry said, 'I think I can use you. I can see you're bright and it looks like you've got a good business head. And, most of all, you know the butchers' trade. I'll make sure there's an opening for you in the Production Department soon enough. Just make sure you jump at it.'

When the job came up a few weeks later, jump at it was the last thing Archie did. He hummed and hawed right up to the closing date. He had often imagined his ideal jobs in production: quality control, production planning, inventory control. But time and motion? Archie knew what that meant in his position. Barry's words after the evening class came back to him: you know the butchers' trade. Poacher turned gamekeeper. He would be loathed on the factory floor for moving from us to them. He remembered Jessie's letters from Wollongong. Her news of Bob at the steelworks – good pay, the hours weren't too long and no one asks what school you went to. How these words had appealed to Archie and helped him make his mind up to come out to Australia in the first place. But he knew it was never about politics. Archie had no interest in labour issues; all he wanted was a fair chance to progress on merit. Unions, them and us, didn't come into it. In the end he went for the time and motion job and Barry Hunter was as good as his word.

It was a first step. Not an office of his own with a telephone on his desk. Not even a suit and tie yet. Just a white coat and a clipboard. It would do for now. When he walked up to the factory on the first day of his new role, he watched the expanse of the Olympic village starting to take shape at ground level. This was a country on the move, Archie decided and, whatever flak you got from the Aussies, it was worth being here if you were lucky enough to be white and British.

When he sat in the hut writing to Nesta that weekend, he felt he was ticking off items on a list in his quest to convince her of his worth. He wanted to remind her of what he'd told her on the ship: that he was Archie Thomson and whatever it took, he was going to make something of himself here, in Australia.

Nesta's letters were more frequent than his, usually he got two, sometimes three, a week. They were short, scribbled affairs though, full of news about her course, the weather, girlfriends and how expensive everything was. And in her latest one, a telephone number. A friend of her landlady's said Nesta was welcome to take an incoming call once a week for no more than ten minutes. Four o'clock on a Sunday afternoon would be best. Nesta's letter said she would be there this weekend waiting for him.

Archie tried to recall her voice, tried to play it in his head like some half-remembered tune. Her smile and the way she said his name: Archee. What would he say to her? How long had it been since he walked down Station Pier with Billy, turning round to look for her on the deck; raising his arm in the hope that at least *she* saw *him*. Nearly four months. A wave of longing came over him. Most of the time he tried to block Nesta out, to concentrate on work and chores and his night school homework. There was no point pining and wondering what she was up to every minute of the day.

On the morning the *Fairsea* had sailed into Port Phillip bay they gave their word to each other. 'We will try to make this work,' they said. Of course, he had still wanted Nesta to say something more, like *I'll wait for you, come what may*. But at least she wrote frequently and always signed her letters *with love from Nesta*. That would have to do. And on Sunday he would call her at four o'clock. Maybe he would tell her about the letter he'd received two weeks ago about the inquiry into Carwyn's death. Or rather, the lack of an inquiry. The letter came on headed notepaper from the British Consulate in Perth; it informed him that the investigation into the incident on board the *Fairsea* was now closed and thanked Archie for his assistance in the matter.

But what he really wanted to tell her about was the Victoria holiday weekend coming up. He would be free from Friday after work until the Monday morning. Would she like him to come to Sydney? He hoped she would.

18

Sydney, 1997

She stops to look at the poster as they leave the arrivals hall on their way to the taxi rank. *The Sinking of the Rainbow Warrior, an opera in one act.* It feels like confirmation, as if she needs it, that the world is changing and she is struggling to keep up. It's a far cry from the old staples in her day. Mozart, Verdi and Puccini made up the bulk of programmes back then. Opera for the masses, designed to pull the crowds in. Designed to help change the country's image too – a more sophisticated Australia. More cultured, whatever that meant. Archie gives her a look which says 'get a move on.'

The taxi driver is from Vietnam. She knows that because his name, Hoang Van Lu, is printed in large black letters on the licence fixed to the back of his seat. Of course, he may well be Australian, she reminds herself. Names don't count, not when it comes to nationality.

Archie settles into the soft, faux leather seat behind the driver. Nesta squeezes her husband's knee, leans forward and cranes her neck between the headrests. 'The Old Harbour View Hotel, please. Just off Lavender Street.'

Mr Lu turns and smiles. 'I know it,' he says. He checks his mirror and pulls out into a slow-moving line of taxis. Late afternoon sun glints briefly on the gear lever.

'So. Holiday?' Mr Lu says to the mirror.

Archie leans back and closes his eyes. Nesta moves forward again. The seat belt cuts into her shoulder. She leans back and raises her voice.

'Sort of.' It feels rude to close down the chat before it's started. 'And you. Are you local to Sydney?'

'Three years,' Mr Lu says, smiling. 'Before that Melbourne. Before that Saigon.'

'And how do you like it here?'

'I like it now. At first, not so good. Very brown. Lots of desert.'

Nesta laughs. The kids have each visited Vietnam recently. So green, they both said. And so cheap. And everyone's so young. 'Well they would be after forty years of war,' Archie had said.

Mr Lu looks like he might be in his early fifties. She wants to ask him what he did when he lived in Vietnam but thinks better of it. Now isn't the time. She moves to take Archie's hand, then stops. *Don't fuss, let him be.*

When they reach the hotel, Mr Lu insists on carrying their bags into the foyer, resisting the attempts of a middle-aged bellboy to wrest them from him. She watches Archie give the taxi driver a bigger-than-usual tip.

*

In the fifth-floor room, Nesta swishes back the floor-to-ceiling drapes and steps onto the balcony. Archie hasn't stinted on the accommodation. Not that he was ever the parsimonious Scot. The view stretches south across Lavender Bay with Luna Park on her left. The sight of the old amusement park brings back memories of happy, let-your-hair-down evenings with Alison, her housemate at university. After dark, they would hop on a ferry at Circular Quay for the short journey under the bridge to the park. The huge illuminated face at the entrance, with its manic smile, loomed larger and larger as the boat approached the quay. Screams and shouts from the rides grew louder above the relentless sound of a pipe organ. By the time they got off the ferry it felt like the park was ready to consume them.

Beyond the harbour bridge, the skyline has changed since those days. Circular Quay is nothing more than a thin line pressed down beneath ever-taller buildings. If you didn't know it was there you would barely see it from this distance. To the right of the quay, a huge white liner is docked alongside the Rocks. Nesta tries to count the number of decks on the ship but gives up. Something comes back to her. Counting ships in the bay at Aden. Another piece of the jigsaw. A small piece of scenery, nothing important.

She can't see the opera house from here, not nowadays. It's somewhere over to the left, beyond more high-rise buildings which cluster around the north side of the bridge. She returns her gaze to Lavender Bay below. It is dotted with small white boats of similar shapes and sizes; they look stylish, sparkling against the blue-green water in early evening sunlight. I would like to be down there, she thinks, just watching the boats bob, listening to the lazy slap of the swell on their sides. Or out on the Manly ferry perhaps, the ocean wind snapping as the boat skirts the Heads.

She remembers the first time they slept together. It must have been quite a few months after they arrived in Australia. There was a holiday weekend in Victoria. Archie travelled overnight on the train to Sydney and she was there when it pulled in at Central Station early on Saturday morning. The last time she had seen him before then was when he turned and waved at the end of the boardwalk on Melbourne's Station Pier. Billy was beside him, his hand on Archie's shoulder. She stood by herself on the promenade deck of the *Fairsea*, listening to the chatter of couples and families. 'Can't wait,' they said, 'it'll be us next. We'll be in Sydney soon enough.' And she felt the weight of being alone drag her down. For two pins, she could have run down the gangplank to Archie just for the sake of his company, for the sake of avoiding her own thoughts.

But by the time he stepped off the train in Sydney that holiday weekend, she had spent several months getting on with her new life. Mostly. She liked her digs in King's Cross and got on well with Alison, who was studying at the medical school. Their landlady, Mrs Nicholson, was easy-going and the house rules were nothing to complain about. And Nesta's own course was absorbing and challenging. Every day, she felt pushed a little harder and, in return, her vocal range expanded, her confidence grew. On most mornings she cut through the botanic gardens to the school of music. She often stopped to marvel at the enormous bamboo plants, their banded stems as thick as a man's wrist. A big man's wrist – like Carwyn's. Always, she pushed the thought away. Every time she walked through the doors of the conservatorium was reminder enough of his absence. At first, there were other reminders of Carwyn but she pushed them away too. What else was there? Weekly letters from her parents, worried sick about their daughter, out of sight and out of reach. Curiously, just one letter from Carwyn's widowed mother who didn't ask her to explain what happened. A small blessing. She simply hoped Nesta was coping with the shock and looking after herself.

It was a warm, bright spring morning when they left the station arm in arm. Archie booked into a cheap hotel in the heart of King's Cross, not far from Nesta's lodgings. She stayed in the street, looking in shop windows. After that, she remembers taking the ferry over to Manly. They exchanged a knowing look when the boat pitched and rolled as it skirted the Heads with the open waters of the Pacific beyond. They walked up the Corso to the crowded beach and spread their towels on the pale yellow sand beneath the promenade wall.

From somewhere, she draws up an image of Archie standing in the shallows as a wave breaks over his knees, the force of it almost knocking him over. 'No wonder it's strong,' he laughed, 'it's come all the way from South America.' That was Archie, always ready with some fact to explain away a moment that needed no words.

They kissed on the beach and in the sea. They kissed again on the ferry back to Circular Quay. When they lingered in the botanic gardens, the sticky, damp heat from the plants made her skin tingle. By the time they reached the street of Archie's hotel they both walked a little quicker. Across all the years she can still sense their urgency. Nothing felt safe, nothing at all, but her thoughts had melted away, overtaken by fear and longing, by an irresistible need to wash away the stains of the past.

Afterwards, while they lay sweating on the damp sheets, she cried briefly. Archie held her and told her everything would be alright. He said they were meant to be together or something like that. She would love to recall her thoughts precisely, just as they were for those few minutes. Was it relief? But it's far too long ago. Nobody can really remember what they were thinking four hours ago, let alone forty years. And she doubts it was simply a matter of a fork in the road – go this way or that. Their lovemaking did push them closer together, though. First Carwyn's death and then this. Perhaps it was all unspoken. Perhaps Archie never said those things at all. Perhaps they each assumed their futures were joined in some way. Nesta has always told herself they made a pact but now she wonders if it was just her. Her secret pact.

Archie joins her on the balcony. She searches his face before speaking. 'It's beautiful, Archie. Thank you.'

'May as well,' he says.

Nesta takes his hand, draws him towards the view. 'Yes, may as well. As they say, you can't take it with you.'

He gives her a blink-and-you'll-miss-it smile, leans his scaly forearms on the polished wood of the balustrade. 'We've done alright, haven't we?' he says.

'And we're doing alright, too.' She takes his hand again, squeezes it lightly. Is now the time? It feels like it. 'I don't want to sound morbid, Archie. Maybe there's never a right time to say certain things. But I want you to know that I don't regret anything.' He keeps looking out at the view so she goes on. 'We've each made mistakes – I guess everyone does. But we've stuck at it, haven't we? Our little bond?'

Archie stares straight ahead. 'I'm scared,' he says. 'Scared and angry. And before you ask, I'm angry with myself. I should have taken more care in the sun. Should have stopped smoking long ago. I'm angry because I can't go back and change it.'

Nesta leans on the balustrade too. Early evening shadows begin to creep across the bay, darkening the water. A faint chill runs through her and she rubs her upper arms. 'No. We can't change the past. And anyway, there's always tomorrow. Let's try to be positive. You've said this Mr Gupta is the best in his field.'

'Yes, but he's not a bloody miracle worker.'

'Well, let's hope he is, Archie. Let's hope he is.' She takes his arm, rests her chin on his shoulder and kisses his cheek.

*

Right now, she would prefer to sit on the balcony with her coffee but the wicker chairs are still wet after the early morning downpour. At home, they haven't had a drop for months. Today of all days.

More than an hour has passed and she is still livid. They had an agreement, she's sure of it. That was the whole point of her coming to Sydney with him – so she could be there when he saw the consultant. But Archie had stage-managed the whole thing. In the hotel room half an hour before the ten o'clock appointment he told her he needed to do this on his own. They spent five minutes arguing and then he was gone. 'I'll walk,' he said, 'now that the rain's stopped. It's only two blocks away.'

Nesta goes out onto the balcony anyway. In the low, grey sky, pale blue smudges appear, spreading like a rash. Spreading like cancer, she thinks. Her watch says eleven-fifteen. How long does a consultation take? An hour? If Archie is to be believed, Mr Gupta already has all the test results and patient history.

The view looks different today. It's not just the weather or the time of day. When they stood here talking yesterday evening there was no gulf between them. She felt their invisible bond wrap itself around them. It always did have an elastic quality, stretching them apart but never snapping; pulling them back together when it mattered most. But now it strains to breaking point. She hates being angry with Archie at this, of all times. She walks back into the room just as the door unlocks and Archie comes in. Her stomach flutters like first-night nerves.

'Well?' she says.

'Give me a minute, will you?' he says, throwing his hands up.

Take as long as you want, she feels like saying, *it's not like it's anything important.* But she bites her tongue. Sarcasm has never been part of her weaponry.

'I'll make us some coffee,' she says. Archie nods and blows out his cheeks. Nesta puts an extra spoonful in the cafetière.

They sit on two easy chairs in the corner of the room and she sets their coffees down on the low, glass table.

'It's not good,' he says. 'Gupta says existing treatments won't work.

He gives me a year at the most. But there is another option.'

'And what's that?' Nesta's cup rattles as she places it in the saucer.

'A clinical trial. It's been going for a couple of years. Twenty per cent success rate so far but it's early days. If it works he thinks it could give me another five to ten years.'

It strikes her that Archie sounds like he's talking about a business deal.

'What have you got to lose, I guess?'

'Just my life, Nesta. Either way, it's just my life I've got to lose.'

'Sorry, I didn't mean it like that. You know I didn't.'

Archie says 'I know,' but it sounds grudging. It's nearly twelve o'clock and they're due to meet Jim at two. Perhaps that wasn't such a good idea. Nesta tries to picture the three of them sitting in a stylish café down in the Rocks. Chatting away, listening intently to what Jim's been up to on his journey across southern Australia. No, she can't see that working.

'Look,' she says, 'you need to say what you want to do. If you need some space to take all of this in, that's fine. I can quite easily cancel Jim.'

'No, no. Let's not cancel Jim.' Archie sounds alarmed.

'Well, in that case, I think it's better if you see him on your own. See how you feel afterwards, you can always arrange for both of us to meet him for dinner if he's free.'

Archie agrees to her suggestion. He looks lost. But then his eyes narrow and he appears to focus on something important.

'What will you do when I'm with Jim?' he says.

'Don't worry about me,' she says. 'I'll find something to while away a few hours.'

While Archie takes a nap, Nesta goes down to reception and picks up some tourist leaflets. There's an exhibition at the state gallery which she would like to see. *May as well get used to it*, says demon thought, *you'll have plenty of time on your hands soon enough.*

19

Sydney, 1997

As I walked down George Street to meet Archie and Nesta, the weekend I spent with them in Adelaide seemed an age ago. Yet little more than a week had passed since I drove away from their house and hit the road for Melbourne.

I listed some of the things I might say to them just in case they asked what I'd been up to. There was my visit to Bob and Jessie in Albury; what I thought of Melbourne and Canberra; my impressions of Sydney. And then there were the things I was sure I wouldn't tell them, like my walks on Mount Buffalo and in the Blue Mountains. And Roz, she was off limits too.

Of course, there was more, much more. Such as what I'd discovered about the pair of them at the archives in Canberra. How they had travelled on the same *Fairsea* voyage to Australia but got off in different ports: Archie in Melbourne, Nesta in Sydney. And then what Roz told me on the phone about the man going overboard somewhere in the Indian Ocean. The man who was on his way to the conservatorium just like Nesta. The man who shared a surname with her. But I still had no plans to broach any of those subjects – how could I? And yet. I recalled Archie's hand pressing my shoulder at the golf club and Nesta's tears on the bluff at Victor Harbor. 'I wish I could tell you,' she said. Perhaps

Nesta was the one to speak to. In the meantime, I had no desire to create an awkward situation, especially as this meeting in the Rocks was arranged only a few days ago. And there was another potential banana skin – would I ask them what they were doing in Sydney? By the time I got to the café I began to wish I wasn't meeting them at all.

I was standing outside when Archie appeared from nowhere and shook my hand. He wore his now-familiar uniform of grey trousers and open-necked shirt under a navy V-necked jersey. I glanced at his feet, half-expecting him to be wearing golfing brogues. We found a bistro table in the shaded courtyard. The place had an old-world feel about it with its pock-marked stone walls and sash windows. Dripping plants in ceramic pots were dotted around the weathered flagstone floor and this morning's rain had left an earthy smell in the air. Even in the trendy Rocks area the café seemed out of place.

A waiter in a dark green apron came over and we ordered coffee. I hadn't eaten lunch so I asked for a slice of carrot cake too. Archie lit a cigarette and smiled but it seemed like an effort.

'So you've made it all the way to Sydney,' he said.

My uncle looked different. His face was grey and worn like an old dishcloth. And why hadn't he mentioned Nesta? Already I was starting to feel irritated.

'Is Nesta not joining us?' I said, hearing a forced lightness in my voice.

'Something's come up. She sends her apologies.'

Christ, it was like a business meeting. I was tempted to say, *shouldn't we minute that?* But I bit my tongue.

'That's a shame. But this is all unexpected anyway. I mean, when I left Adelaide, I had no idea you were going to be in Sydney at the same time as me.'

'Neither did we,' he said, looking intently at a plant pot on the ground.

The waiter brought the coffees and cake and left the till receipt in a shot glass. There was murmured conversation from a couple at a table behind Archie. Then the sound of a metal tray clattering somewhere inside the café. My head throbbed. I willed myself not to say anything and ate a forkful of cake slowly.

In the end I gave in and asked some dull question about their hotel. I was determined not to launch into some opinion about the places I'd been. *Don't give him ammunition to shoot you down.* But he surprised me by asking about my research so I talked for a while about Walter Avery and his adventures, his lies and omissions, my search for the truth.

'He sounds like quite a character,' Archie said and fingered the lighter on top of his cigarette packet. 'I guess we've all got stories to tell about making our way in Australia. Our journeys.'

'I expect you must have an interesting story to tell.'

Archie laughed and his face coloured a little.

'How long have you got, Jim?' He looked away for a few seconds then turned back sharply. He took a deep breath and his face came alive, all furrows and lines. His eyes shone. I was looking at a different Archie, the one I had hoped to meet. Even now, I can still picture that look as he stared at me.

'Maybe it's time to let you into a few secrets,' he said. 'Dispel a few myths that have been going around the Thomson family for as long as I can remember.'

I took my time, not wanting to sound too eager. 'Well, I'm certainly keen to listen but only if you really want to tell me.' I held my hands up. 'I'm sorry if you thought I was prying when I asked you things back in Adelaide. I can't help being a historian. We're all nosy buggers, I guess.'

Archie laughed again and lit another cigarette. He told me how my mother and the rest of his sisters used to tease him. They said he was the lucky one, missing the worst of the hardship during the depression and escaping service in the war. The world was his oyster, they said, and he was going to make his fortune one day.

I picked at the crumbs on my plate and said, 'I used to love hearing about you when I was growing up. It all seemed so exotic. Australia. And that book you gave me. I spent hours poring over it, looking at the photos.'

We finished our coffees and Archie insisted on paying the bill. He suggested we go for a walk and said there was something he wanted to show me. We strolled up George Street for a minute or so until Archie hailed a taxi. It was a short ride but he said the walk was too long for him these days. Five minutes later we got out on Macquarie Street and entered the park near the phone booth where I'd spoken to Roz the day before.

'These are the botanic gardens,' Archie said in a mock tour guide voice. 'I take it you haven't been here yet.'

'I've passed them once or twice but not really gone in.' I didn't have the heart to tell him.

The afternoon sun had dried the paths and benches but the gardens were quieter than when I visited the previous day. Archie led me along a shady winding path through lush, tropical plants with huge fronds and stems slick with algae. I smiled when we emerged into sunlight. Archie sat on a bench near a statue. A hunter stood on a plinth. He was dressed in an old-fashioned jacket, and trousers with gaiters. His right hand was cupped to his ear and his head was cocked slightly. In front of him were two gun dogs, one sitting on its hind legs, the other standing; both of them strong and alert. It was an unusual subject for the location and I studied it for a while. A hunter standing with his dogs in a park in the centre of Sydney. Listening, waiting for a sound. But what made me smile was the building behind him across the lawns.

'Strange-looking place, isn't it?' Archie said.

I agreed.

'It's called the Sydney Conservatorium of Music.' He turned to me. 'It's where Nesta studied when she came out here in fifty-five.'

This was difficult but I had to play along. 'Really,' I said, or something like that. And then he told me things I didn't know. I listened and tried to erase from my mind images of ships' names and passenger lists; tried to erase feelings of guilt about my time at the archives in Canberra. Archie was starting to tell me his story and I had to trust him.

He talked about what drove him to come to Australia in the first place. How, after leaving school, he tried to settle for life in a Britain bounded by limited opportunities. 'Of course the war changed everything,' he said. But increasingly he realised those changes would take decades to benefit the likes of him. His sisters had told him he was the lucky one but he reckoned the really lucky ones hadn't been born yet. 'It's your generation,' he insisted, 'that's benefited from all the social and welfare and education changes. But the irony,' he said, 'is you're the ones that don't seem to understand just how lucky you are.'

I could have argued with him in so many ways but what was the point? My uncle was talking about his past and that was all that mattered.

There were no strong ties to family, he said, and certainly none to Edinburgh or Scotland. It made it easier to leave when there was nothing really holding him back. But I thought I heard a small quiver in his voice when he told me he never saw his parents again after they disappeared into the gloom on the platform at Waverley station.

'My brothers, all four of them, came back from the war unscathed.'

'So, weren't they the lucky ones too?' I said.

'They were unlucky to be born when they were. And lucky to escape with their lives, with their minds and bodies intact,' he said. 'But it was like they'd had a whole lifetime's worth of adventure and fear crammed into six years of war. When they came home they just wanted to live out the rest of their time as quietly as possible. You can't blame them.'

'But Bob took a chance by coming out here?'

Archie laughed. 'He took a chance on finding a quiet life in Australia, the one he couldn't find in Leith. Bob had nothing to lose. And like me, he never felt held back by family ties. Or Scotland, for that matter.'

'I saw them in Albury,' I said. 'Visited their home. They seemed content with their lot. And their family. So many of them.'

Archie nodded but didn't say anything. I asked if he saw Bob often. He looked away, seemed to study the statue of the hunter and his dogs.

'As you've discovered, Albury's a long way from Adelaide,' he said. 'And to be honest, Jim, we don't have a lot in common. I know it seems odd to the Scottish Thomsons. They think: two brothers thousands of miles away in Australia, they must be bosom buddies. But it's a ten-hour drive to Bob and Jessie for a start.' He paused to look at a galah which had landed on the hunter's head. 'And they don't like Nesta.'

I imagined Bob and Jessie sitting comfortably at a one-armed bandit in their local RSL club, a couple of schooners of beer within easy reach. And then Archie, his photograph on the wall at his golf club. Mr Thomson, that's what Jock the barman had called him. Jock the barman, Bob the brother, it was all the same really. How so many of us travel down different paths. If Archie didn't have a lot in common with his brother and his wife, where did that leave Nesta?

Archie leant to one side and fished his cigarettes and lighter from his pocket. 'Bob went straight to the steelworks in Wollongong. Nesta went *there*.' He nodded towards the conservatorium, a cigarette in his mouth as he cupped his hand round the lighter.

'I get the picture,' I said. And then I risked a little more. 'But you didn't come out here to marry an opera singer, did you?'

'No, I certainly did not. But it's the best thing I've ever done. And you know why?' He didn't wait for my response. 'Because Nesta helped my career. She made me, how can I put it… she made me interesting by proxy. When I was climbing the ladder – sales manager, then regional manager, right up to sales director and so on. We'd do the introductions at business meetings and conferences and the like. "And are you married, Archie?" they'd say. I'm talking about board members, export trade officials, government ministers, potential Japanese customers, you name it. "Yes," I'd tell them, "my wife's an opera singer." You'd be amazed how it changes the way people treat you. Suddenly, you're not just another businessman in a suit.'

His words hit me like a bad smell. I wondered if he'd ever told Nesta how he felt about her. Perhaps their experiences were mutual but I doubted it. Somehow, I couldn't see Australia's arts establishment being wowed when Nesta told them her husband was a director of a canned food company. I struggled to find anything to say and Archie still hadn't spoken about how they met. He leaned over the arm of the bench and stubbed out his cigarette in a flower bed.

'And was it love at first sight?' I laughed.

He looked embarrassed. 'You know how we met?'

I felt like he was teasing me. Of course I didn't know. 'On the ship?'

'How, I said. Not where.'

He told me a story about Nesta being robbed in a souk in Port Said. How he grabbed the young thief and retrieved Nesta's purse. And then he let the boy go.

'Why?' I thought I knew the answer but I asked anyway.

'Not to impress her with my compassion if that's what you're thinking. No, I let him go because things were dangerous back then. It was the year before the Suez crisis. Nasser was in power and the French and the British were living on borrowed time. Of course, the Egyptians still wanted our money. But the atmosphere in Port Said was tense. I didn't fancy holding onto a young boy in the middle of the souk while we waited for the local police to arrive.'

I wasn't convinced. 'And you worked all of that out in an instant?'

Archie looked amused. 'Are you doubting my word?'

'No,' I lied. 'It just sounds remarkably cool-headed. And brave, I suppose. I mean grabbing the boy in the first place.'

'Sometimes you have to be brave, Jim.'

His statement cut me like a knife. My uncle seemed to rip open my feeble defences until he looked right into the heart of me. I could have kept quiet or changed the subject but it was out before I knew it.

'I wouldn't know,' I said. 'It's something I try to avoid.'

'You've been brave enough to come to Australia on your own. And drive all the way from Adelaide to Sydney. There are plenty of people who couldn't handle that.'

'But that's easy. It's just getting on a plane and driving a car and checking into hotels. It's not... it's not...'

'It's not what? Facing up to people? Taking responsibility for your actions? Making tough decisions? Is that what you mean?'

His words felt harsh, abrasive like sandpaper, but I let him go on.

'You probably won't remember this,' he said. 'It was a long time ago, you couldn't have been more than seven or eight. I was on a business trip to Europe. The whole thing was very full on but I managed to grab a night in Edinburgh in the middle of it. Short notice though. I told your mother I'd come round for a couple of hours in the evening. When I arrived it was just her, your dad and your Auntie Ida. You were nowhere to be seen.'

Something jolted in my head and suddenly the scene appeared, fully formed. How had I forgotten it? Across that passage of time, came the trembling, the wanting to be sick, the sound of my mother's voice. Walking downstairs, already failing to hold back the tears. 'Here he is, Archie,' my mother said, 'your nephew. Jim the Coward. Jim the Cry Baby.'

Archie's voice cut through the dreadful memory. 'So your mother called you down from your room and called you names. Said you were in disgrace because you'd hit a wee girl in the eye with an arrow. She said you'd run home to hide. That you wouldn't own up to it. I remember you standing in a corner of the living room trembling, your lip going, tears streaming down your cheeks.' He looked up and away towards the harbour bridge. 'Yes, she can be a hard woman, your mother.'

What's the point of fighting tears? Just to prove you're a man? The tears will always win in the end. As they should. So I let them come as I sat there on the bench. But there wasn't so much. I filled a couple of tissues blowing my nose and then I was done.

'Feeling better now?' I heard tentative laughter in Archie's voice. 'Look, I know we're all different. You probably think I've got where I am by being ruthless, by using people. And maybe that's right up to a point. But some of it, especially in the early days, was about gritting my teeth and getting on with it. I never wanted to have regrets, to wonder what might have been.' He sat upright and folded his arms. 'You know, I used to imagine lying on my death bed and going over...'

He collapsed into a fit of phlegm-filled coughing. It was my turn to look the other way. When he had finished, Archie shifted across on the bench and spat noisily into the flower bed.

'Sorry about that,' he said. 'What was I saying?'

'You were talking about your death bed.'

We sat in silence for a while. Perhaps we both needed a breather. I looked at the conservatorium and then scanned left towards the harbour bridge. North or south? Even after several days in Sydney I still struggled. We were facing north, I decided. The Pacific Ocean was out there somewhere to my right. All the way to South America. In two days' time I would be heading north up the coast to Port Macquarie. I started thinking about Roz but Archie's voice brought me back.

'I imagine you've been wondering why Nesta and I are in Sydney. Why we didn't mention it the other weekend. Well, as I said in the café, back then we had no idea we'd be here. The thing is, Jim, I'm dying. I've got terminal cancer. Skin cancer. Secondaries too. I came here to see a specialist, the number one guy in Australia. But there's no chance. Apart from being a bloody lab rat for some dodgy treatment. I'm not prepared to do that. And I don't want a slow, lingering death either. So, you see, Jim, I want you to help me.'

He rested his hands on his knees. I stared straight ahead but kept snatching looks at his hands. Veined, sunspotted, translucent. I imagined the cancer spreading, eating through tissue, leaving only the bones of the man. He smelled of death. And then he told me his plan.

*

Nesta seemed nervous that evening. She kept touching her cutlery and glancing round at the other diners as we waited to be served.

The restaurant was busy – the location ensured that. It was right on the edge of the harbour between Circular Quay and the opera house. Through floor-to-ceiling windows we looked out on the silvery harbour bridge, yellow lights of traffic pulsing across it like an army of luminous ants. And in the foreground, ferries large and small criss-crossed the bay, taking people to and from the city's coves. Just for that evening Sydney felt like the centre of my universe.

I made all the usual comments about the view and the stylish decor. The prices on the menu were a new experience for me. Was Archie pushing the boat out? He ordered a bottle of Maclaren Vale chardonnay. 'Not from my estate,' he said, 'but close enough.'

Nesta excused herself, saying she was going to powder her nose.

Archie leaned forward across the table. 'Forget what I said earlier.'

'About what?'

'About my plan. I've changed my mind. You were right. It's not fair on Nesta and the kids. So forget I ever said it.'

'I'll try,' I said and relaxed a little.

While we ate, Archie controlled the conversation in his usual way. 'Nesta thinks I was trying to impress her in Port Said,' he said. 'Told me that earlier. All these years and I never knew.'

I looked at her and smiled. She grinned and shook her head briefly.

'Well, impressed or not,' I said, 'something must have clicked between you.'

'And was that it, then? I mean after Port Said did you… did you get it together?' I felt my cheeks burn. 'Sorry, I could have put that better.'

They exchanged a quick, unsmiling look.

'Not straight away,' Nesta said. 'Let's just say there were a few bumps in the road.' She twisted off a claw from the lobster and set about it with her crackers.

'So you found Canberra useful, Jim?' she said, not taking her eyes off the claw.

I hesitated, then told them how I'd been distracted from my academic research. How I was fascinated by the materials they held on post-war migrants in the National Archives. Displaced people from Europe. And the Assisted Passage Scheme, of course. Nesta seemed more interested than Archie. 'What sort of materials?' she asked. I tried to speak lightly and explained about the passenger lists, what information they held – ports of disembarkation, destination addresses, that sort of thing.

'Really?' Her voice went up a pitch or two. 'And is that information publicly available?'

'Some of it,' I said. 'But you need to know what you're looking for.'

After leaving the restaurant we walked slowly along the promenade towards Circular Quay. Archie said he was tired and they would get a taxi on Young Street. I noticed a large ferry heading east and asked if they knew where it was going.

'To Manly,' Nesta said. 'It goes out by the Heads so it needs to be bigger. I remember the first time I went on the Manly ferry.'

She squeezed Archie's hand, laughing. 'Do you remember it, Archie?'

His eyes looked moist and he nodded, the hint of a smile. We hugged and shook hands before they got in the taxi. Archie waved as they drove off and I waved back. I never saw my uncle again.

*

Back in the hotel I lay exhausted on the bed, letting the day's events wash over me. My walk in the Blue Mountains a few days earlier seemed like an awful long time ago. I tried to bring back the feelings I had when I sat on the rock overlooking the gorge but Archie and Nesta kept butting in, their words and looks buzzing around me.

I can't say I was shocked by Archie's news that he had terminal cancer. But I was angry, I suppose. I remembered their scornful laughter in the restaurant in Victor Harbor when I mentioned the hole in the ozone layer over Australia. Had they known about his diagnosis then? Surely they must have done, in which case their reaction was macabre. And then there was Archie's so-called plan. Sitting on the bench in the botanic gardens, he explained to me calmly how he had no desire to die slowly and painfully. 'But there's the issue of insurance,' he said. That was the problem for him. Money. He said nothing about the effects on his wife and children, let alone his own legacy. I listened, appalled and fascinated as he tried out on me the options he was considering. Like a door-to-door salesman showing me his wares. 'What do you think?' 'Which one do you like best?'

And he wanted it done as soon as possible which was where I came in. He needed a witness to say it was an accident. A 'disinterested party' was how he put it. 'Sorry, Jim, but you don't stand to gain a penny from my death.' His laugh was mirthless.

But I stood up to him. Perhaps some of his speech about bravery rubbed off on me. Backfired for him, I guess. 'Think about it,' I said. He'd already been diagnosed with terminal cancer. An accidental death, however well executed, would look suspicious. There would be investigations, inquests, God knows what. Nesta wouldn't be getting a cheque in the post any time soon. 'And what about her and Ewan and Hannah? Have you no regard for their feelings? They're the ones who will have to live the rest of their lives with it hanging over them.'

'Take your time, Jim,' he said. 'Give it some more thought.' I told him to do the same. And then in the restaurant he said to forget it. Forget he'd ever suggested it.

I stretched my arms, gripped the top of the headboard and laughed. What Archie said about the bow and arrow incident had been a shock. Something was unlocked in my deepest memory vault, something buried for decades. The effect of his words was cathartic; my tears were too. I was sure that was why I stood up to him about his outrageous plan. And it worked. I felt like I had really influenced him.

My thoughts turned to Nesta and her brief shake of the head in the restaurant which seemed to say, 'not now'. Was there something she wanted to tell me? And why only her, why not Archie too? He seemed disinterested but I suppose that wasn't surprising. Archie had his forthcoming death to contemplate. Perhaps in the botanic gardens he'd said his piece.

*

The chirping phone woke me just after eight. It was the first time I'd slept through the alarm since my first few days in the country. I took a moment then picked up the receiver. Nesta's voice sounded bright over the phone. 'I want to show you some real Australian art,' she said. Archie was exhausted and needed to rest. Something told me this was about more than art.

The walk through Hyde Park in the cool morning air helped to wake me up properly. I met her outside the Gallery of New South Wales at ten. The façade was classical Greek in style. It reminded me of the National Gallery in Edinburgh, only the stonework here was brighter, like desert sand. Inside, if you ignored the artwork, the place could have been anywhere in the English-speaking world. Stuffy, colonial and depressing.

'Ignore all this,' Nesta said, waving her hand dismissively as if reading my thoughts. She led me through some rooms of European art then down two flights of stairs into a strikingly different gallery. The walls were white, the floor a shiny grey which seemed to throw light onto the huge, vibrant paintings, each one hung with elbow room to spare. At the far end of the room stood a dense collection of wooden totems like an indoor forest.

'Welcome to the Yiribana Gallery,' she said with a hint of pride. 'It only opened last year. Can you believe it? It's taken till the end of the twentieth century to get a permanent collection of indigenous art on display.'

By the time we finished touring the gallery my head was throbbing. Too much at once. But I knew I wanted to come back. We headed for the café. I suspected it was time to get down to business.

Nesta didn't bother with preliminaries. She talked about Archie's diagnosis and his refusal to join the clinical trial. 'I can't blame him,' she said, 'he wants better odds than he's being offered.' Her manner was so matter of fact that I found myself joining in, sympathising as if we were talking about an unattractive business proposition. And then she turned to her main topic: what I'd found out in Canberra. Archie's health was merely the warm-up act, it seemed.

'So what did you find out about us, Jim? I can tell you found something.' My aunt looked tired and anxious but her eyes were demanding.

I mumbled an apology before setting out my case. After what she said on the bluff, I was curious about how they'd met. Perhaps my words sounded hollow because I went on to say how they seemed an odd couple in many ways. I said something like business and art being strange bedfellows. And then I tried to stop digging a bigger hole for myself. I told her about searching the records in the archives and discovering that they both travelled on the same *Fairsea* voyage. But I couldn't be sure they'd met on the ship, I said, not until Archie told me yesterday.

'And was that all you found?' she said, a tense smile on her lips.

Surely she was fishing but fishing for a reason. I swallowed hard.

'You mean about the man who went overboard? The man with the same surname as you? The man who was also going to the conservatorium?' I didn't mean it to sound like she'd been found out. My mouth felt dry. I picked up my coffee cup but it was empty.

Nesta's face looked like it might crumple. But she composed herself and leaned back in her chair.

'I'm surprised you were able to access that information.'

'I'm sorry,' I said. 'I saw his name scored out on the passenger list, just below yours. I couldn't help myself.' I told her what I told Archie. 'I'm a historian,' I said. 'We're nosy buggers.'

'I think we should go for a walk,' she said and grabbed her bag.

We sat on a bench in Hyde Park under a long thin shadow cast by Sydney Tower. Nesta told me about Carwyn, a family friend, she called him, who just happened to be going to Sydney at the same time as her. To teach music, in his case. She said he was known in Cardiff as a bit of a drinker but to avoid making a fuss with her family, she agreed to travel with him to Liverpool. Her parents seemed to think Carwyn would provide some kind of protection. Once on board, she avoided him as much as possible which wasn't difficult since he spent most of his time in the bar.

'Anyway,' she said, 'a storm whipped up somewhere east of Aden and Carwyn went overboard.' There had been an investigation, of course. Someone had seen him staggering out of the bar just before it happened.

'And that's all you need to know,' she said.

'Who knows about this?'

She hesitated. 'Just Archie and me. And Carwyn's family, of course.'

'Not the Thomsons?'

'No.'

'Not Ewan and Hannah?'

'Why should they?' I thought I heard a threat in her voice.

'But – if you don't mind me asking – what's the big deal?' I knew I could have phrased it differently but my exasperation got the better of me.

She pushed her cup and saucer to one side and leaned towards me. 'Look, Jim. Australia was a much smaller place back then. We… I mean I…didn't want to arrive in the country with this accident hanging over me. Sometimes we bury the past and over time it stays buried. That's just how it is. I'm sorry, Jim, I've got more than enough to deal with right now.'

She stood up abruptly and shouldered her bag.

We walked slowly across the park to the taxi rank on Macquarie Street. Nesta asked how much longer I was staying in Sydney. I told her I would be on the road to Port Macquarie in the morning. 'But I'll call you when you're back home,' I said. We hugged awkwardly before she got into a taxi. She gave me a quick wave and a faint smile before the car was swallowed by traffic.

As I walked back across town to the hotel, I thought of Roz properly for the first time in days. Tomorrow was Thursday, a week since we made our agreement.

20

Port Macquarie, 1997

Early next morning I left Sydney and drove north over the harbour bridge. The city was half-asleep, waking slowly in a thin, watery mist. The place looked different from two nights ago when it had sparkled and shone. But it didn't pull me back at all. I'd had my fill and was ready to move on. It was far too early to call Roz before I left the hotel just after seven. Our week of cooling off had ended. We agreed that I would call her today but all of that would have to wait until this evening, after I reached Port Macquarie five hours up the coast.

I was back in pursuit of Walter Avery and trusted him to keep me company, to keep my mind off Roz. As I mentioned before, they'd had enough of Walter's repeated crimes in Sydney and sent him up the coast on a steamer to Port Macquarie. The penal out-station was a prison within a prison, a place of banishment in a land of exile.

Walter is scathing in his memoir about the conditions at Port Macquarie. The jail was full of one-armed, one-legged and blind men, he said, more infirmary than penal settlement. Unsurprisingly, he didn't adapt well to the widespread thievery, drinking and cruel pranks. Nor did he take to the hard work of breaking stones every day, especially when overseers were only too eager to mete out floggings to slackers.

Walter decided to flee which was easy enough to do. The prison's only wall was the bush. He claims to have walked out of the settlement one day, confident he could find his way south and get a passage back to England. And this is where my interest lay. He tells a story about spending several months in the bush, surviving the first few weeks on roots and wild nettles until he was discovered by a group of Aboriginal people who took him in and became his 'most dearest friends'.

According to colonial records, many of the local Aboriginal people were vigorous convict hunters, being rewarded for their catches with small amounts of tobacco and sugar. So Walter's tale, like many of them in his memoir, seems unlikely. He says he was discovered eventually by a squad of soldiers who were doing a routine sweep of settlements on the lookout for escaped convicts. In Port Macquarie, however, I wouldn't be poring over state or national records; there was nothing like that in the small town. I would be taking another approach, looking for a different type of recorded history.

The landscape changed after I left Sydney's northern limits. I had got used to the flat plains between Adelaide and Melbourne and the rolling pasture from Albury to Sydney. Crossing the bridge over the broad estuary of the Hawkesbury River, the land seemed to become older and wilder despite the marinas and riverside restaurants. The forest looked ancient and thick, indented with muddy creeks, gullies and secrets. It was tempting to veer off into the bush on a side road but I kept on driving.

By nine o'clock I was well past Newcastle and starting to feel hungry. Half an hour later I pulled off the highway into Bulahdelah. By now, these little towns all looked the same to me with their wide, frontier-style main streets, rows of cars and utes parked nose to the pavement. I stopped at the bakery for a pie and a coffee and stood outside looking up at the huge blue sky. For the first time since I arrived, I wondered what it would be like to live here in Australia. Not in the cities, that seemed like such a waste. No, I meant out here close to the bush or out in the ranges where you could smell and taste the place. But I pushed these idle thoughts away. Home isn't a country, after all.

*

The man shook my hand and introduced himself as Fenwick Mitchell. He was shorter than me and stocky, with a patch over his left eye. Grey hairs sprouted from both his ears. He wore a pair of patterned beach shorts and his legs were smooth like polished wood. And he had the widest smile I've ever seen. We sat at a table on the verandah of the Birpai Land Council building not far from my riverside hotel.

Fenwick talked about the history of his people, the Birpai. How they lived in settled villages along the riverbanks and around the lakes, long before the British invaded. 'We farmed the country with fire,' he said, 'like all of us do across Australia. The rivers, creeks, lakes, swamps and lagoons made it easy to control the spread of fire. Of course, some things have changed,' Fenwick said, waving his hand towards the ocean. The coastal fringe where they used to fish and gather shellfish is now two hundred kilometres out to sea. 'We live *with* the land, not *off* it,' he said, 'but I expect you know that.'

I listened and waited until he seemed to have finished, resting his palms on his thighs.

'And when the British came?' I asked.

Fenwick gave me a look of resignation. 'We made a stand but what chance did we have? You can't stop the tide, can you? Many people were shot and killed. They gave us fever, they poisoned us with arsenic. All because they wanted our land. They wanted the trees, the *woolia*. Cedars. Red gold, they called them. And then they took our children.'

I wanted to say sorry but the words wouldn't come.

'Anyway,' he said, 'tell me about your research.'

When I'd finished talking about Walter Avery and his claims about being taken in by Aboriginal people, Fenwick sat upright and squared his shoulders.

'There are many stories of prisoners being taken in by our people,' he said. 'It wasn't all about being tempted by the white man's sugar and tobacco. As you will know, our oral history is handed down by the elders. We have funding for a major project to record that history and we're making good progress. But there's still much to be done. And you say that you have other examples of when this Walter Avery lied or embellished things.'

'It's a long shot, I know.' I held my hands up in defeat.

'Don't give up hope before you've started,' he laughed. 'And we're not the only ones from around here. There's a more advanced project to record the history of the Thungutti people who come from further north.' Fenwick stood up. 'Just give me a moment.'

He disappeared into the building and returned a few minutes later followed by a woman. She was small and wiry, with short dark hair. Late fifties perhaps.

Fenwick introduced her as Rosalyn. He said she was leading the Thungutti project, working with the elders further upstate in Bellbrook. I shook her hand, it felt thin and bony. Rosalyn told me she came across many stories like Walter Avery had described. 'Often, the prisoners would leave a token for the people who had looked after them,' she said.

'What sort of thing?' I asked.

'A pocket ripped from a coat, a neckerchief, a chain with a cross, that sort of thing,' Rosalyn said. 'But mostly buttons, brass buttons. There were no names for these people, though. No names that could trace them back to their prison records.'

Rosalyn went back inside. I thanked Fenwick for his time, gave him my email address and the number for my hotel. 'And thank you for sharing your people's history,' I said.

'No worries,' he laughed, 'the more who know it the better. Pass it on,' he said.

I walked back to the hotel. Perhaps it was down to my mood but Port Macquarie wasn't doing anything for me. It seemed full of soulless motels and squat, featureless shops and cafés. If the town had a centre worth seeing, I hadn't found it yet.

The clock in the hotel lobby said six-fifteen. It was time to call Roz. She was bound to be home from work by now. I couldn't put it off any longer.

'Well?' she said. Her voice sounded expectant.

'Well what?'

'What have you decided?'

'Me? It's not just me, you know.'

'Oh, get on with it,' she said, laughing.

I hesitated and took a deep breath. 'I want you to come to Port Macquarie. As soon as you can.'

'What, for a dirty weekend?'

'For a serious weekend. Because I… because I just want to see you.'

I counted five breaths before she spoke again.

'I'd best pack a bag then,' she said.

*

It was one of those evenings when I couldn't settle. I had dinner at a pizzeria by the marina but ate barely half of it. Afterwards, I walked along the concrete promenade, the shore lined by a break wall of quarried stones. Perhaps some of them had been broken way back in Walter's time. The path was dimly lit with streetlights as it meandered past a holiday park; its wire fencing made it look like a prison camp. Raucous laughter came out of the darkness from unseen groups of people; the smell of meat on barbecues. And all the time, the water shushed and slopped along the break wall.

My thoughts flitted over so many things. The woman, Rosalyn, whom I'd met earlier; how she reminded me of Roz, an older version. Which made me think about Roz's year doing research in Papua New Guinea and the Torres Strait islands. What prompted her to do that? I hadn't asked.

I skipped to Archie and Nesta, what each of them had told me. The robbery in Port Said and their first meeting. Nesta's story of the man, Carwyn, being lost overboard out in the Indian Ocean. I was relieved that my snooping was out in the open, at least with Nesta. I was frustrated too. It wasn't that I didn't believe them but what they'd told me felt like mere fragments. In the park, my aunt seemed to suggest there was more to tell. And underlying all of it was Archie's news. I made a mental note to call Nesta on Sunday evening.

But mostly, I thought about Roz. What made me say what I did on the phone? And what the hell was I going to say to her on Saturday? A dirty weekend, she said. A joke, I know, but all I really wanted was certainty.

*

I spent most of Friday sorting through my notes and catching up on work emails very slowly in an internet café. It was late on Saturday morning when Roz arrived. I met her at the airport. We'd argued on the phone about how she was going to get here. She couldn't take Friday off work and anyway, driving four hundred miles was out of the question. 'You'll have to fly via Sydney,' I said, 'and I'm paying.' In the end, she gave in when I admitted the British Arts Council were the ones who were really paying.

When she came through the arrivals door we hugged and kissed like it meant something. And then we pulled away. All of a sudden I felt shy and thought Roz did too. I'd booked a separate room for her in my hotel, she insisted on that. And I liked that about her, her one-step-at-a-time approach, her need for an escape route. 'Just in case,' she said.

The day was clear and sunny, a mere breath of wind off the ocean. We sat outside for lunch at a large restaurant overlooking the marina. Roz turned her chair towards the sun and brushed a fly from her summer dress. Port Macquarie looked better already. Roz said she'd never been here before. 'I don't think you've been missing much,' I said.

'Don't be too hard on it,' she said, 'you haven't seen the Gold Coast yet.'

We talked about the old penal colony and speculated about the town – maybe it was just a legacy place. It hadn't grown much over the years. I mentioned what Fenwick had told me about the local timber. 'And shipwrecks,' Roz said. 'I think it's why it never developed as a port; there's a big sandbar in the estuary.'

She asked about Archie and Nesta. I told her about Archie's diagnosis and what they'd said about how they met. 'So, the information about Carwyn was useful then,' she said.

'I wish I could let it go,' I said. 'Sometimes I get fed up with myself. I spend too much time with my head in the past.'

'You and me both.'

'Sorry, that was insensitive of me.'

'No worries. But you're right. All this time we spend dwelling on the past. Sometimes I think we should learn more from Aboriginal people. Our concept of time is so linear. They seem to have a much better sense of the circularity of time. Of what's important and what's not.'

We paused while a waiter brought our salads with a bucket of fries on the side.

'I'm famished,' Roz said, dipping a couple of fries in the little pot of mayo.

Her necklace glinted in the sun – a gold chain with a brass button hanging from it.

'That's an interesting necklace. It looks like an old button from a coat.'

'It is. Mum gave it to me on my tenth birthday.'

I hesitated. 'Do you mind if I ask you something? About your mum.'

'Go on.'

'What did... sorry... what does she look like?'

'Blonde, at least she was back then. Solid, big boned. Nothing like me. Why?'

'Just curious.'

We ate in silence for a while.

'Maybe it doesn't matter where we come from,' I said. 'All of my grandparents were dead before I was born. But I know quite a lot of family history so I guess I'm lucky in some ways. They all seem to have settled in the same area a long time ago.'

Roz wiped her mouth with a paper napkin. 'Apart from your uncles, of course. Dad's family moved up north from Sydney when he was young. Mum... Mum was adopted, I think.'

After lunch we drove up to Settlement Point and took the little car ferry, like a floating bridge, to the north shore of the Hastings River. The afternoon sun felt hotter now. We drove along the unsealed coastal road for a while and parked up beside a gap in the dunes. The beach seemed to go on forever. Long enough for us to talk about everything. And long enough for us to say nothing as we walked on the hard, flat sand, the turquoise ocean breaking frothily over our feet.

Eventually we reached Queen's Head. We sat at the edge of the beach, below the bluff. Roz rummaged in her beach bag for two peaches which she'd bought at the quayside. A solitary pelican skimmed the shoreline and lowered itself gradually into the shallows.

'I think he's looking for a new home,' Roz said.

'Or maybe she just needs some space.'

'It's definitely a male.'

'How can you tell?'

'By the way he looks. Full of himself.'

'Hey, we're not all like that.'

'I know,' she said and kissed my cheek.

'Come on,' I said. 'Let's have a swim. I haven't been in the Pacific yet.'

I stood up and grabbed her hand. We ran down the beach laughing, splashing into the rollers as they broke on the shore.

On the way back we stopped at a roadside café and bought a couple of pies which we scoffed in the car.

'I could get used to these pies,' I said.

'You'll miss them when you get home.'

I wiped a piece of pastry from Roz's mouth.

'You're very solicitous,' she laughed.

'Look at us,' I said. 'Thirty-three years old and behaving like kids.'

'I don't care. I've waited a long time for this.'

'Me too.'

We wiped our mouths and kissed. It was one of those times when nothing else matters, nothing at all. The world could take care of itself.

'I don't think I'll be needing that room tonight,' Roz said.

'If you're sure?'

'It'll be fine.'

And it was, it was much more than fine.

*

We cried at the airport the following evening. Time had slipped by without us noticing its endless background ticking.

I still remember that mixture of feelings when Roz walked through the departure gate, her holdall slung over her shoulder. There was such an instant, deep sense of loss. How could I give so much in a short space of time only for it to be ripped away? But there was resolve too. A steeliness I'd never experienced before.

As Sunday wore on, we had confronted our situation. We stood for ages on the small balcony of our room, overlooking the marina.

Roz told me she couldn't leave Australia. 'I feel close to Mum here,' she said, 'and I can't ever give that up.' I talked about my own mother. Just past her seventieth birthday and finding her feet in a new world of sheltered living. As an only child, I felt a lonely responsibility for her. But she was young enough to make a fresh start; she still had two older sisters in Edinburgh and a group of long-standing friends too. And it wasn't as if I popped round twice a week. Edinburgh was a good five hours drive from Sheffield.

Then there was my career to consider. The academic job market was increasingly global. Australia had tough immigration policies but my research expertise would count for something. I knew there would be opportunities if I was willing to look for them.

But more than anything there was Australia itself. I told Roz about my musings when I'd stood outside the bakery in Bulahdelah. 'Bloody hell,' she said, 'we'd end up playing bowls and spending our money on the pokies.' I laughed but it didn't lighten my mood. What the hell did I really know about this country? I'd only spent three weeks here. Really, I was nothing more than a tourist with an interest in convict history.

And then I ranted about the blokey culture, the casual racism, the endemic sexism, the rubbish on television, the obsession with sports I didn't like, the pathetic news stories about some MP fiddling his expenses.

'And Britain's not like that?' Roz said when I'd finished.

'It's different.'

'Sounds to me like you're talking yourself out of it.'

Looking out across the bay, Archie's words came back to me – what he'd said about my generation being the lucky ones. How I'd wanted to say that having too much choice wasn't something to feel fortunate about. I heard my uncle laughing at me and then his voice was serious. 'Coward,' he said. Then my mother joined him and they chanted the word together like a pair of taunting children.

I turned to Roz. Her face looked fragile.

'I'm sorry,' I said, 'I was miles away.'

'You'll be miles away soon enough.'

'Only for as long as it takes to find my way back here.'

We held each other until my arms ached, my nose pressed to her hair with its scent of peaches.

*

I called Nesta when I got back from the airport. She said Archie was adamant about not taking part in the clinical trial. As soon as they'd got home Archie asked Ewan and Hannah to come round. He explained the situation to them. 'They both took it well,' Nesta said, 'but no doubt I'll be the one who gets to hear how they're really feeling; they won't know how to talk to Archie.'

In two days' time I would be heading home on a flight from Sydney. I felt sick and restless. If only I could fast forward by six months or a year when I hoped everything Roz and I planned had fallen into place. I tried to imagine the pair of us, out there somewhere in this vast country. But the vision was faint, as if seen through a thin curtain rippling in a breeze.

I know things don't happen just because you want them to. You have to make a plan and try to stick to it. Something else Archie said came back to me, about gritting your teeth and getting on with it.

21

Adelaide, 1998

'The Kaurna Cultural Foundation? Are you sure?' Nesta wonders if the woman at the bank hears the scepticism in her voice.

'I'm sure,' the woman says.

'And it started in nineteen seventy-five?'

'That's right.'

Nesta thanks her and ends the call.

With her pencil, she puts a tick against the entry on the bank statement. She stares at it, willing the words and numbers to come to life, to provide an explanation. One hundred dollars every month for more than twenty years. She feels pleased and cheated at the same time, but mostly cheated. Half-formed questions tumble in her head. *Why did you do it, Archie? What for?* But Archie can't answer them. He died six months ago and probate has only just been completed.

All his other incomes and outgoings are clear enough and expected, although some of the amounts are surprising. For as long as she can remember they each kept separate bank accounts; plus one joint account for the mortgage and shared domestic bills. Archie never asked about her finances and she did likewise. But this? She had no idea.

When she stops to think about it, she can't remember Archie ever saying anything disparaging about Aboriginal people, not in her presence at least. But she can't remember him saying anything empathetic or positive either. It's the only shock she's had since her husband's death and, in a way, it's a pleasant one. He might have been giving money to the One Nation Party for all she would have known. All the same, it's unsettling. The ground beneath her feet doesn't feel quite so solid anymore. If he kept his regular donations to the Kaurna people a secret, what else did he hide? What else is out there that she doesn't know about?

Something Archie said comes back to her. It was not long before he died, just before the morphine began to make him incoherent. 'Carwyn's death was my great fortune,' he said. 'You wouldn't have wanted me otherwise.'

It was a simple statement of belief, on the face of it. Archie thought he got lucky – Carwyn's death helped create a bond with her that might not have happened otherwise. But it nags at her. Over the years she has often wondered what really happened that night, out there in the stormy ocean. And she has always reaffirmed her belief that Archie told the truth. Let it go. The only two people who know the truth are dead. If Archie had any more secrets, he has taken them to his grave, just as Carwyn did. Might she do the same? Or does she need to unburden herself? It's too late to tell Archie but perhaps there's someone else.

She comes back to the monthly donation. Yes, of course she will maintain it for now. Money is the least of her worries. And the children are well provided for, Archie saw to that too. She makes a note to speak with Winnie McMahon, the Kaurna elder, about funding more generally. There is always more to be done.

*

Nesta sits at the mosaic table, slips off her sandals and rests her feet on the liver-coloured tiles. She raises the glass to her lips then stops to check her watch. Ten to six. Close enough. She takes a generous slurp. I hope she's not doing it out of sympathy, she thinks. Allie, who heads the Adelaide Festival Corporation, has just asked her to chair the Music Organising Committee. Surely Allie must believe she's capable, otherwise it would be too much of a risk.

She had her final session with Louise after the festival meeting. Is that why she's starting in on the wine before six o'clock? A little reward for finally putting the past to bed with her counsellor. Since Archie died she has rather missed the secretive nature of the meetings with Louise. Their rendezvous used to have an illicit thrill about them but recently they've become a chore. Like a long walk in the hills where you start off all bright and motivated but by the end you just want the bloody thing over with. To be fair to Louise, the past six months have been more about dealing with bereavement than raking over the past. But there's a limit to how long you can spend doing either. There comes a point when you simply have to get on with living. Demon thought got its way in the end and has been chucked in the bin – job done.

Louise had rounded off the session by talking about next steps. 'You might like to consider writing some things down,' she said. 'We've covered so much ground. I don't want you to lose sight of what you've achieved. And the children, you've still not talked with them about the voyage. They might appreciate knowing a bit more about their father.'

Nesta won't talk to Ewan and Hannah. Neither of them has really shown the slightest bit of interest in how she and Archie first met. Why force it on them now, only to risk being met by more indifference or worse? But she's sick of hiding things, sick of guilt, sick of carrying this burden. So who could she tell? Clearly, not Louise. Nesta has had over a year to tell her counsellor everything but she's fallen short. Hasn't quite managed to get over the line, as they say.

Her thoughts turn to Jim, and what she told him last year in Sydney about Carwyn. What is it they say about politicians these days? Being economical with the truth. In her case it was a long way from being a full disclosure of the facts. The whole thing had been a mixture of lies, half-truths and omissions. Distracted by Archie's health, she had no time or energy to tell her nephew the real story, even if she'd wanted to. And Jim's prying did feel rather intrusive and insensitive at the time. But at least he has shown an interest in her story, and Archie's too, of course.

Archie told her about the conversation he had with Jim in the botanic gardens. It was as close as her husband got to a deathbed confession. How Archie tried to persuade Jim to help him fake an accident. 'Do away with myself' was how Archie described it to her.

According to her husband, Jim dissuaded him and he was grateful for it. Me too, she thinks. Yes, perhaps her nephew is the best person to understand what she has to tell.

She laughs. Jim has proved himself to be quite the dark horse. Who would have thought it? Her nephew taking the plunge and moving out to Australia to live with a woman. Good for him. And Canberra of all places. It wouldn't be her choice and apparently it wasn't Jim's either. 'But needs must,' he said, when he and Roz spent the weekend in Adelaide a few weeks ago. One step at a time. She caught his tentative look at Roz when he said that.

Roz seems pleasant enough. Lively. Wouldn't have thought she was Jim's type though. Not that they stayed long enough for Nesta to get to know her properly. That will take time. But she didn't say much about her family, seemed a bit shifty when asked. Perhaps she's harbouring family secrets. Nesta takes another generous slurp of wine. Aren't we all? She laughs. Aren't we all?

I'll write to Jim, she decides, and feels excited at the prospect. It's a long time since she's written anything other than official letters.

*

The letter takes her a week to write until, finally, she's happy with her fourth draft in pencil. For a moment she thinks about typing the final version but rejects the notion. The stylish white paper with its faint ruled lines calls to her. Writing the letter properly will provide authenticity, as if stamped with her personal seal. She sits at the table in the conservatory. Warm spring sunshine filters through the glass as she begins to write.

> *Dear Jim,*
>
> *It was lovely to see you the other week and to meet Roz too, of course. I thought she came across as considerate and lively and you both seem very happy together. Ewan and Hannah thought so too. I do hope we will stay in touch regularly. And not just on the phone. I'm sure Canberra must have changed for the better since I last visited. It would be good to find out sometime.*

Anyway, I imagine you're already wondering why on earth I'm writing. I've been thinking about when I met you in Sydney last year. It was the day after Archie's visit to the consultant. We went to the Yiribana gallery and afterwards we sat in Hyde Park. As you know, I had a lot on my plate back then. Archie's news had rather overwhelmed me. I told you about Carwyn – the man who went overboard on the Fairsea during our voyage to Australia. I must admit that I missed out a few things and I've been feeling quite bad about that lately. So let me try again.

As I think I told you, Carwyn was a family friend and he was going to Sydney to take up an appointment as a music teacher at the conservatorium. My parents were concerned about me making the journey on my own, and I felt quite anxious too. Eventually, Carwyn changed his plans slightly so that we could travel on the same voyage. I didn't know Carwyn at all. He was in his late thirties so quite a bit older than me. At first, we got on well enough, swept up in the excitement of this big adventure. Every day we had lunch and dinner together. After we got into the calmer waters of the Mediterranean, we went to the evening film show and danced to the live band in the sun lounge. I enjoyed Carwyn's attention. The fact that he was older gave me a thrill. He began to try things on a bit – your generation would laugh. Pecks on the cheek when we met, exploring with his hands when we danced. I tried to make light of it.

Then one night, before we reached Egypt, I got drunk while we were dancing in the sun lounge. I honestly don't know how it happened. Perhaps Carwyn was plying me with double gin and tonics. After the band had finished, he persuaded me to go up to the boat deck with him – to look at the stars, he said. He put his arm around me and began kissing my neck. I barely remember what happened after that. Inside me a desire for more was fighting with a desire to stop. I tell myself that the alcohol tipped the balance. Afterwards, all I remembered was a feeling of desolation, a desperate feeling of loss. I cried silently all night in the dormitory. Soiled goods, that's what my mother would have said. In the morning…

She lays down the pen for a moment, remembers standing in the shower trying desperately to scrub herself clean.

…my feelings had changed to anger. Anger at myself, anger at Carwyn. I wanted to confront him but my sense of guilt held me back. The ship docked in Port Said and the pair of us made our way to the souk. Our silence seemed to drown out the endless noise of people and traffic.

I think Archie told you that we first met in the souk there. How, while I was looking at some fabrics, Carwyn standing next to me, a young boy snatched my bag. Archie just happened to be there, watching. He grabbed the boy and recovered my bag. And then the boy slipped away. When Carwyn and I rushed over I sensed that Archie was pleased with himself. And I sensed his interest in me too. Carwyn was in a difficult position. He had to thank Archie for rescuing my bag but he appeared threatened by him.

Carwyn told Archie we would meet him in the ship's bar that evening to thank him properly. I hated Carwyn's use of 'we'. Like he owned me. On our way back to the ship I told him how much I regretted what had happened the night before. I remember how he stopped on the quay, turned to me and said, 'Don't be so hasty, Nesta. Just remember, I have your reputation in my hands.'

No part of me wanted to go along to the meeting in the bar but not going would be unfair to Archie. I arrived late and after a few pleasantries, Archie made his move. He said something about congratulating me and Carwyn on being an item. Of course, I was furious and turned on Carwyn. He protested that he'd said no such thing. And then all of a sudden Archie was gone, making his excuses and saying he would leave us to sort things out. I raged at Carwyn. What the hell had he told Archie? He insisted he hadn't told him we were a couple. Insisted he said nothing about what happened between us the night before. But I refused to believe him. In the end I told him I wanted nothing more to do with him.

Much later, long after we were married, I wondered about how calculating Archie had been. More than once, when we were rowing about something, I accused him of lying about what Carwyn had said, that he'd made it up as part of his strategy for making his own move on me. Perhaps I wanted to believe this version – just for the convenience. Of course, Archie flatly denied it. Always did.

When we docked in Aden, Archie and I spent some time together. We went ashore, visited the market and had lunch somewhere. Yes, I felt odd but it was also an escape from all that had happened. I remember us each buying a pair of tiny Arabian slippers and posting them to our families. As we walked back along the quay towards the Fairsea, I saw Carwyn staring at us from the deck. And then when we boarded, Archie stomped off downstairs, muttering something.

While I was on my way to the dormitory, Carwyn appeared from nowhere and grabbed my hand. He pushed me into a recess and pressed me against the wall. I could smell he'd been drinking. 'Butain!' he hissed. (In case you don't know, the word means whore in Welsh.) He said he would ruin me when we got to Sydney, how he'd tell everyone at the conservatorium that I was nothing but a cheap whore. He came out with a stream of other insults – I expect you can imagine the sort of thing he said. And then I hissed: 'I wish you were dead!' He stood there looking blankly at me and I ran off down the stairs. I never saw Carwyn again.

Not long after we left Aden the weather changed. The wind got stronger and more and more people spent time in the dormitories, only going up on deck briefly for meals. I was one of them so it wasn't too difficult to avoid Carwyn. I said I never saw him again but he filled my thoughts day and night. Trapped on the ship with him. Trapped by his knowledge of what we'd done, of what I had allowed to happen. I did wish him dead.

The next time I saw Archie was when I came out of the doctor's surgery a couple of days later. They had just told me about Carwyn's accident. The nurse was ready with a reassuring hand on my arm. But the men – the doctor and the First Officer – were cold. I felt they were accusing me. I imagined them repeating Carwyn's filthy insults.

I muttered, how had it happened? The First Officer said a young Scotsman had been the only witness. Archie Thomson's his name. I remember him raising one eyebrow and leering at me as he said, 'I understand you're acquainted with him.' They made me feel tainted. Tainted and dirty. So, you can perhaps imagine what state I was in when I closed the door behind me and saw Archie standing there.

We hurried off to the rear of the ship and found a quiet bench. Archie told me his version of what happened. At the time I believed him and I kept on believing him. He said he was standing at the rail when Carwyn rushed at him from nowhere. Archie ducked, the ship ploughed *sideways in the gathering storm and Carwyn somersaulted overboard. It was an accident, Archie said. A terrible accident.*

Be careful what you wish for – that's what people say, isn't it? And my wish had been granted. Whatever went on between us, Carwyn didn't deserve to die. I know that, have always known it. But, there were actions and consequences on both sides and there's nothing I can do to change any of it.

Jim, I imagine there are many thoughts racing through your head – not least, why the big secret? And why is she telling me this? At first, there was no big secret. Archie was in Melbourne and I was in Sydney. But once Archie moved to Sydney and we got together properly, we decided to keep quiet about meeting on the ship. People at the conservatorium knew I had travelled to Australia with Carwyn and they knew about his accident too, of course. Admitting that Archie and I had met on the journey would complicate things, set tongues wagging. It was easier to say we met in Sydney so that's what we did. Sometimes we just laughed and said it was all very mysterious. And so it has remained.

Burying the past suited me in other ways, too. You see, I never told Archie about what happened with Carwyn that night on the boat deck. Hiding it from Archie meant hiding it from myself too. I hope you can understand that.

She pauses. How much should she tell? No more, she decides.

Not long before he died, your uncle said to me, 'Carwyn's death was my great fortune. You wouldn't have wanted me otherwise.' And he was right, in a way. But Carwyn's death benefitted me, too. He took our secret to his grave, and my past with him was wiped out. It forced Archie and me together – created a lasting bond between us. Who knows how each of our lives would have turned out had it not been for Carwyn?

I've often wondered: if I could go back, would I change what happened to Carwyn? And always, my answer is an emphatic no. That's a hard thing to come to terms with – that a man's death was in my best interests.

Anyway, I've said it all now, Jim. I'm sorry to unburden myself to you like this but I needed to do it. Of course, I should have told Archie

*all about Carwyn a long time ago but it's too late for that. You're the only
one in the family who has ever shown a genuine interest in hearing the
real story so I hope you don't mind.*

*I hope they're making you feel welcome at the university. And that
you and Roz are settling into life together in Canberra. It must all be very
exciting for both of you.*

*Life here is busy. Sometimes I think I've taken on too much with all
this volunteering. But I mustn't complain. A lot of the work is rewarding
and most days I wake up full of energy. Long may it continue.*

After giving it some thought, she signs the letter: *with much love, Nesta.*

Some secrets are not for sharing. Nesta remembers arriving in
Sydney, knowing she was already two weeks late. A week went by, then
another week. She began to make discreet enquiries – carefully worded
adverts in newspapers; reading the noticeboard at the doctor's surgery
when she went along to register. Money wasn't a problem. Eventually,
she gathered all of her courage and made an appointment. Nothing in
her wants to go back over the details. All she ever sees is the dim room
and its brown linoleum floor. Think of something else. She survived,
she was fortunate – that's all that matters. By the time Archie came to
Sydney on that first holiday weekend she felt safe enough to remove all
traces of the past and their bond was sealed.

She stands up, stretches her back and walks out to the terrace.
The lowering sun sparkles between the leaves of the blue gum, casting
mottled light on the tiles. If Archie were still alive, he would probably
be at the golf club. But she misses him all the same. Misses knowing
that he'll be home later. Misses the prospect of him being here ever
again.

She is left with memories; some so clear she can almost live them
once more; others fading like a half-forgotten dream. Nesta laughs
quietly to herself and returns to the conservatory looking for her diary
with its appointments, with its lists of things she must do this week.

22

Adelaide, 2018

The softness of his voice sounded odd coming from this bear of a man with his double chin, a scarf of fat wrapped snugly round his neck. He stood frozen in front of so many people, his hands gripping the lectern like a zimmer frame. I hadn't seen my cousin for over ten years and from where I sat it looked like the passage of time hadn't been kind to him.

This was my fourth funeral in the past two years and I had begun to judge them, to score them I suppose; compare and contrast, hand out points for attendance, for the quality of speeches and the jollity of the wake. And broader questions. Did the funeral do the person justice? Was it a fitting send off, as they say? For me, this one counted more than the others; even more than my mother's funeral a year earlier, just before her ninetieth birthday. There had been no more than a dozen mourners at the crematorium in Edinburgh that day, reflecting the smallness of our family, my mother's age and something else – her lack of connections. By comparison, Trinity Church in Adelaide was rocking. Someone must have pulled strings along the way to get the venue because Nesta had been no churchgoer. I guessed there must have been two hundred or so people in attendance and even more at the swanky hotel reception later. I thought my aunt would have been pleased.

Nesta's death was expected. She had struggled with throat cancer for the past couple of years, a struggle she was never going to win. The last time I saw her was about six months ago when she came to stay with us in Canberra for a few days. It was just before her final course of chemotherapy. She showed great interest in Caitlin's piano grades. 'Take your time,' she said, 'don't let Mum and Dad force you into taking exams when you don't feel ready.' Roz and I laughed and protested, we've never been the pushy types.

My aunt had visited us regularly over the past twenty years, ever since she wrote me the letter. Her frankness created a bond, a kind of instant closeness that often comes from sharing confidences. I felt privileged.

On her last visit to Canberra, I remember taking a walk with her down by the lake, our final walk as it turned out. It was late autumn. Red and yellow leaves, on the trees and on the ground, softened the landscape. The sun was piercingly bright and there was a slight chill in the air. Nesta wore a stylish, red down jacket, a bobble hat and huge sunglasses. My aunt appeared strong and steady despite the cancer and her age – she had just turned eighty-five. She took my arm as we walked.

'You're still here,' she said, giving me that toothy grin. 'I thought you would have moved years ago.'

I laughed. 'You say that every time you visit us. And every time, I tell you the same thing. We're settled here.' I raised my free hand. 'And I know what you're going to say. *But it's Canberra!* And, as usual, I'm not going to make great claims for the place. But there are practical reasons – work, obviously. Neither of us are likely to find something better at our ages. And we bought our house at the right time, long before the market went crazy. You ought to see the prices in Red Hill these days. We'd be lucky to afford a shed in someone's garden. And there's Caitlin to consider, of course. Fourteen is never a good time for children to be uprooted. But enough of all that. Anyway, you're one to talk. You've been in Adelaide for God knows how long.'

'Nearly fifty years,' she said and scuffed some leaves with her foot. 'I feel like I'm part of the city and the city's part of me. We've kind of grown together.'

Nesta's words came back to me as I scanned the room at her funeral reception. So many people in smart clothes, talking noisily, taking generous sips from their glasses. And laughing. Laughing loudly and smiling. The opera crowd, the arts festival crowd, the Kaurna crowd. They were all here. What a pity Nesta wasn't around to see it. Squeezing past bodies on my way to the buffet, I caught snatches of conversations. *It's a shame. She never did get a lead role, did she? Such a hard worker, she never stopped after Archie died. He was a ten-pound Pom, I believe. I heard they met each other in Sydney.*

I scoffed a few sandwiches and grabbed another glass of wine. It was time to find my family and do the rounds. First, I spoke to Alison, Bob and Jessie's eldest daughter, now in her early seventies. I asked about her mother. Alison said she was doing just fine in the care home she'd moved to a few years ago. 'Still on course for her maiden century,' she laughed. Only four years to go. It didn't surprise me. Jessie had always seemed much stronger than her husband. Uncle Bob passed away after a second stroke just before his eightieth birthday.

Looking across at Hannah on the far side of the room, I took a deep breath. It would have been easier if my cousin had been on her own but Wayne, her husband, was sticking close. He owned a large Ford dealership and, despite his age and burgeoning stomach, wore the sort of clothes designed for a younger generation of used car salesmen. I loathed the man. Wayne was the main reason why Nesta always came to visit us in Canberra. It was just better that way and if meeting up with Hannah and Ewan was some kind of collateral damage then so be it. Frankly, not seeing my cousins was no great loss. We lived in the same country but we inhabited different worlds.

On her regular visits to Canberra, Nesta would sound off for an hour or more about her children and their partners. 'Where did I go wrong? I can't believe they're really mine.' That kind of thing. 'I blame myself up to a point,' she'd say. 'Yes, I should have been there for them more when they were young. But nevertheless. Their lives are just so… so empty!' She would stare at Roz and me then, her face a study in amazement. We nodded, murmuring nothing words, unwilling to join in the character assassination. 'Family is family, after all. And you're so lucky with Caitlin,' Nesta would say, even though she knew our daughter was adopted. 'Nature and nurture,' we'd reply, 'it's a bit of both.'

Roz would usually leave the room then, mentioning some task she had to be on with. 'Better that,' she said, 'than getting angry or upset with Nesta.' Whatever their problems, at least her family still existed. Nesta had never abandoned them, had she? Only once that I knew of. When he was a toddler, she'd left Ewan with Bob and Jessie for the best part of a year while she toured the Far East with the opera company. But she came back, that's the important thing. Roz's mum has never come back. And I guess we stopped searching a long time ago. Roz still makes up her stories of what her mother is doing in her unknown life. 'It keeps me sane,' she says.

Luck was on my side at the wake. Wayne seemed to have moved elsewhere. Ewan and Hannah were alone together. I walked over to them. 'Good speech,' I said and clapped my cousin on his broad back. He smiled and nodded, his neck fat wobbling. I made small talk with them for a few minutes and then I asked about Nesta's ashes. 'We haven't thought of that yet,' they said. 'How about the bluff at Victor Harbor?' I suggested. 'Maybe give it some thought. Your mum loved it there.' They both looked surprised. 'Really,' Hannah said, red lipstick marks on her teeth. 'Well, I never knew that.' I could have said, *And that's the least of what you don't know about your mother. And you know why? Because you were never interested enough to ask*, although I doubted if Nesta would have told them the whole story. Instead, I simply thanked them, said I'd be in touch, made my excuses and left.

I checked my phone in the hotel foyer. No text from Roz, no more news on the bush fire. It started yesterday in Pierces Creek about ten kilometres west of our house. Sparked by a burnt-out car, the fire service said. I'd seen the smoke and flames this morning from the plane. We agreed that Roz would stay home, just in case.

It was mid-afternoon and I had an hour before I needed to head back to the airport. I took off my tie, slung my jacket over my shoulder and crossed the university footbridge. The railings looked new, all glossy, green painted metal. And a strange tubular sculpture, strung with chicken wire from which hundreds of padlocks hung. On the north side of the bridge I stopped to watch a solitary pelican nestling on the riverbank. Had more than twenty years really passed since I sat not far from here watching one of these birds? For all I knew, it was the same one. I tried to remember what I felt back then. Underneath the jet lag there had been a deep sense of anxiety. A restlessness too, a constant search for how to be and where to be. I laughed quietly. How different I felt now. How much my life had changed in those few weeks – coming to Australia, the chance meeting with Roz. Was it as simple as that? I thought of Archie and his iron will to make something of himself out here. 'He grabbed life with both hands,' Nesta said. I had envied him, his courage to do it all in the first place. Maybe some of that stuff rubbed off on me. But I like to think my approach has been a whole lot kinder to others than Archie's seemed to be. Who knows.

There was more to it than simply grabbing hold of life, though. Somewhere along the way, I had a reckoning with the past. I stopped searching for truths that some people take with them to their graves so that all we're left with are stories. I still love the past but I don't rush to it for comfort or hide from its dark secrets.

My phone buzzed. A text from Roz saying the bush fire was under control and did I want her to pick me up at the airport later. *Of course I do*, I replied. A warm feeling coursed through me as I crossed the bridge. I said a loud goodbye to the pelican as it nestled comfortably on the riverbank. And a whispered farewell to Archie and Nesta too. It was time to go home.

Acknowledgements

Thanks to Maxine Linnell– a few, well-chosen words of encouragement made all the difference. Thanks also to Bridget Walsh for your reading and suggestions on the early chapters.

Huge thanks to Elaine Ramsay and Jean Rawle for your invaluable feedback, good humour and, above all, your commitment in staying with it to the end.

Finally, thanks to Eleanor and Harry for your patience throughout and for going along with my wishes!